BLUES IN THE

BLUES IN THE NIGHT

Dick Lochte

This first world edition published 2011
in Great Britain and in the USA by
SEVERN HOUSE PUBLISHERS LTD of
9–15 High Street, Sutton, Surrey, England, SM1 1DF.

British Library Cataloguing in Publication Data

Lochte, Dick.
  Blues in the night.
  1. Ex-convicts – Fiction. 2. Organized crime – California –
  Los Angeles – Fiction. 3. Serial murder investigation –
  Fiction. 4. Suspense fiction.
  I. Title
  813.5'4-dc22

ISBN-13: 978-0-7278-8108-3 (cased)

All Severn House titles are printed on acid-free paper.

Severn House Publishers support The Forest Stewardship Council [FSC],
the leading international forest certification organisation. All our titles that
are printed on Greenpeace-approved FSC-certified paper carry the FSC logo.

Typeset by Palimpsest Book Production Ltd.,
Falkirk, Stirlingshire, Scotland.
Printed and bound in Great Britain by
MPG Books Ltd., Bodmin, Cornwall.

For Michael Laughlin, friend,
bon vivant and all-round gent

Paris

When the gunfire began, Modi Sarif, who'd been double-timing down the Rue de la Reyne, clutched his briefcase to his chest and threw himself to the grimy sidewalk. Hearing laughter, he blinked open his eyes and raised his head cautiously.

Several schoolboys, unkempt wraiths in baggy black, were posed at the open doors of a cafe, observing him with typical youthful scorn. Sarif saw that, in the café beyond them, others of their ilk were playing an electronic game that had apparently been the source of the 'gunshots'. On its display panel was the animated, muscled figure of Captain Combat, the comic-book soldier of fortune who seemed to have captured the hearts and minds of teenage boys the world over.

Sarif rose, brushed off his dark blue suit jacket and trousers and glared at the smirking youths. 'Idiots!' he shouted. 'Wasting your euros on noise and bright lights.'

The boys did not bother to reply. They merely drifted back to their game, no longer amused by the little man standing on the sidewalk hugging a briefcase, his knuckles scraped and bleeding.

Sarif glared at them in frustration. He wanted to give the insolent little bastards a demonstration of what was in his briefcase, to wipe the sneers from their pasty faces. To show them that he, unlike their make-believe Captain Combat, possessed the real power of life and death.

Another time, perhaps.

He began walking again, pausing momentarily to investigate the stinging sensation on the back of his hands. Flecks of blood peeked through the scrapes. *The bastards, with their fucking game.* He wondered if he needed some kind of inoculation. The area was so unclean.

His destination was in the next block, a red brick two-story building, surprisingly kempt for the neighborhood, that might have been taken for a residence or perhaps the office of a doctor with an upper-class clientele. A polished brass plaque above the doorbell read, '*Le Galerie Honore*. By Appointment Only.'

He had an appointment.

He pressed the bell and a reassuringly no-nonsense buzzer sounded inside the gallery. Almost immediately, the door was opened by a freshly barbered, pink-faced man in his middle years, his solid body caressed by a tailored suit of dark gray. A white shirt, canary-yellow tie and buffed, black bluchers completed his attire. 'Yeah?' he asked, as if the answer were of no earthly importance to him.

A fucking American, Sarif thought. Of course it would be an American, the money they were offering. If any race were more loathsome than the French, it was the Americans. But, unlike the froggies, they had money and they didn't mind spending it, even with their economy in free fall.

He gave the fucking American his name. The fucking American took his time before stepping aside. 'C'mon in,' he said. 'I'm Corrigan. You're late, sport.'

'A few minutes. The underground . . .'

'We like to call it The Metro,' Corrigan said as he locked the front door. 'And it works pretty good, last I noticed. Moves right along.'

'I . . . exited at the wrong stop.'

'Did you, now?' Corrigan said.

Sarif took a few steps down the hall. To his right was the gallery's main display room. The Bokhara on the floor. The walls filled with art. The perfect indirect lighting. The exquisitely placed vases with freshly cut flowers. The ambiance made him a bit heady.

'C'mon,' Corrigan ordered, walking past him toward the rear. 'And try not to touch anything. Your mitts are bleeding.'

Bleeding and painful.

Sarif told himself this was the price one paid for venturing into a crude and unpleasant country where the men smelled of perfume and the women walked about without underwear.

He followed Corrigan down the hallway and through a door into what appeared to be a large garage that was also serving as an office, workroom and storage space. A gunmetal gray desk was against one wall, its surface cluttered with invoices and other papers, dirty coffee cups, a cellular telephone, a computer – dark at the moment – and the machine Sarif had been expecting to see.

Crates and packing materials were stacked in one corner. Piles of sawdust and wood shavings had been swept near a large round trash bin. A sliding, metal exit door had been built into the far rear wall. A dusty, gray van was parked facing the closed door.

The rest of the room was unpainted drywall, decorated by framed prints. Empty frames of varying sizes and styles hung on black metal hooks protruding from the wall that separated this area from the gallery.

As Sarif crossed the room, he stepped on a sheet of bubble wrap, the resulting pops causing him to hop nervously. This provoked a chuckle from a tall raw-boned man, younger than Corrigan, whom Sarif hadn't noticed leaning against the wall to his left. Another fucking American, Sarif assumed, judging by the man's crew cut and rumpled, ill-fitting conservative dark suit.

'Mr Sarif seems to be a little goosey,' Corrigan said to the other fucking American. 'He looks like he damaged himself on the way here.'

'I . . . stumbled in my haste.' Feeling awkward and uncomfortable, Sarif quickly opened the briefcase and withdrew an unusual-looking handgun. Small and glossy gray, it seemed toylike, even with a thick circle of flat black metal wrapping the tip of its barrel. He held it out to Corrigan.

'Mr Drier will take that,' Corrigan said, indicating the other American. 'He's the expert.'

Drier pushed away from the wall and ambled over to Sarif. His unblinking green eyes continued to stare at the little man as he picked up the weapon. 'Light,' he said. 'Uses a standard silencer?'

'Just one of its many attractions,' Sarif said.

'Full load?'

'Oh, yes.'

Drier took a few seconds to fit the pistol in his big hand. He pointed it at a colorful print of LeRoy Neiman's *Sinatra at the Sands* that had been taped to a thick roll of pink fiber-glass insulation.

'Sorry, Frank,' Drier said and fired the weapon.

The sound it made was a subdued pop, like the opening of a beer can, accompanied by a jagged circular hole in the Neiman print removing Sinatra's snap brim hat and the top of his head.

'On the mark, Cap,' Drier said. He hefted the gun. 'I'd give it a ten.'

Corrigan took the gun from him and carried it to the desk.

Sarif watched anxiously as Corrigan moved the gun toward the device he'd noticed on the way in. Dr Abelard had had one just like it in his lab, a Garrett Super Scanner, a top of the line metal detector.

When the weapon was a few inches away, the Super Scanner suddenly emitted a loud squeal, startling Sarif.

Corrigan glared at him.

Blinking, feeling a shortness of breath, Sarif looked from the metal detector to the weapon. He relaxed. Smiling weakly, he said, 'The, ah, silencer.'

Corrigan nodded, unscrewed the silencer. He moved the pistol toward the device again. As confident as Sarif was of the weapon's molecular structure, he experienced a moment of panic.

What if . . .?

But no. This time there was blessed silence.

Corrigan grinned. 'Well fucking done, Mr Sarif.'

'My mission is to please. If you are satisfied, then, perhaps . . .'

'You want your lolly. Of course you do.' Corrigan circled the desk. He rested the gun on top of the scattered invoices and bent down to retrieve an aluminum case from the floor.

He placed the case beside the gun, snapped it open, showing Sarif that it was jam-packed with neatly bound, small denomination euro banknotes.

Sarif's damaged hand seemed to have a will of its own, reaching out to the bills. With his fingertips nearly touching them, Corrigan snapped the lid of the case shut. 'There's still one little thing.'

His throat dry, Sarif nodded. He withdrew a tiny, green felt bag from his briefcase and offered it to Corrigan.

Puzzled, Corrigan accepted the bag. He shook it and a dull-gray coin the size of an American quarter fell on to his palm. On it, the upper torso of a bearded man stood out in bas-relief. 'What the hell is this?' the gallery owner asked.

'What you paid for,' Sarif replied, still focused on the aluminum case.

Corrigan raised the coin and squinted at it. Muttering, he took it to the cluttered table and shoved the papers around until he uncovered an antique magnifying glass not unlike those usually associated with Sherlock Holmes. He used it to examine both sides of the coin. 'I'll be damned,' he said, smiling.

He held the coin and magnifying glass to Drier who pushed himself off the wall and accepted the items.

'He's a cutie pie, that Doc Abelard,' Corrigan said, turning to Sarif. 'Who's the old bird in the engraving?'

'Dr Abelard did not say.'

'The coin *is* one of a kind, right?'

'Of course,' Sarif said, hand on the aluminum case now, drawing it toward him. 'All records and notes have been destroyed.'

'Good.'

'Along with Dr Abelard.'

'Come again?' Corrigan asked.

'I set fire to the lab. Everything is ash.'

'Including Abelard?'

Sarif had the case opened and was too concerned with counting its contents to notice Corrigan's face. 'Of course,' he said, as if he were discussing the weather. 'As soon as he gave me the coin and his assurances, I slit his Limey throat. He squealed like a pig.'

Corrigan picked up the pistol, replaced the silencer. 'A genius like that,' he said, 'you kinda wonder what other useful shit he might have had on his drawing board.'

Sarif continued to count his money. 'We will never know,' he said.

'Precisely my point, you stupid Arab son of a bitch.'

The words and the anger behind them got through to Sarif. Blinking rapidly, he said. 'I, sir, am Egyptian.'

'That's better?' Corrigan asked.

Sarif, clutching his euro notes, was starting to reply when the bullets lifted him off his feet and hurled him against a stack of frames, scattering him and them to the floor.

Corrigan walked across the room, reached down and yanked the packet of currency from the dead man's fingers. He didn't have to break the fingers, so that was one good thing he could say about the slimy little weasel. He returned the banknotes to the briefcase and snapped the lid shut.

'Egyptian,' he said.

'I'd have done that for you, Cap,' Drier said.

'The gun was in my hand,' Corrigan said.

He slipped the engraved coin back into its felt pouch and handed it and the pistol to Drier. 'They go with the canvasses, Leonard.'

The door buzzer sounded.

Corrigan glanced at the monitor attached to a metal brace over the hall door. He smiled at the sight of the visitor standing on the stoop.

'Think of some inventive resting place for Mr Sarif, Leonard. But be sure you dig the ceramic bullets out, first. Wouldn't want to confuse the Sûreté.'

He moved quickly to the front door. There, he paused to fix the knot of his tie, straighten his cuffs and pat down the hair at the back of his head. Satisfied with his appearance, he twisted the bolt lock free and opened the door to what, in his Yalie years, he used to refer to as 'an F. Scott Fitzgerald wet dream'.

Angela Lowell was an ice princess in her late twenties. Blonde, dressed for success. *Grace Kelly playing a Rosalind Russell role,* Corrigan thought. He had to remind himself that the stunner entering his shop was too young to know who the hell Rosalind Russell was. She might not even know who Grace Kelly was.

'Ms Lowell, an unexpected pleasure,' he said.

'I just wanted to make sure that everything was set for the flight tomorrow, Mr Corrigan,' she said, leading him to the display room.

She could have phoned, Corrigan thought. Dare he hope

that her visit might be an invitation to . . . something? 'We're all set,' he said.

'Could I take one last look at my selections?'

Corrigan realized her selections were in the back room with the freshly dead Mr Sarif. 'I'm afraid they're already crated,' he said. 'Not having second thoughts?'

'No. I just wanted to see them again.'

Corrigan gave her his most charming grin. 'You'll have years and years to do that.'

'Assuming I remain . . . employed by the purchaser.'

'Hold out for visitation rights,' Corrigan said.

She smiled. Damn. Bottle that smile and you could put Pfizer right out of the Viagra business.

'I don't suppose you'd want to spend your last evening in Paris with a middle-aged art dealer,' he said, 'who just happens to know a great little four star restaurant on the Rue de Varenne?'

'That's sweet of you, but I'm meeting friends.'

'Lucky friends.' Laying her would have been the icing on the cake, but since that option was off the table, he saw no reason to prolong his hard-on. 'Well, you've got an open dinner invitation on your next visit,' he said, leading her to the front door.

Before exiting, she turned to look at him. 'It must be so stimulating,' she said.

'Beg pardon?'

'Being constantly surrounded by all this wonderful art.'

Corrigan cocked his head. 'Yeah. Stimulating . . . and frustrating,' he said.

'Frustrating?'

'Sure.' He smiled. She probably thought the smile was for her, but actually he was thinking about the dead self-proclaimed Egyptian in the back room. 'You know the old saying: "Art is forever, but life is so damn short".'

Los Angeles

ONE

'Jee-zus,' Wylie said. 'He's giving it to her good.'

Mace stared at the grinning young idiot sitting beside him at the window and wondered if he might be suffering from Attention Deficit Disorder. They were in darkness, in a room on the top floor of the Florian Apartment Hotel, a U-shaped, three-story building a block above Sunset Boulevard.

Wylie had his night vision binoculars trained on the wing of the building across the way. Mace guessed that he was barely into his twenties. Six feet tall, a couple inches shorter than Mace and maybe twenty-five pounds lighter at one-sixty-five to one-seventy. Greenish-blonde mop of hair showing black at the roots.

There was enough light from the moon and the Florian's glowing pool in the courtyard below for Mace to make out the head of a blue and red serpent tattoo poking above the neckline of Wylie's loud Hawaiian shirt.

At Pelican Bay prison, Mace used to watch an old con named Billy Jet stick needles full of dye into the flesh of some of the other cons. There wasn't much else to do there, except get tats or watch other guys getting tats. As far as Mace knew Wylie had never served time, so the snake didn't make any sense to him at all.

The second floor window occupying Wylie's attention wasn't the one they were there to watch, but that point seemed to be lost on him. He licked his slightly feminine lips and said, 'Oh, ba-bee, don't use it up all at once.'

Mace stubbed out his cigarette and picked up his binoculars. He aimed them at a set of windows directly across the way. The main room of the apartment was still empty. The subject was somewhere to the right, probably in the bathroom, since no light had gone on in the bedroom.

'Shee-it,' Wylie said, 'this waaay beats the beater flicks on cable all to hell. I'm ready for a little hormone fix, myself.'

Mace sighed.

'Whoa. Watch out for Mr Back-door Man.'

'If I didn't know better,' Mace said, staying focused on the subject's apartment, 'I'd take you for some snot-nose kid on his first trip to what they laughingly call a gentleman's club.'

'Oh, yeah?' Wylie said, obviously stung. 'Well . . . go fuck yourself.'

'You're the one who's turned on,' Mace replied calmly.

'What turns you on, big man?' Wylie said heatedly. 'Little boys?'

Mace watched the subject enter her living room dressed in a robe, rubbing her blonde hair with a towel, her face shiny from night cream. She crossed the room and moved just past the wide window and out of view.

'Pro work,' he said. 'That turns me on.'

The subject walked back into his line of sight carrying a thick book. A coffee-table book. Probably an art book, Mace thought. He'd been told she was an art appraiser, an artist herself.

He liked the way she moved, a graceful glide. He couldn't see her feet, but he imagined they were bare, luxuriating in the soft texture of the carpet.

'You saying what? That I'm not a pro?' Wylie asked, more hurt now than angry.

'I'm saying you should concentrate on the job.'

The subject turned out the living room light. Mace started a countdown. One hundred. One hundred and one. One hundred and two. One hundred and—

A light went on behind the bedroom drapes.

Mace lowered his binoculars and placed them on the table. 'She's tucked in,' he said.

Wylie was glaring at him. 'So you don't think I'm a pro, huh?'

In point of fact, Mace thought he was a hopeless jackass. He'd formed that opinion as soon as he'd laid eyes on him at LAX that afternoon. But he didn't know how long they'd be cooping, so he said, 'Right now, I'm jet-lagged, bone-tired and pissed off at the world in general. If Paulie Lacotta gives you a paycheck, you're a pro. OK?'

Wylie still wasn't happy. 'I'm pro enough to stay out of the joint,' he said, half to himself.

'Good point,' Mace said, letting it slide. 'OK if I fade for a while?'

'Do what you want,' Wylie said, raising the binoculars. 'You're the pro.'

There were two beds in the room. One was filled with Wylie's crap; a black plastic shell, ear phones, a razor, a head set, various plugs and wires, candy bars, rubbers, a Dopp Kit bulging with colognes and creams.

Mace sat on the other bed and started taking off his shoes.

'Yo, Mace,' Wylie said, shifting moods gracelessly. 'We might as well make this as homeboy as we can. You stay off my back, I stay off yours. OK?'

'Sounds like a plan,' Mace said, stretching out. 'Give me a couple hours and I'll spell you.'

'The bitch isn't goin' anywhere. What's the harm if I grab some Z's, too?'

Mace stopped the sarcastic reply that came immediately to mind. 'You never know what a subject will do,' he said. 'If she cuts and runs while we're snoozing, Paulie will see to it we both get lots of rest.'

'You know Mr Lacotta a long time, huh?'

'Long enough,' Mace said, closing his eyes.

TWO

At roughly eight fifteen the next morning, Paulie Lacotta slipped his SL55 into a visitor slot in front of the Florian. He was about to open his door when he saw a yellow Mustang convertible departing from the bi-level parking garage to the left of the apartment hotel. The top was down and the driver's blonde hair flowed in the wind as the car zoomed past.

He'd be damned if convertibles weren't made for blondes to drive.

He wondered where she was headed at – looking at his watch – eight sixteen in the morning. Well, he figured he'd know soon enough. Wylie's company Lexus sedan had just emerged with screeching tires to follow after the Mustang.

He pried himself free of his car, a stocky guy wearing two-inch heels that almost brought him to six feet. He was wrapped in a Zegna suit worth a couple thou, cut to emphasize his shoulders and hide a thickening waist. His nut-brown face had once been slick-handsome, but it was starting to sag at the jowls.

That morning while shaving he was thinking it just might be Botox-and-tuck time. Youth must be served, after all.

He circled the front building at a jaunty clip, strolled past the pool where two wrinkled old duffers were puffing through their morning laps. No hot babes in bikinis that early, if ever. The Florian was not exactly a Girls Gone Wild operation. It was a well-run apartment hotel with some permanent guests who enjoyed its full-service facilities and close proximity to the stores and restaurants on Sunset Boulevard and transients – mainly theater actors, artists and musicians from the Other Coast – who prized its vaguely Bohemian atmosphere, the harmless eccentricities of its friendly staff and the fact that each 'suite' included kitchenettes for them to cook their own food.

Paulie, in his Sam Goldwyn-like way, had concluded that he wouldn't have been caught dead living there.

He took the rear stairwell at a brisk pace, paused before a door on the third floor and knocked. 'Me,' he said.

He heard the lock sliding away.

When the door opened, he stepped in to find Mace, dressed in clothes that looked like he'd slept in them, his feet bare. Holding a coffee mug. It had been nine years since he'd last seen the man. Dave Mason looked harder now. Tougher. A little weather-beaten, but that figured, him living in swampland.

Lacotta opened his arms. 'C'mere, you son of a bitch,' he said, grinning.

Mace put his coffee mug on a table and accepted the inevitable bear hug.

When Lacotta was through physically bonding, he took a backward step and gave Mace a head-to-toe. 'You're looking money, amigo.'

The tan. The hug. Now 'money' and 'amigo'. Jesus Christ! Mace bit his tongue and said, 'You too, Paulie. Really living la vida El Lay, huh?'

Lacotta beamed proudly, as if Mace had paid him a high compliment. 'You know it, dude.' He turned to the windows. 'My girl been behaving herself?' he asked.

'So far.'

Lacotta scanned the room. He moved to the nearest bed and tested the mattress with a finger poke. 'We've seen worse, huh?'

Mace supposed that was true. He took his mug over to the stove for a refill. 'Coffee?' he asked.

'Hell, no,' Lacotta said, wincing. 'That caffeine shit stains the teeth. Sours the stomach. Coffee'll kill you quicker'n cancer.'

Mace toasted him with his mug and took a sip.

'How's my boy Wylie doin'?' Lacotta asked.

'Out tailing the subject.'

'They were leaving when I got here. What I want to know is what you think of him.'

'The snake on his neck makes close shadow work a little tricky. People tend to remember things like that. You know, start to wonder, wasn't there a guy with a snake walking behind me this morning?'

'The fucking kid's body looked like the Sunday funnies. We got most of it lasered off, but the doc said he couldn't do anything with the snake. Something about the ink. He offered to turn it into a birthmark, like the Russian guy, what's-his-name, had on his head. Wylie's not exactly up with that. What do you think?'

'I think you're losing it if you're coming to me for cosmetic advice.'

Lacotta ducked his head in a nod of agreement. 'What else about him?'

'If the subject decides to go for a stroll, he'll be OK, as long as it's on the Strip or Hollywood Boulevard. If it's Beverly

Hills or Brentwood, that lousy hair-dye job and the beach-boy shirt might stick out more than the snake.'

'I don't suppose you could call shit like that to his attention?'

'You're beautiful, Paulie,' Mace said. 'Not only do you bring me in cold and saddle me with a green punk, you want me to play mentor.'

'The kid's a legacy. His old man was Leo Giruso.'

'Leo, huh?' Mace said. 'That figures.'

'Leo was goddamn loyal.'

'Get a dog. They're smarter.' Mace took a sip of coffee. 'How'd the kid wind up with the name Wylie?'

'I dunno. Read it in a book, maybe?'

Mace rolled his eyes.

'OK, so you don't like the kid,' Lacotta said.

'It's not him. I don't like this whole set-up.'

'Hey,' Lacotta said with a little heat behind it. 'You did me a good thing a while back, but I figure I kinda made up for it. Your old man kept his business going in Louisiana, right? Some kinda canning operation . . . where exactly?'

'Bayou Royal.'

'And didn't I put some dough aside for you every year you were at Pel?'

'That you did.'

'So now I ask you for a little help and you bust my balls?'

Mace moved to the window and frowned out at the bright morning. 'What's with this Lowell woman anyway?'

'Since when you start asking questions like that?'

'Since I started sitting around an empty apartment with a dim-bulb kid, peeping in windows like some bathroom idiot.'

Lacotta got to his feet, pouting a little. 'Yeah, well, like Bobby D used to say, we all gotta serve somebody.' He shifted from foot to foot. 'Aw, hell. Angie and me . . . it's personal, OK? I wanna know what she's up to. Can you handle that?'

'What are you expecting her to do?'

Lacotta shrugged and shook his head. Not much of an answer.

'You wanna grab some breakfast?' he asked.

'No, thanks. I don't know what I do want, but it's not breakfast.'

'Well,' Lacotta said, 'you find out, you let me know.'

THREE

Night two.

Wylie was at the window of the darkened room, presumably on guard. 'Damn,' he said, 'bitch dropped the blinds on me.'

Mace was in the kitchenette, washing down a cold Mexican dinner with a bourbon and water. He placed a half-eaten taco on its Styrofoam bed and hurried to the window, picking up his binoculars.

The subject was clearly visible in her apartment, standing before an easel, painting. 'What the hell are you talking about?' he asked Wylie. 'She's right there. No blinds.'

'Yeah, I know. She's cool. I was clockin' the naked bi-atch one window over. Full frontal, doing her Pi-lat-tease.'

Mace sighed and walked back to the kitchenette. He dumped the remains of his Tico Taco dinner into the dispose-all. 'Where's that list of places she went today?' he asked.

'Why? It's just bullshit stores.'

'Humor me.'

Wylie plucked a small pad from the pocket of his flowery shirt and held it out with thumb and forefinger.

Mace took it into the bathroom, closed the door and turned on the lights. He flipped the pages of the pad until he found what he wanted. Even in Wylie's crabbed handwriting, the names of three business establishments were clear enough.

He turned off the light and went back into the darkened bedroom. 'Tell me again what went on,' he said.

'Nothing went on. She had her errands. She parks the 'Tang and runs in. Comes out with her stuff. Cruises to the next place. Parks the 'Tang, goes in. Like that.'

'And you didn't see what she did inside the shops?'

'Christ, no. She was in and out like The Flash. I barely had time to park. Why you making such a big fucking deal of it?'

'Don't mind me,' Mace said. He pulled his jacket off the back of a chair and headed for the door.

'Were you goin'?' Wylie asked.

'I need some fresh air.'

'Fresh air? In *this* fucking city?'

'Keep watching the window,' Mace said. 'Hers.'

'Where you really goin'?'

'Cigarettes. You need anything?'

Wylie shook his head. 'You gonna be gone long?'

'Hour, maybe. You know what to do if the subject leaves her apartment?'

'I gotta tell ya. I'm so raked by your "the subject" bullshit. Use her fucking name or call her a bitch or whore or what the hell.'

'You don't want to use names,' Mace said. 'And you do want to keep it impersonal. So, with your permission, she's "the subject". OK?'

Wylie shrugged. 'It's so fucking *spy movie.*'

'Call her what you want,' Mace said. 'Just keep your eye on her.'

'Yeah, yeah,' Wiley said.

FOUR

Although walking seemed to be frowned on in LA, Mace thought it preferable to getting the rental out, bucking traffic and then trying to find a parking place. Actually, the Sunset Strip had changed so drastically since he'd last seen it, he didn't even know where you could or couldn't park any more. Too many signs. 'One Hour Parking, 8 am – 6 p.m.' 'No Parking 6 pm – 10 p.m.' 'No Parking Anytime.' The address he wanted wasn't more than five or six blocks away.

He moved with purpose down the Strip, maneuvering around the late-night dawdlers – hookers, pimps, members of the glitterati who'd dined fashionably late, tourists looking slightly lost and anxious, slackers with nothing better to do.

He put himself in the tourist camp.

His destination was an address in the middle of the block. Nine years ago, when he'd been a resident of the city, it had been home to a vegan health restaurant called 'The Elegant Eggplant'. Now there was nothing elegant about it. Or remotely healthy. The building had been painted black long enough ago for wind and weather to have softened the color to an ugly mottled gray. A red neon sign identified it as 'Honest Abe's Coffee Empourium'. A cardboard sign, stuck in the display window added, in hand lettering: 'Tonight: Jerry Monte, Saturday: Super Slam.'

A youthful crowd, mainly female, formed a line that continued down the block as far as he could see, not too many of them listening to the poetry and jazz blaring from a pair of speakers attached just under the club's roofline. Thanks to a groping couple, Mace found a narrow gap in the queue and headed to the entrance where a closed door was being guarded by a giant with arms like tree trunks hanging from his muscle T-shirt. He was the standard-brand bald bouncer except for the five precious stones weighing down his right ear lobe and the heavily mascaraed eyes, which he turned on Mace with some suspicion.

'I'm an old friend of Abe's,' Mace said.

'So are they,' the bouncer said, indicating the queue.

'Tell him Mace wants to see him.'

The bouncer studied him for a beat. He took a few extra seconds to look past him to prove he was no pushover. Then he turned, opened the door and ducked inside the club.

The people in line glared at Mace. He ignored them and did his best to ignore the blather coming from the speaker.

When the bouncer reappeared, he said, 'Abe's at the rear.'

The night air had been cool enough, but inside the shadowy club it was freezing, even with the place packed with young customers. They didn't seem to notice their chattering teeth as they stared reverentially at a pale poetess who was sharing the tiny stage with a poodle. The poetess was rapping about the beauty of watching dogs fuck.

Mace headed for a table at the far end of the room where a gaunt man sat grinning at him. Back in the day, Honest Abe Garfein had pushed his resemblance to the sixteenth president of the USA to the max by wearing chin whiskers, a stovepipe hat and a black suit. Having moved past Lincoln's longevity by at least a dozen years, with the sagging flesh and wiry gray hair to prove it, Abe had evidently decided to drop the impersonation. Clean shaven and wearing a Tommy Bahama shirt that provided nearly all the color in the room, he had morphed into another familiar figure, the crazy neighbor from the old *Seinfeld* TV show.

He held out a nut-brown hand that Mace assumed was for shaking. Instead Abe used it to slap Mace's hand, a gesture that surprised and annoyed him.

'High five,' Abe said, trying to explain the slap.

Mace shrugged and took a seat at the table. 'A little chilly in here, don't you think?' he said.

'Some like it hot,' Abe said, 'I like it cold. Anyway, it's a coffeehouse, Mace. People drink more coffee when it's cold.'

'Looks like it's working for you.'

'I always knew being a history buff would pay off. Welcome back to the Fifties.'

'I'd heard the Strip was dead,' Mace said.

'Not if you can give the customers something TV and movies no longer provide.'

'That would be . . . ?'

'Literary pretension,' Abe said. 'It's bringing in the green. I'm thinking of expanding the brand a bit. Remember the old Brigston Studio? It's been sitting there collecting dust and rats since Brigston shuttered it back in the Nineties.'

Actually, Mace not only remembered the studio; he and Paulie Lacotta had crashed the party old man Brigston tossed on the lot, the night he pulled the plug. But he didn't feel the need to mention this to Abe, who, in any case, was more interested in telling his own story.

'Well . . . this . . . guy I know just bought the studio. Laid down the hard cash with the idea of turning out pornos for the on-demand and home video markets. And, of course, the Internet. I thought I might just buy a little piece of his action and try the Cecil B. DeMented trip, produce a few myself.

'There are a couple of flies in the ointment, of course. Hi-Def and, worse, Blu-Ray. The few performers whose skin can stand that kind of scrutiny demand more money than Julia Roberts. It costs almost as much to have the warts and pimples and the goddamned tats removed by CGI. The government is starting to demand the use of condoms. Hell, disease has everybody so spooked you can't even get a decent anal penetration shot these days.'

His watery eyes must have registered that Mace had tuned out. 'But you didn't drop by to hear about pen shots. What can I do for you, old friend? I'm still serving the body as well as the mind.' He nodded toward the bar where a young woman, dressed like a freshly scrubbed high-school student, was looking their way, expectantly. She smiled at Mace and placed her thumb between her lips, pushing it in and out.

Mace turned to Abe. 'What I need is information,' he said. '"I've been out of the loop awhile.'

'Heard you went to live in the bayous with your old man after Pel. Guess that Katrina thing was pretty rough?'

'People forget the Rita thing came first. What that didn't wipe clean, Katrina took care of. And then came the BP oil spread.'

'Jesus. Bet you wished you'd been back high and dry inside Pel, huh?'

'Not really,' Mace said. 'You'd know if you'd ever been inside.'

Abe's face registered embarrassment. A fleeting gesture. 'How can a humble whoremonger be of help?' he asked.

'I'm hoping you're still the go-to guy when it comes to what's going down in the city.'

'A living, breathing Google on El Lay, that's me. Enjoying the fruits of the age of information.'

'I need some background on a woman.'

'Ah, romance.'

'Not exactly,' Mace said.

'If she works the city I'll know her.'

'She's no pro. At least, I don't think so. Her name is Angela Lowell. Blonde, twenties, trim. Lady exec type.'

'Tits?' Abe asked.

For some reason the question annoyed Mace. 'A pair, would be my guess,' he said.

Abe furrowed his brow and stared at the cup of coffee in front of him. After a few beats, he unfurrowed and shook his head. 'Don't think I know the lady. Sorry.'

Mace took Wylie's pad from his pocket. 'You familiar with these places: The Leather Derby, The Honeymoon Court Drugs, The Inpost?'

'Dress shops, shoe shops, a drug store. What about 'em?'

'I was hoping you could tell me,' Mace said, pocketing the pad. 'Legit? Fronts? Connected in any way?'

'It'd help if you told me what's on your mind.'

'Only confusion,' Mace said.

A waitress in short skirt, black stockings and a baggy sweater approached their table.

'Something to drink, Mace?' Abe asked. 'Coffee, cider, Perrier?'

Mace shook his head, no.

'Nothing for us, honey,' Abe said to the waitress. 'But ask Teddy to keep an eye out for Jerry Monte. He's late as usual.'

'Who's this Monte?'

'Jerry Monte? Jesus, Mace, welcome to the world. He's the new Justin Timberlake.'

'Who?'

Abe blinked. 'Let's try the new, white, hetero Michael Jackson, may God rest his soul. Jerry Monte's music gets millions of downloads. His movies top the lists and his computer games are everywhere you look. He created Captain Combat.'

'*That* Jerry Monte,' Mace said. 'Never heard of him.'

'Well, he's why this place is packed. The kids don't come out to hear Miss Dirty Knickers over there.'

Mace looked at the poetess who was carefully enunciating every word of an excruciatingly amateurish piece of poetic self-exploration. Buried in her doughy face was his faint memory of a rosebud-mouthed starlet.

'If this Monte guy is so big time, what draws him here? The girls?'

'Most of the showbiz cretins come in to read because it

makes them feel intelligent,' Abe said. 'But Jerry's got money in the club, not that that removes him from the cretin list.

'So, do you want me to try and turn something up on Miz Lowell?'

'You get a line on her, you can reach me at The Florian. I'm registered there under Wylie.'

'You still on Paulie Lacotta's team?' Abe said.

'Why do you ask?'

'The rumor was you took your fall for him.'

'You know how rumors are,' Mace said.

Abe had a comment but forgot it when the club went suddenly silent. His eyes shifted to the entrance where two very black walking slabs of beef had just moved past the bouncer. 'And heeeeere's Jerry,' Abe said, standing. 'I gotta go meet and greet. Stick around for the show. He'll probably be reading from Charles Bukowski or maybe Rod McKuen. One of the greats.'

'I've gotta run anyway,' Mace said. 'I'm susceptible to frostbite.'

'Mind leaving by the rear?' Abe asked, pointing to a back door. 'Jerry sees you walking out, he'll take it personally.'

'What'll he do? Cry?'

'No. He'll probably get his two associates to make you cry.'

Mace glanced at the two bodyguards.

'Actually, he's not that big an asshole. But it'll probably piss him off and he'll vent out on me.'

'Rear door it is,' Mace said. 'If Paulie or anybody else asks, you haven't seen me. OK?'

'You can trust me, Mace. Honest Abe,' he said as he moved off to meet the new pop wonderboy.

Mace had a vague feeling that he'd made a mistake coming to Abe. He'd always been a stand-up guy, but people changed. He watched the lanky aging entrepreneur approach the shorter, younger newcomer and do that hand-slap bullshit.

What the hell. If he had been stupid to seek Abe's help, it was too late to do anything about that now. And what was the worst that could come of it?

He made his exit through the club's rear door.

FIVE

Abe's mind was spinning as fast and erratically as a Tijuana roulette wheel. Had he kept a game face or had Mace been able to read a reaction to the bitch's name?

No. He'd been cool. He was Abe, for Christ's sake.

He put on his fixed grin and moved in past Jerry Monte's two beasts of burden to high five the tanned, diminutive superstar who was dressed in the tattered, soiled style known as homeless chic.

'Jesus, it's like a meat locker in here,' Jerry Monte said. 'I can see my breath.'

'I'll bring it up a few degrees,' Abe said, though he had no intention of doing so. He liked it cold.

'Some crowd, huh?' Jerry Monte said. His spiked jet-black hair had been given a blueberry tint since their last meeting. 'My net geeks got everything goin'?'

'We'll be blasting broadband in exactly fifteen minutes,' Abe said, hoping it was true. He left that end of things up to the Geek Chorus, the two sullen men and one sullen woman who worked for Monte and handled the Empourium's web site and its accoutrements. They usually got the job done.

'There's this freaking incredible poem this broad works at the Hyatt in Orlando tipped me to. It's called 'Tyger, Tyger, Burning Bright.' That's t-y-g-e-r. By this dude named William Blake.'

'Bobby's dad?' Abe asked, and was immediately annoyed with himself for snarking at the wrong time and at definitely the wrong person.

But he need not have been concerned.

Jerry Monte was oblivious to the sarcastic nature of the question. 'I kinda doubt it,' he said. 'This Blake's from, like, ancient times. A, what do you call it, an ancestor of Bobby's, maybe. Anyway, he's written this mind-blowin' masterpiece.

I got Blaine and Richards workin' on a melody. But I'm giving it a lyrics-only try-out tonight.'

'I'm looking forward to it,' Abe said.

Monte scanned the room. 'Angie pull a no-show again?'

'She left word saying she was sorry,' Abe said, wondering if Mace's ignorance of Monte had been a put-on. 'She promised to tune in, though.'

Monte shrugged. He winked at a brunette at a table to their right. 'I think I see a stand-in,' he said.

The brunette looked to be possibly twenty-one, pretty in a semi-Goth way. Black blouse and short skirt. Black lipstick and fingernails. But no piercing or tattoos that Abe could see. She was sitting with two other girls, also attractive, but not quite as promising.

'Hi, ladies,' he said, approaching their table. 'I'm Honest Abe, proprietor and master of revels. Welcome to the Empourium.'

The brunette's name was Katie. Her two friends were Joanie and Tess. They seemed friendly enough to bring the category 'new meat' to mind.

'Jerry likes to have the most beautiful ladies present right in front of the stage,' he said. 'It inspires him to . . . greatness. So, allow me to invite you to the *numero uno* table.'

'We're fine here,' Katie said, surprising him.

'Oh, Katie,' Tess said. 'It'll be fun.'

'Fun it will be,' Abe said. 'And you'll get to meet Jerry.'

Katie raised an eyebrow. 'Do Jerry's "inspirations" usually pay a cover charge?' she asked.

Abe felt a little frisson at the bitchy and yet flirtatious way she asked the question. 'Of course not,' he said. 'Nor will they have to pay for drinks or . . . anything that may please their fancies.'

'Well, hell, girls,' Katie said, 'what have we got to lose?'

Abe led them to the empty front table where he introduced them to Jerry. In his practiced manner, the entertainer made a big thing about meeting Joanie and Tess, but turned the charisma ray on full for Katie who seemed to be wearing her invisible shield.

That wasn't terrible, Abe thought. Jerry liked a little fight.

Still, if Katie didn't succumb to the celebrity's dubious charm, there was no sense in his sticking around to take Jerry's inevitable abuse. He wished the ladies well, mentioned to Jerry that it was five minutes to showtime, and departed to the relative quiet of his upstairs office.

The Geek Chorus had installed a cutting-edge entertainment center that included a large high-definition plasma screen covering the better part of one wall. Currently on display was the web site, featuring a still shot of the brightly lit stage below. The logo – a white coffee mug featuring an Al Hirschfeld-like pen and ink caricature of Abe – bounced in one corner of the screen, continually sloshing its caffeinated contents. An incessantly blinking Day-Glo green message implored net surfers to 'Stick and Click here for Live From the Empourium Stage – Jerry Monte!'

There was a narrow drawer under his desktop that he slid toward him, exposing a white keyboard with black numerals and letters. He pressed the key numbered 'F3'. The image on the plasma wall-screen changed slightly to a live feed of the stage area, complete with ambient noise. As the actress hired to introduce Jerry moved to the mike, the Empourium T-shirt stretched taut against her football-sized implants, Abe's thumb began to play with the toggle switch the Geeks had been thoughtful enough to attach to the keyboard. It moved the room camera in a side-to-side pan and activated its zoom lens.

At his bidding, the image on the monitor closed in on Katie. She was watching Jerry leap onstage. Abe couldn't read the expression on her face, but it did not seem to be adoration. This lifted his mood, but only temporarily. He continued to focus on the woman, ignoring Jerry's stirring rendition of 'Tyger, Tyger.'

He was worried about Mace. Dropping in out of the fucking blue, asking about Angie. The man was a wild card and Abe was not a fan of wild cards.

On the big screen, Katie smiled. Her show of disinterest seemed to be shifting. Blake's poetry? Probably not. Score another for Jerry.

Abe sighed. This was not going to be one of his better nights.

SIX

Heading down the corridor at the Florian, Mace heard a moan coming from his and Wylie's room.

He paused at the door with the key in his hand, straining to listen.

Another moan. A grunt. Rustling.

Mace stepped away from the door. He located the switch for the overhead hall lights and clicked them off.

In darkness now, he pulled the gun from his belt and returned to their door. He carefully inserted his key in the lock, turning it quietly and easing the door open.

There was enough moonlight for him to see Wylie and a plump woman banging away on the cot.

The woman's bloodshot eyes popped open and she saw him standing there with the gun. She didn't say a word, but she stopped writhing under the skinny boy.

Wylie didn't seem to notice her sudden passivity. More likely, he simply didn't care.

Temporarily ignoring them, Mace moved to the window. The drapes were blocking the view into the Lowell apartment, but he could see a shadow indicating movement in the room. He turned back to the couple.

The plump woman watched his armed approach fretfully.

She still said nothing.

Mace wondered if she were mute.

Wylie's snake tattoo stretched from his neck down his back, curving at his waist and disappearing toward his lower stomach. Mace pressed the gun to a spot just above the snake's tongue and below Wylie's left ear and said, 'Bang, you're dead.'

Wylie made a noise like 'Gah,' and pushed in on the woman.

'Feeling better now?' Mace crooned. He grabbed Wylie's left ear and gave it a nasty twist. Then, continuing to twist, he forced the screaming boy off the woman.

'Lemme go, you fuckhead.'

Mace obeyed the request, pushing him on to the foot of the bed. He tucked his gun behind his belt and said to the naked woman, 'Out.'

'But I . . .' she began, not mute after all.

'But nothing.' He picked up her discarded clothes and six-inch pumps. Gripping her by a fleshy arm, he yanked her from the cot.

'Hey, wait a goddamn min—'

Before she could get to her feet, he was dragging her across the carpet to the open doorway. She tried to kick and bite as he pushed her into the darkened hall. 'Be good, or there'll be cops here,' he said. 'You'd like that, right?' He threw her clothes and shoes to her and slammed the door.

Wylie was sitting on the roiled cot rubbing his ear. 'You're a real asshole,' he grumbled.

'And you're a real pro,' Mace said. 'Yes you are.'

There was a soft knock at the door. 'My money,' the plump hooker whined.

Mace picked up Wylie's pants and found his wallet. 'How much do you owe her?'

'Fifty.'

There were two fifties and several twenties in the wallet. Mace took a fifty and a twenty, opened the door and held the bills out to the woman who already was back in her working girl outfit. She snatched them from his fingers.

'Keep the change,' he said and closed the door on her.

When he heard her mumbles fading in the direction of the stairs, he relaxed a little and left the door. He sat down at the table by the windows and stared at Wylie who was slipping on his rumpled khaki pants over bright red boxer shorts with giant mosquitoes on them.

Trying to ignore the shorts, Mace said, 'I don't suppose you noticed when the subject closed her curtains?'

Wylie didn't reply. He stared at Mace, rubbing his ear.

Mace picked up the binoculars and aimed them at the Lowell apartment.

'She was over there painting, last I looked,' Wylie said.

'When was that? A half hour ago?'

Wylie didn't answer.

The light was out in the Lowell living room, but there was shadowy activity in the other room now.

'The broad's probably making Z's,' Wylie said.

'Not quite,' Mace said, resting the binoculars on the table. 'How much did you tell your whore?'

'What?' Wylie was deeply offended. 'Nothing. Jesus, what do you think I am?'

Mace stared at him.

Withering, Wylie said, 'It's this place. Everybody was getting off but me. For all I know you were out layin' pipe.'

A glob of plastic on the rug emitted a light that caught Mace's eye. 'What the hell's that?' he asked.

Wylie scooped up the glob. 'My Crackberry,' he said. 'Musta fallen out of my pocket.' He pressed a button that extinguished the light. 'Don't tell me you never seen a Blackberry?'

Mace didn't answer.

'What kinda cellular you use?' Wylie asked, zipping up his pants.

'I don't.'

'No shit? How do you fucking . . . communicate?'

'I use those,' Mace said, pointing to the wall phone. He moved to the window and sat down, staring at Angela Lowell's now dark apartment.

Wylie picked up his shirt and put it on, leaving it unbuttoned over his concave, hairless, snake-tattooed chest. 'You, ah, gonna tell Mr Lacotta about the hooker?'

'Where's the percentage in that?'

Wylie nodded. He moved to the kitchenette counter where a bottle of Jack Daniels rested beside a couple of tumblers. He cracked the bottle. 'Thirsty?' he asked.

'Sure.'

Wylie put a couple of inches of whiskey into each tumbler. He walked to the table and sat, shoving one of the tumblers toward Mace.

Mace shot his.

Wylie followed his lead. 'Mr Lacotta says I got a future in the corporation.'

Mace said nothing. He raised his empty glass. Wylie hopped

up and retrieved the bottle. He splashed more liquor into their tumblers. 'I figure, guy's gotta have a plan, you know,' he said. 'I mean, shit, this town'll carve you up a hundred different ways you don't have a plan.'

'What's your plan?' Mace asked.

'I figured it out in upper school. Hell, that musta been three years ago. Had a lot of time to sit around, figuring things out, while these assholes kept yakking away about world history, Shakespeare and shit like that. Mr Lacotta had already told me he wanted to do something for me when I finished up. On account of my old man. You know him? Leo Guriso?'

'I met him once,' Mace said.

'He was OK. I mean he treated me and my mother OK. Just didn't know what the fuck, you know? I mean, he bought his suits at Sears. Always smelled of garlic and Old Spice.'

'Didn't have a plan,' Mace said.

'Exactly,' Wylie said. 'He was like . . . strictly blue collar. Anyway, Mr Lacotta offered. He's got a big firm, Mount Olympus Industries. Important contacts. And he needs a guy to do investigation stuff for him. Big-business private eye, right? It sounds fine to me.'

'How long you been with Mount Olympus?'

'Uh, eleven months, a couple weeks.'

'You like it?'

'Got me a title: Security Consultant. My own office. Check every other week. Free time to screw off. OK, so Mr Lacotta's on my ass to go to a fucking hair stylist and he made me burn off most of my tats. Still a fucking good deal.'

'What kind of work has he had you doing?'

Wylie thought about it. 'Checking up on personnel, mainly. Looking at the daily reports from the hired guards. Some background checks, which bore the crap out of me.'

'What was the gig before this one?'

'Gettin' the goods on one of the dudes in accounting. Found out he was ass-deep into online poker and "borrowed" thirty thou – transferring it from Olympus' slush account – until he got even. The jag-off.'

'Do much surveillance work?'

'Some. A while ago, me and this other guy, Jamey Scalise, was keepin' tabs on cars comin' and goin' at a place up near Frisco. Big fucking joint. Commingore.'

'Commingore Industries?' Mace asked.

'That's the one. They make weapons. Guns, missiles and shit.'

'Right.'

'The way things are going these days, not a bad business to be in,' Wylie said. 'I figure Mr Lacotta's interested because he and the big boss, Mr Montdrago, got some deal cookin' with 'em.'

Mace didn't bother asking what the deal might be. Paulie sure as hell wouldn't have given Wylie that information. 'See anything interesting while you were clocking the place?'

Wylie shrugged. 'All we did was copy license plate numbers and turn 'em in. After a couple weeks, we got the word to come back home. My next surveillance job is this one.'

Mace wondered if there might not be a connection between the two gigs.

Wylie poured another shot into Mace's tumbler, then his own. 'Anyway. I really need this job. I mean, if you told Mr Lacotta about the hooker . . .'

'Forget about it,' Mace said. He downed the whiskey, cleared his throat and said, 'Get some sleep. I'll roust you at four.'

Wylie nodded and moved to the bed. He dropped his pants, giving Mace another look at the ridiculous mosquito boxers. He sat on the bed, winced, and pulled a used rubber from under his thigh.

Mace leaned forward. 'Oh, lemme get rid of that for you,' he said.

Wylie held out the contraceptive.

Mace turned away from him, shaking his head sadly.

SEVEN

Angela Lowell was asleep, her blonde hair fanned out on the pillow. The thick art book she'd been reading lay nearly submerged in the bed's thick down duvet.

Mace stood beside the bed, watching her. She was only partially covered by the duvet. He found her, in peaceful slumber, to be the most beautiful woman he had ever seen. Achingly beautiful.

Her right arm was raised high on the pillow. Her full right breast had freed itself from the beribboned neckline of her sheer nightgown.

Something – an intake of his breath, a slight shifting of air current – caused her to stir.

She opened her eyes. And looked directly at him.

She smiled at him. For some reason this did not surprise him in the least.

He bent toward her and she lifted her arms to welcome him, to enfold him. Playfully, she pulled him down on top of her.

The mere touching of their lips ignited her. Her fingers tightened on his back. She breathed heavily, drawing him toward her with an urgency he, too, was feeling. Her tongue, hot and hard and pointy-tipped, slipped into his mouth.

She began tearing the clothes from his body. First the white shirt, then the belt. Fingers fumbling.

He tried to help, but, almost angrily, she insisted on doing the job herself.

He lay down on the bed and watched her remove his clothes.

She seemed fascinated by his erection. Lovingly, she began to caress it.

He moaned. He had not been with a woman in such a long time . . .

He heard his name being called.

'No,' Angela shouted, her lovely brow wrinkled in anger. 'Not now.'

She rose up and straddled him, working frantically to place him inside her. He arched his pelvis, feeling the velvety softness yield—

'Mace,' Wylie hissed in his ear. 'You gotta get up.'

Mace awoke from the dream to a room filled with sunlight. Just a few seconds more . . .

'What the hell's so fucking important?' he asked.

'Mr Lacotta just crossed the courtyard,' Wylie said.

Mace swung his legs around. The nub of the carpet scratched his bare feet. He was still groggy from sleep. And the goddamned dream. 'What time is it?'

'Almost ten,' Wylie said, the statement punctuated by a knock at the door.

'Why didn't you wake me earlier?'

'No reason to. She . . . the subject don't look like she's goin' anywhere,' Wylie said on his way to the door.

Paulie Lacotta entered, giving Wylie a manly punch on the arm. 'How's the boy?'

'Fine, Mr Lacotta.'

Lacotta turned to Mace, who was still sitting on the edge of the bed, yawning. 'You keeping banker's hours, Mace?'

'Mace had the late watch, Mr Lacotta,' Wylie said. 'Just hit the sheets a couple hours ago.'

'Drop by for breakfast, Paulie?' Mace asked. 'We're running a special on cigarettes and booze.'

Lacotta said to Wylie, 'He always this funny in the morning?'

Wylie didn't know what to say. 'He just woke up. He's—'

'What's on your mind, Paulie?' Mace asked.

'Why don't you wash your face and comb your hair, Mace. We'll go for a little sunshine.'

'Considering it's you,' Mace said, 'I'll even brush my teeth.'

EIGHT

'**N**ow this is beauty,' Lacotta said as he and Mace strolled through Griffith Park. It was green and tranquil, bathed in midday sunlight. 'Nothing like your friggin' hurricane-crazy Louisiana.'

'Nothing like.'

As they passed a field, a softball landed at Lacotta's oddly tiny feet. He picked it up and tossed it back into the game. Immediately, he began rubbing his shoulder. 'What do you do with yourself back there?'

'Rebuild. Hunt. Fish. Read books. Listen to the news, mainly the weather. Every now and then I wrestle an alligator, just to keep fit.'

'No jobs?' Lacotta asked.

'Not the way you mean it.'

'Guess you're doing OK since you sold your old man's cannery.'

'Cost of living's a little lower in Bayou Royal than here.'

'Those seven years at Pel Bay – guys go bad in there,' Lacotta said.

'Guys go bad out here in your sunshine,' Mace said, annoyed. 'What's on your mind, Paulie?'

Lacotta looked at him, squinting, maybe from the sun. 'You've changed. Maybe it was Pel Bay. Maybe fighting Mother Nature in the bayou. You're not the Mace I knew.'

'I'm older.'

'Thirties turned you curious, huh?'

'I get it. You've been talking to Abe. Honest Abe.'

'Since when did you get so chummy with pimps?' Lacotta asked, continuing his stroll.

'He owns a coffeehouse now,' Mace said. 'Makes movies.'

Lacotta snorted. 'Maybe. But he's still a pimp. And you put my friggin' business on the street.'

'Not much I could tell him, considering I don't know anything,' Mace said.

'Why can't you just do like I ask and not worry about it?'

'You know goddamn well I've never done business in the dark,' Mace said. 'Secrets make me nervous. There's enough going on in this city to confuse me as it is. I feel like fucking Rip Van Winkle without his glasses.'

'Culture shock,' Lacotta said. 'I read an article about it once, in *Vanity Fair*.' He gestured toward an empty park bench. 'One of the old Bush Must Go issues.'

When they were seated, looking out at the softball game, he said, 'I suppose I been playin' it a little too close. When I told you this was a personal matter between me and Angie, I wasn't being straight up. I guess you figured that, huh?'

'It did occur to me that you might not be paying me a couple grand a day to eyeball Angela Lowell just because she dumped you.'

'I guess I never was the jealous type,' Lacotta said. 'Not that I'm Joe-Don't-Care, exactly. Remember the Irish broad who worked at On the Rox? All that red hair and a body that—'

'Let's take it one romance at a time,' Mace said.

Lacotta smiled at him. 'You know what used to piss me off about you, Mace? You always knew what I was thinking before I did.'

'Not always,' Mace said.

'Yeah, well, spilled milk. Look, the deal with me and Angie, some of it's personal and some of it isn't.'

'Tell me about the "isn't,"' Mace said.

Lacotta shifted on the bench as if the subject matter was adding to his physical discomfort. 'Angie and me, we were getting along just fine until right around the time the trouble started.'

'You want me to ask what trouble?' Mace said. 'OK. What trouble?'

'I had this deal in place. A little out of my league, but with the potential of moving me into the bigs. I swear, the payday was gonna impress even my prick uncle, Sal.'

'What happened?'

'It turned to shit and the next I know, Angie is suddenly

unavailable. About the third "sorry, but I'm busy that night", I went a little nuts, like I do. Getting her back in my bed was the only thing on my mind. I even asked her to marry . . . Hell, I tried everything short of kidnapping her ass.'

'Why stop there?'

'It's too much like rape, which is sick. Oh, I get it. That was a joke.'

'Not much of one, I guess,' Mace said.

'Anyway, I gave it my best shot, but she was no longer interested. Once I finally calmed down and accepted defeat, I went back to being my usual cynical rat-bastard self. I mean, nobody with an ounce of smarts believes in coincidence where money is concerned.'

'You figure she helped the deal go south,' Mace said. 'Only you don't have any proof. Is there anything particular that you hope we catch her doing?'

'Remember Tiny Daniels?' Lacotta said.

'Hard to forget anything that big that wasn't floating in some parade. He still angling for your job?'

'Not any more. He's been on his own for a while.'

'And here I thought *I* was special, getting out with my head still attached.'

'Even more amazing, the fat fuck was cutting all these deals on the side while he was still working for us. With the Russkies. The Colombians. The Chinese. For all I know, the terrorist crowd. No morality whatsoever. Sal nearly had a fucking coronary when he found out. But he just let Tiny stroll.'

'Sal Montdrago suddenly get religion? Mace asked.

'The Mighty M gets religion about the time the Holy Ghost gets his own talk show. What happens, Tiny says he has some heavy insurance in place that can bring down the corporation and make Uncle Sal do the Gotti. Maybe it's a bluff, but it's keepin' the fat man alive and wheezing in his own little six-mill tear-down out by Point Dume.'

'And how does this relate to Angela Lowell?'

Lacotta squirmed again on the rough bench. 'I get word Angie's keeping company with Tiny. So you see my position?'

'Starting to.'

'Did she have anything to do with the deal fuck-up? Has Tiny taken over the project? I got to know the answers before my uncle gets back in town and starts asking me the questions. That's why I need you, Mace. Somebody I can trust.'

'What's the project?'

Lacotta frowned. 'You're better off not knowing.'

'How much does Wylie know?'

'Bupkis. He doesn't even think about what he doesn't know, 'cause he's my man. He reports to me. We got a rigid line of communications at Mount Olympus now. Very streamlined. Very smooth.'

'It doesn't sound that way,' Mace said. Feeling suddenly restless, he rose from the bench. Reluctantly, Lacotta followed. 'Suppose Angela Lowell is cozying up to the fat man, what happens then?'

'Whadyamean?'

'Is it the last we see of Angela?'

'No way,' Lacotta said. 'This is just an information thing. Once I know what's what, I'll know how to get my tit out of the wringer.'

That didn't make sense to Mace. There was more to the story. He was about to press for it when a tall black man in a long black coat, apparently one of the homeless army, staggered toward them.

'You gen'mens got a dollah you kin spare?' he asked.

Lacotta gave the man a hard, get-the-fuck-away glare.

Mace put his hand in his pocket and Lacotta said 'Don't do that.'

Mace got out his wallet and removed a dollar. He handed it to the black man who accepted it with a grin. 'Thank you, suh.'

He held the bill out to Lacotta. 'Heah. This fo' you.'

'I don't want your friggin' money,' Lacotta said.

'It's fo' you. A dolla' to blow me.'

'What?' Lacotta couldn't believe his ears.

'Man say you a dollah blow job. Heah's the dollah.' He tucked the bill into Lacotta's coat pocket, crushing the white display handkerchief.

Furious, Lacotta grabbed the black man's coat collar. 'What man said that?' he yelled.

Grinning, the black man slipped a hand into the pocket of his long coat and brought hand and coat and maybe something else up near Lacotta's mid-section. 'The fat man. He say, "Bye-bye, asshole".'

With amazing speed, Mace kicked the black man's ankle causing him to stumble away from Lacotta just as the gun in his pocket went off.

Lacotta yelled and stepped back. Mace moved closer to the black man, his hand controlling the gun in the pocket, holding it aside as he head-butted the man.

Blood gushed from the black man's broken nose. He tried to pull free, but Mace held the hand trapped in the coat. 'Lemme . . . LEMME,' the man wailed as Mace spun him around, forcing the trapped hand into a position where the wrist could do nothing but break.

When it did, Mace yanked the freed weapon from the over-coat pocket.

He swatted the man's head with it, sending him to ground. There, it was easier to use his shoe. He was kicking the man in the head when he felt someone grab his arm.

He spun around, fist cocked for the punch, and saw it was Lacotta. Even then, he almost let loose.

Lacotta backed away, a bit unnerved. 'Let's get outta here,' he said.

Mace blinked.

The park was in silence. The ballplayers, the dog walkers, the strollers were all frozen in place, staring at them. The only thing in motion, as far as Mace could see, was the black man staggering away, cradling his broken wrist and spitting and snorting to clear the blood from his nose and mouth.

Lacotta approached warily to take the gun and slip it into his pocket. He led Mace by the arm to the parked car. He said, 'Still got your temper, I see.'

'Seems like,' Mace said, though it had not manifested itself in years. There'd been one time, during his first week at Pelican Bay. But not in the next seven years on the yard there. And not in flare-ups in the meanest bars a man could find in Cajun Louisiana. Just two days back in LA and he'd gone off. What did that tell him?

Mace got into the car.

As they drove away, he asked Lacotta. 'You hurt?'

'Naw. Maybe some burns on the suit, which is goin' direct to Goodwill.' Lacotta grinned, then started laughing. Soon he was laughing so hard tears appeared at the corner of his eyes. 'I told you not to give that fuck the dollar, didn't I?' he said between bursts of nervous laughter.

NINE

S tanding in front of The Florian, Mace watched Lacotta's Mercedes glide away heading for the Strip. After the encounter with the gunman in the park, he realized he was operating at about eighty percent of normal, but his reflexes were off enough to make him feel uncomfortable. The midday warmth had his clothes sticking to his body. If he were home, he could strip and dive into the bayou to cool off and clear his head. He thought about the Florian pool. Swimming trunks hadn't been at the top of his packing list. He supposed it wouldn't be that hard to find a pair for sale in LA.

His mind was on the therapeutic effect of a mile-long swim as he passed the entrance to the Florian's parking garage. Which may be why he didn't hear the clicks right from the jump. He was almost to the iron gate leading to the pool when he noticed the sound.

He did an about-face, scanning the area.

Nothing. No motion. No sound.

He took another couple of steps toward the pool gate.

This time, he was waiting for the click and was able to get a directional fix on it. There were only three vehicles parked in that section of the garage. The Jag sedan and the Lexus RX were sealed up tight. The grape-colored Cherokee with a bashed in front right fender had its windows rolled down.

Mace double-timed it into the garage and the Cherokee to find a panicked man stretched out across its front seats on his back, clutching a camera to his chest. The car was a mess of fast food containers, plastic pop bottles, rumpled clothes. The man was in his forties. Bald. His nervous eyes were tiny and slightly slanted. They, his off-white color, roman nose and high cheekbones suggested an ethnic mix too complex for Mace to sort out, even if it mattered. He was wearing faded brown cargo shorts and a yellow T-shirt emblazoned with the question: 'Who Directed WILD SEX IN THE COUNTRY?'

Seeing Mace at the passenger window, he tried to slide under the steering wheel.

Mace yanked the door open, grabbed one sandaled foot and dragged the man out of the vehicle. The man's head hit the side of the car and the garage's cement floor, but he held the camera protectively.

Mace pried it from his fingers.

'Th-that's my property,' he whined. 'Shit, I think I chipped a tooth. And my fucking head . . . I'm gonna sue your fucking ass.'

Mace ignored him. He was trying to make some sense of the camera.

'Be careful, goddamnit,' the man said as he got to his feet, using the car to steady himself. 'That's eight grand you're holding.'

'How do I get the film out?' Mace asked.

'The . . . film?' The man looked like he didn't know if he should laugh or cry. 'There's no film.'

'What'd you do with it?' Mace asked, stepping toward him.

The man backed up, bumping against the Cherokee. 'There's no film,' he screamed at Mace. 'It's a digital . . . an EOS-1D. Top of the line.'

Mace looked from him to the camera. 'The photos are on a disc or what?' he asked.

'A Fat32 memory card.' He reached out a hand. 'I can show—'

'No. Tell me.'

'OK.' He talked Mace through the camera's image playback set-up. 'Hit that button,' he said, 'the photo can be magnified as much as twenty-five times. At eleven point one megapixels, you can—'

'These six shots of me all you took?'

The man hesitated, then said, 'No. I took twelve, total.'

'How do I get rid of them?'

'Key that command.'

'This one? "Erase all?"'

'Oh, Jesus, no. I got over fifty shots in there. Even some of Gaga without the wig. Please. Just delete the snaps I took of you.'

Mace started on that, going one at a time, to make sure.

'I can never figure you fuckers out. It's all publicity, man. I don't get why guys like you and Clooney try to take my fucking head off. I don't get in your face like some. I respect your space. Still, you guys throw shit at me. Hit me. Bounce my head on concrete. I can't even get health insurance any more . . .'

Mace was barely listening to the guy. When he was finished deleting his photos, he handed over the camera.

The man took it eagerly, cuddling it like it was a favorite pet. 'You guys think we're all lowlifes, right? Bottom feeders. Fuck you. We make you guys.'

Mace didn't know what the hell the man was going on about. 'Who told you to take my picture?'

There was an aluminum case open on the Cherokee's back seat with two cameras nestled in foam rubber pockets. The photographer placed the EOS-1D in the remaining pocket. 'Told me? Nobody told me. It's just what I do.'

Mace saw that the question asked on the front of the man's T-shirt was answered on the back. 'I DID.' He grabbed the man's shoulder and spun him around.

'C'mon, buddy. Leave me alone, for Christ's sake. You got what you wanted.'

'Who told you to take my picture?'

The man looked genuinely puzzled. His free hand moved toward his pants pocket. Mace stopped it.

'What's your fucking problem?' the man whined, trying to release his wrist from Mace's grip. 'I just wanna give you my card. OK? Just my fucking card.'

Mace released his wrist.

Slowly, he removed a worn, overloaded wallet from his pocket. He fished a bright yellow card from it that he handed to Mace. 'I'm Simon S. Symon. Like it says there. Proprietor of ShootOnSite. That's me. I take candid pictures of celebrities.'

'This is supposed to make me like you more?' Mace said. 'Who told you to take my picture?'

'Listen to Mister Me. Like you're the reason I'm here.'

'Talk straight.'

'The night man at the Florian's an old bud, so he phones me real late to tell me some guest just blew through the lobby with Deidre Lindstrom. They're stoned. Feelin' each other up, almos' goin' down on each other right there in the lobby.

'So I grab a few hours of snooze and here I am. A shot of Deidre looking hungover will be worth maybe two grand, three. But the guest, some kinda TV exec from back East, ain't a guy. Now that hikes the price of the photo considerably. That's the guest's Audi across the aisle. They gotta show up sooner or—'

'You took pictures of *me*,' Mace said. 'Why?'

'You're somebody, right? Got that don't-fuck-with-me look. To me that says photo op. My guess is TV, right? I can't keep track of everybody on the box, what with cable and all. But you TV pricks are the toughest to get along with. And we make you guys.'

Mace stared at Simon S. Symon, trying to decide if it was worth knocking him around a little to make sure he wasn't bullshitting. The sound of heels clicking on concrete made the decision suddenly moot.

Mace glimpsed someone at the far end of the garage.

Simon S. Symon had already grabbed his camera.

But it wasn't Deidre Lindstrom and her lesbian exec from back East. It was Angela Lowell, dressed for summer in tight white slacks and a black silk blouse.

Mace moved between the Cherokee and the SUV. 'Fifty bucks for a couple of good clear prints of her,' he whispered to the paparazzi.

'No prob,' Symon said.

'I gotta run. Pick up at the address on your card?'

'Yeah,' Symon said, busy getting Angela in his frame.

Mace headed toward his leased Camry Hybrid, hopping over car bumpers to avoid Angela's line of sight. He was sliding under the steering wheel by the time she drove past.

Backing the Camry from its stall he saw Wylie running full out from the stairwell carrying a small laptop. 'I got her,' Mace shouted to the boy.

'What about this?' Wylie held up the laptop.

'I don't need it.' In point of fact, he had no idea how the tracking device hidden in the Mustang's trunk worked.

As he drove past the Cherokee, he was annoyed to see Symon aiming his camera at Wylie.

TEN

Angela Lowell couldn't find a coin for the meter.

Sitting several parked cars back on Melrose Avenue, in a loading zone, Mace watched her root through her handbag, then duck back into the yellow Mustang, probably to rifle the glove compartment. Finally, she gave up the search and decided to risk the ticket.

She literally ran into a shop with the enigmatic name of Slick.

Unless she returned to feed the meter, indicating she would be spending some time there, he wouldn't bother following her inside.

From his angle he couldn't see anything on the storefront to indicate what sort of goods or service Slick provided. Its Spartan display window offered few clues. Just a white plastic tree on Astroturf. Colorful little squiggly things were hanging from the tree's otherwise bare branches. Mace counted three customers, male, going into the store before Angela emerged with a package the size of a large book under her arm. She tossed it casually into the rear of the Mustang and slid behind the wheel.

He let her enter the traffic flow along Melrose before nosing the Camry out. As he drove past Slick's window, he discovered that the squiggly things hanging from the tree were contraceptives.

Angela's next stop was on Hollywood Boulevard. Triple

Tech, an ultra-contemporary aluminum Quonset hut, with a chrome and neon facade as understated as a slot machine and about as appealing. She found a parking space directly in front.

Mace backed into the only other open slot, eight or nine cars down. Facing the street, he was able to watch the Mustang and Triple Tech's front door in the Camry's rear-view. This time, it took no imagination to figure out what the place was peddling: computer games and other electronic crap.

In less than five minutes, she emerged with a small bag of what he presumed were expensive non-essentials. She surprised him by walking away from the Mustang, heading for a flash clothes store named Cruise Line. In its window, two male mani-kins, dressed in yachting gear, lay spooning on a wooden deck chair, while a third, wearing a US Navy officer's cap and a thong stood at a ship's wheel with a martini glass in one hand.

Returning to the Mustang with arms full of merchandise, Angela took her shopping expedition to Honeymoon Way, an unassuming semi-commercial street between Sunset and Hollywood Boulevard. She parked at an old, brick building that housed two presumably separate enterprises, the Honeymoon Drug Store and Schlesinger's Gun Shop.

Mace was growing restless. His watch told him he'd been following her for nearly an hour and it seemed to have been a waste of time. As far as he could tell, the woman was just shopping. As he watched her stride into the drug store, her body language gave no suggestion of anything out of the ordinary.

But the store was another matter. Its lighted display window featured an assortment of aloe lotion bottles in front of a card-board diorama depicting a woman slathering her naked, lobster-red sunburned back with the stuff. An innocuous-seeming display. But it blocked a view of the shop's interior. As did the frosted glass panels of its old-fashioned wooden front doors.

It was as if Angela Lowell had walked into a dark cloud and faded away.

The set-up seemed . . . suspicious. He supposed the cloudy glass may have been used to ward off direct sunlight. But the dark green awning that covered both doors and display window should have taken care of that. Was there a reason they were hiding the interior of the drug store?

Was this assignment fucking up his head? He was afraid he knew the answer to that one.

He concentrated on the opaque glass panels, saw or imagined vague shadowy motion in the store. Finally, he took a deep breath, exhaled, shook his head and got out of the car.

An old-fashioned bell tinkled as he entered the Honeymoon Drug Store. The place was a throwback to the days before chain superstores. Black and white tile floor, high ceiling, wood and glass counters. Boxes and bottles neatly shelved against the walls. There was even a small soda fountain, dark and unused. At the rear of the room a middle-aged druggist in a crisp white coat was talking to a boy wearing cargo pants and a Lakers T. The boy was carrying a skateboard under one arm. A few elderly Hispanic women were studying a cosmetic display to his left.

It reminded Mace a little of the drug store his father had used, where he had spent so much time on medication runs during the old man's last days. In spite of the association, he'd liked that store. And he would have liked this one, except for one thing. Angela Lowell wasn't in it.

Mace moved to a postcard rack. Idly pawing an assortment of glossy ultra-ugly photos of LA by day and night, he scanned the store, convincing himself that she wasn't behind a counter or display.

Puzzled and annoyed, he exited the store. He turned to give it one last look, took a backward step and bumped into someone.

It was Angela Lowell, hurrying to her car. She seemed angry.

'Sorry,' he said.

'It helps if you look where you're going,' she said, continuing on to the Mustang.

Feeling like a fucking idiot, Mace stood there watching her get into the car. Finally, he pried his feet from the sidewalk and went back to work.

The Mustang led him to Sunset Boulevard, where a traffic light stopped them just as, to their right, Hollywood High had ended its school day. A group of pierced, tattooed, spike-haired, tattered-bloused schoolgirls were thumbing a ride. They caught Mace staring at them and waved their hands. A female student with hair the color of flamingo feathers and a voluptuousness that seemed advanced for her years placed a hand under one partially-exposed breast as if offering it to him.

Just what I need, Mace thought, shifting his glare from the girl to the Mustang.

To distance himself further from the delights of statutory rape, he pressed on the Camry's dash panels, hoping to uncover the car's cigarette lighter. The Camry had its good points, chief among them being anonymity. At first glance it looked like half a dozen other charcoal gray sedans. And he liked the keyless ignition system and the hybrid engine's silence that allowed you to lurk unnoticed with the motor running. But there was a lot of crap he found unnecessary, like the LED monitor on the dash that kept a running tally of gas consumption. And the panels hiding necessities like ashtrays.

And the goddamned cigarette lighter.

A metal door flipped up, exposing a plug for a cellular phone and the lighter. He got a cigarette going, then punched on the radio and began scanning past the rap, rock and Spanish-speaking stations. The traffic opened up and as the Mustang made a turn on to Sunset, he settled on a shock-jock show.

It was stop-and-go along Sunset in the shadow of the giant ego stroking billboards. One of them, devoted to Jerry Monte, featured the superstar and blossoming poet standing on a windswept mountain top in tight black leather pants and a flowing open white silk shirt. The caption read: 'The Legend Continues.'

On the radio, a female call-in was complaining that her husband 'was lucky if he got it up twice a week.'

'Maybe you should slip a little blue pill into his oatmeal, honey,' the jock suggested with a leer in his voice.

'I tried that,' the caller said, whining now. 'All it did was give him the added excuse of a headache.'

'OK, then you gotta slip the dude a roofie, babe. I'm a big believer in love chemistry.'

'Shit,' Mace grumbled and snapped off the radio.

He drove in angry silence, filling the car with cigarette smoke that the air conditioner battled but could not defeat. His discomfort and increasing depression almost made him miss the Mustang's sudden burst through an opening in the traffic.

Cautiously, he followed the yellow convertible's lead, squeaking through a changing traffic light.

The Mustang continued up Sunset past the Florian, past the Strip with its shops and bars and restaurants. Past Honest Abe's Coffee Empourium which looked dreary and deserted in the sunshine.

The traffic fell off as they cruised beside UCLA where students walked and jogged, evidence that there were still some pockets of normalcy in the city.

Crossing over the San Diego Freeway, Mace relaxed a little and tried the radio again, this time giving the FM band a spin. He settled on a jazz station broadcasting from Long Beach. He wasn't what you would call a jazz lover, but it served his mood as the drive continued.

Gliding easily along Sunset's snake-like turns, he tried to figure out how Angela Lowell had exited the drug store. She'd been coming from the direction of Schlesinger's Gun Shop. Were the two stores connected? He hoped so, because that meant she may have had business in both. If, on the other hand, she had gone out the back of the drug store and into Schlesinger's through its rear, that would suggest she'd spotted him tailing her and was now aware of his presence.

Even in the air-cooled car, he felt a drop in the outside temperature as they approached the ocean. The Mustang turned on to the Coast Highway, heading north.

Another few miles and both cars passed under the Malibu sign. Eventually they left the Coast Highway at Wildlife Road heading in the direction of a strand of beachfront mini-mansions in a gated community called Point Dume Estates.

The high-end homes had been built in the Eighties to fill the needs of the excessively wealthy, television and film folk in the main, who, for unspecified reasons, were unable to secure residency in The Colony. The Dume Estates crowd could rest assured that they were in the second most elite section of Malibu and that their ridiculous monthly mortgage payments were buying them privacy from the common herd, if not from fire, high tides, rodent infestation and septic tank malfunctions.

Mace followed the Mustang, staying what he thought was a safe distance behind. But he was caught off-guard by how close the Estates's security gate was, once you turned south off Wildlife on to Dolphin Way.

The Mustang was barely two car-lengths from him, stopped at a white booth with an orange roof that resembled the tile roofs on the beach front homes resting beyond and below. He braked, but it was too late. Angela Lowell may not have seen him. She could have had her eyes on the gate being raised and, that completed, the road ahead. But the guard standing just outside the booth was facing his way, giving him the Ray-Ban once-over.

That couldn't be helped.

Mace put the Camry into reverse and began engineering a U-turn away from the gate, conscious of the guard focusing on him and the car. He was a big man, black, wearing a brown uniform and a sea-green helmet. He said something and a second uniformed guard, this one white, appeared from behind the booth.

Mace had to blink to make sure he was seeing properly. The white guard seemed to be riding a big motorized two-wheel scooter, rolling his way at surprising speed.

The white guard yelled out, 'Sir . . . ?'

Mace ignored him, as much as you can ignore a guy on a motor-driven scooter shouting at you. He straightened out and drove off, following Dolphin Way to Dume Drive. Making the turn, he took a final look back and saw the white guard, standing atop his scooter, turning it in a slow circle, eyeballing him.

ELEVEN

Mace picked up a late portable lunch at The Malibu Country Mart, an upscale mall in the vicinity. He was heading for his car, scowling because he'd just paid fifteen dollars for a cup of coffee and a Swiss-cheese sandwich, when he saw a pack of paparazzi pressing in on a young brunette wearing big sunglasses and a tiny summer dress. Mace had no idea who the girl was, though he gathered her name was 'Gigi,' since that was what the monkey-like photographers were shouting to catch her attention.

She didn't seem to be aware of their existence, but her bodyguard, a black mountain of muscle with a communication device screwed in his right ear, was struggling to keep from swatting the scruffy interlopers from their path. He looked hot and uncomfortable in his gray suit and he kept repeating, 'Stand back, please,' as if it were a mantra that he didn't really believe in.

Part of the passing Malibu parade.

Mace carried his overpriced lunch to the Camry and returned to Wildlife Road, parking half a block before Dolphin Way where he could dine while observing the traffic leaving Point Dume Estates. He lowered the car's windows and took advantage of the cool ocean breeze.

For a while, he entertained himself by studying the sea birds as they rode the wind currents. But after nearly an hour their graceful glides began to have a hypnotic effect. His eyelids were at half-mast when he heard someone clear his throat with a pointed 'A-hem!'

He jerked awake to see a man standing near the car, staring into his open window. The guy was in his forties, a British stereotype, complete with off-white silk suit, ascot and brush moustache. Smiling genially. Not at all threatening.

'Help you?' Mace asked him.

'My friends and I would love for you to join us.' A British accent, no surprise. He made a graceful gesture with a thin, pale hand, indicating a baby-shit-yellow limousine, the ugliest color Mace had ever seen, parked on the opposite side of the road.

'It's hideous,' the Brit said, 'but the interior amenities are excellent. And one has the advantage, while seated inside, of not being able to see very much of the exterior.'

The reflection of the sun on the limo's windows effectively kept Mace from getting a sense of who the Brit's friends were, exactly. The open rear door didn't show much more, other than a foot or so of dark brown rug and tan leather seat.

'I'm pretty comfortable right here,' he said.

'Aren't you the least bit curious?'

Mace was. But not enough to get into a limo with strangers, even if he'd had a gun, which he didn't. 'You'll have to do better than that,' he said.

The Brit sighed. He stared up at the sun and winced. 'We were wondering why you're parked here?'

'Any reason why I shouldn't be?'

'That remains to be seen,' the Brit said.

Mace reached out suddenly and pressed the Camry's starter. The car came alive almost immediately. But before he could move it into drive, he felt cold metal pressed against his neck.

'Don't be rude,' the Brit said. 'I must insist you join us.'

Mace turned off the engine.

The Brit hopped back to avoid the car door should Mace attempt to swing it into him. He held his weapon steady and professionally while Mace got out of the car. As the two of them walked across the road to the mustard limo, Mace was able to see enough of the back of the driver's head and neck to tell he was a black man wearing a white shirt, a black coat and sunglasses. He faced straight ahead as if his only interest was in the open road.

Before entering the vehicle, Mace looked in at the other passenger. He blinked, and then looked again. What he thought he was seeing was a huge cowboy hunched forward on the leather-covered rear seat as if in eager anticipation. But it wasn't the man's western gear – the well-worn Levis, boots, a battered and sweat-stained Stetson – that made him doubt his vision. The Hollywood cowboy's face was a duplicate of the twenty-something Elvis Presley's, complete with sleepy eyes, curled upper lip and droopy jaw.

As Mace got into the car, the Presley lookalike drew back, pushing as far away as possible. Then, with his lip curling even more contemptuously, he performed a smooth quick draw from his elaborately stitched holster.

Mace paused, staring at the six-gun pointed at his chest.

'Holster your weapon, Timmie,' the Brit said.

'Why should I?' The cowboy Elvis seemed to be mocking the man, imitating his accent. 'You've got a gun.'

'I'm the elder. That means you have to obey me.'

Timmie returned his six-gun to its holster and folded his arms, staring forward, pouting.

Mace sat, trying not to brush against him.

The Brit took the remaining seat and pulled the door shut. 'All in, Sweets,' he shouted to the chauffeur.

Mace heard the locks engage. He saw no release buttons on the doors. It was probably why the Brit had put away his gun. As long as the driver was in control of the doors, Mace wasn't going anywhere.

Sweets put the limo in motion and the Brit asked Mace, 'Might I take a peek at your billfold, old man?'

'You boys have a very classy mugging style,' Mace said, handing over his wallet.

The Brit gave its contents a quick study. 'Mr Mason is it? Do tell us what you find so alluring about this part of Southern California.'

'What's not to like?'

'We were thinking you may be interested in a resident of Point Dume Estates.'

'Don't know a soul there,' Mace said.

The Elvis cowboy whipped his gun out again. 'Liar, liar, pants on fire,' he said, and jammed its barrel into Mace's side. It hurt.

'Timmie!' the Brit said. 'Put the gun away.'

Timmie the Elvis cowboy glared at him. 'He told a lie. You punish me when I tell a lie,' he said. Then, with an elaborate twirl of the gun he plopped it into its holster.

'He's very intuitive,' the Brit said to Mace. 'Of course, even I know you're lying.' He leaned forward and said loudly enough for the chauffeur to hear, 'Sweets, plug in the name "David Mason", Louisiana driver's license EQ3256987.'

He repeated the license number and returned the wallet to Mace who stuck it in his pocket without much thought. He was too intrigued by the chauffeur. The more he saw of him the more familiar he seemed. He shifted to get a better view, but the chauffeur turned his head away. His mouth was moving. Possibly mumbling to himself, but more likely taking to some distant party via a hidden device.

'You could save us time and effort, Mr Mason, if you simply told us why you were parked where we found you.'

'I was about to take a snooze,' Mace said.

The Brit sighed again. 'Perhaps you could tell us the name of your employer?'

'I'm self-employed. But I'm not working now. I'm on vacation.'

'He-e's fib-bing,' Timmie said in sing-song. He leaned closer to Mace and whispered. 'Do not lie to Thomas. My brother can be mean. He won't let me eat chocolate.'

Mace looked at the Brit whose name was apparently Thomas. 'Timmie's your brother?'

For a moment Thomas's face seemed to soften. But only for a moment. 'When Timmie was born, an attendant at the hospital made a mistake,' he said. 'One thousand cc's of something or other, instead of one hundred. I was six at the time. Unaware of how that little mistake might affect both our lives.'

'He good for anything besides comic relief,' Mace asked.

Timmie's huge right hand suddenly grabbed Mace's throat and began to squeeze.

Mace gasped and clutched at Timmie's fingers, trying to pry them free.

'TIMMIE!' his brother shouted. 'LET HIM GO!'

Timmie didn't obey.

His fingers were like iron, unyielding. Within seconds, Mace felt his strength and his life ebbing away.

Then, suddenly, the hand was gone and he slumped forward experiencing a hot flush as his blood started to circulate again. Timmie was happily playing with a Rubik's Cube that his brother had used to distract him. His large fingers, the same ones that had nearly choked Mace to death, were moving the sections of the Cube quickly and efficiently.

'Sorry about that, Mason,' the Brit whispered to him. 'But you mustn't nettle him. He may be mentally challenged but physically he's . . . well, you've experienced his strength.'

'Were you talking about me?' Timmie asked. He tossed the Cube back to his brother, its puzzle solved. 'What were you saying?'

'Your brother says you're very strong,' Mace said.

'I am. I am . . . like Superman. I have a Superman costume I wear sometimes. Don't I, Thomas?'

'Yes, you do.'

'No Batman costume?' Mace asked.

'Batman is ugly,' Timmie said. 'Superman is handsome. Like Timmie. I have a lot of costumes. I make movies.'

'Silence, Timmie,' his brother said.

Mace leaned back against the seat and waited for the pain in his neck to subside.

The limo zoomed along Sorrel Canyon Road though light traffic.

Then, suddenly, the driver spun the wheel and Mace became aware of a plaster cast on the man's right hand and wrist. And he knew where he'd seen Sweets before. In Griffith Park, where Sweets had tried to kill Paulie.

The limo made a right turn and began traveling on a macadam full of more potholes than Sweets was able to avoid. Mace had had a vague idea of where they were, but this road wasn't on his memory map. It may not have been on any map.

At first, eccentric plaster and wood houses dotted the landscape, trucks sharing their gravel driveways with old cars in need of paint and patching. But, after a couple of miles, the macadam was replaced by a plowed dirt road that was so narrow Mace wondered what might happen if they met another vehicle coming the other way.

Maybe Timmie would get out and lift it over the limo.

There was nothing but foliage out there on either side. No sign of human life, nor any of the accoutrements of human life, such as electricity or phone landlines. Not even barbedwire fences or private-property signs.

'Where exactly are we?' Mace asked.

'Just a nice quiet country road,' Thomas said.

'Where are we headed?'

'That depends on you, actually.'

The rough road bounced them around. Timmie did not seem to be enjoying the jouncing. 'Make it smoother,' he said.

'Pretend you're riding a stagecoach,' Thomas suggested.

Timmie grinned. 'Goin' to Deadwood.'

'You're right about him being intuitive,' Mace said.

'He's many things,' Thomas said. 'Some good, some bad.'

'You're talking about me again,' Timmie said. 'What?'

'Your brother was saying you can do many things,' Mace said.

'I can.'

'But he said you're not strong enough to kick that door open.'

'I did not say that, Timmie. Do not kick—'

Timmie had already smashed his boot against the door, jarring it from its frame.

'Don't you dare . . .' Thomas said.

But his brother booted the door again, this time flinging it open. The limo's forward thrust swung it back in place and, giggling, Timmie kicked it open again, this time knocking it from one of its hinges, so that it dragged along scraping against the road, stirring up dust.

The rear of the limo was filled with wind and noise and Timmie yelled, 'This is fun,' and tried to move over Mace to get at the other door next to his brother.

'NO. NO. DON'T,' Thomas shouted.

Pinned to the back seat by Timmie's massive body, Mace used the opportunity to slide the six-gun from the big man's holster. Thomas' gun was trapped by his linen coat, which was, in turn trapped by his brother's legs. He struggled to pull the weapon free.

'Leave it,' Mace said, pointing the six-gun at Thomas.

Thomas ignored the threat. 'Do you think I'd give him real bullets?' he said.

Mace aimed the gun at Thomas' face and pulled the trigger. Click.

'Give me my gun,' Timmie said.

'Sure,' Mace said and smashed the gun's barrel against Timmie's cheek.

The giant wailed. A tiny cut on his cheek opened up and Timmie touched it. When he saw the blood, he stopped crying. His face turned red and he scowled and began waving his arms. He rolled backward on to his brother.

Mace felt a large boot heel digging into his right shoulder. He brought the gun down on the big man's ankle. With a screech, Timmie straightened his leg, pushing Mace to the side of the car near the open door.

Mace took it from there.

The limo had slowed because of the rough road. Mace checked to make sure there were no upcoming trees, threw the empty gun at the giant and dove through the door.

He pulled his arms close to his chest and let his legs go limp, hitting the mud and scrub grass hard. When his body settled, before the pain could take over, he forced himself to get to his feet and run into the foliage.

The limo seemed to be driving on, the door still hanging open, leaving a cloud of dust.

Groaning, he weaved through the bushes and high grass. He barely thought about the other living creatures that might be sharing the canyon with him. Snakes. Wildcats. Cougars. He'd survived a boyhood among coral snakes, water moccasins and alligators. He'd take any or all over having to stand within arm's distance of Timmie.

He figured the limo driver was probably looking for a place where he could turn around. Then they'd drive back, maybe searching for him, maybe not. His plan was to hunker down within earshot of the road, wait for them to pass and then hike out.

It wouldn't be pleasant.

He wasn't dressed for a hike and his shoes were not made for it. And there was some pain. His right shoulder ached. Right elbow. Left knee.

He rotated the shoulder, straightened his right arm. No breaks.

So far, so good.

He hadn't taken more than a few steps when he heard the limo returning.

He ducked down, well out of sight and listened as it drew closer.

And stopped.

He held his breath.

'MR MASON?' It was Thomas. Surely he didn't expect a reply.

'WE ONLY WANT TO TALK!'

They waited a minute or two, then the limo's engine revved and rolled on.

Mace stood up slowly, in time to see the mustard-colored vehicle moving away, raising a wake of dust.

Only want to talk? He hoped to hell that was a lie. Otherwise he'd put himself through a lot of crap for nothing. It was definitely bullshit, he decided. They didn't have to drive up a deserted country road just to talk. And he'd already had a sampling of Sweets' way with words.

He decided to screw caution and save himself some scratches and tears by using the road. But there was the possibility that he might hike around a curve and find them parked, waiting for him. So he decided to rest for an hour or so. He figured the childlike Timmie wouldn't let them sit still any longer than that.

He found a comfortable spot on the ground beneath a tree and went to sleep.

He woke over an hour later, sweaty, filthy and sore. He stood, stretched and worked his limbs, then started walking. He was surprised that there wasn't more pain. Tomorrow, probably.

He paused to slap dust from his coat, but that didn't improve anything, so the hell with it. He draped the coat over his shoulder, Sinatra-style, and continued walking until he hit Sorrel Canyon Road. There he tested the generosity of drivers on their way in the direction of the ocean.

He didn't see the mustard limo again.

TWELVE

Night fell before he was offered a ride by a big Hawaiian with a Charlie Chan moustache-soul patch combo and heavily muscled arms that extended from a wife-beater sweat that read 'He IS The Way.' The rear of the man's dust-caked, powder-blue van was filled with yellow pamphlets that Mace guessed carried some religious pitch since the driver had holy pictures stuck to the dash, along with plastic statues of, if he remembered his catechism correctly, Jesus, Mary and Joseph.

Another clue came from the van's radio, a music show that billed itself the Christian Top Twenty Countdown.

During the short run to Wildlife Road, Mace was amazed by the facility with which Christian songwriters were able to find rhymes for 'Jesus,' though, for the most part, 'sees us,' 'frees us' and 'please us' filled the bill.

'That yo' cah?' the Hawaiian asked, indicating the Camry parked by the side of the road.

Mace could see no limo of any color lurking anywhere in the vicinity. He told the Hawaiian that it was indeed his car. 'About that canyon where you picked me up . . . ?' he said.

'Sorrel Canyon? Yeah?'

'Around fifteen miles east of PCH, there's a road that angles off to the right. Any idea where it goes?'

The big man shook his head. 'All I know, Sorrel takes me from the I-10 to PCH. Them side roads, nothin' but distractions. Like strayin' from the true path.'

'Well, thanks for the lift, friend,' Mace said, getting out of the van.

'Peace be with you, brudda. Let the Lord Jesus Chris' shine his light into yo' soul.'

'Back at you,' Mace said.

The van turned and headed off in the direction of the Coast Highway. Mace watched it until it disappeared into the dark.

He did not get into the Camry.

Instead, he walked the short distance toward Dolphin Way. He had no particular plan. He'd check on the guards, see what they were up to. Then he thought he might scout a little, maybe find a footpath down to the beach that avoided the security post.

The section of the road by the gate was brightly lit, as was the gatehouse.

He saw no sign of any guards, which was odd. If you were paying top dollar for the security of a gated community, especially one as exclusive as this, having guards there at night made more sense than having them during the daylight hours.

Maybe they'd been called away?

He supposed that happened every now and then. Somebody might get drunk and rambunctious. Kids might get loud enough for the nearest neighbor to complain. There could be medical emergencies. Heart attacks. Maybe a bit of spousal abuse. Hell, maybe even a theft. But wouldn't one guard stay put, to keep out the riff-raff and raise the gate for arrivals or departures?

Strange.

He moved quickly past the empty gatehouse and entered Point Dume Estates.

It would have been nice to know which of the estates had been Angela Lowell's destination. At least he had the yellow Mustang to clue him in. If she was still there.

The car was parked some distance from the security shack, beside a high, smooth wall, painted a pastel pink. A few feet away, the wrought-iron gate to the property was hanging open a few inches.

Mace approached the gate. He looked in at an overgrown garden; its flowers adding perfume to a chilly breeze off the ocean. He entered the grounds cautiously, not liking the creak of the gate. He moved down a flagstone walkway, scanning the foliage for some sign of motion. All he saw were leaves, ruffled by the ocean breeze, shimmering in the moonlight.

Beyond the plant life was a modern beach home, all stone and metal and glass.

The two-wheel security scooter stood sentry before the pebble glass front door. The guards had been called here. But where were they?

Mace stood still, closed his eyes and listened.

There was the comforting roar of the surf, the flutter of leaves, the distant cry of a gull, faint highway-traffic noise. Nothing else. The neighbors were too far away for him to hear, or too quiet or too absent. Not a sound came from inside the stone and glass home. Not from the guards. Not from anyone.

Suddenly, a light began to flicker at a window to his left.

He moved there silently in a crouched position, staying lower than the sill. A sound came from the room, the deep growl of a dog. Curious, he rose enough to peek through the window.

What he saw shocked him.

A huge dog stood in the center of a large room, shimmering ghostlike in a column of light that appeared to emanate from the animal itself. It was the biggest mastiff Mace had ever seen, almost the size of a pack mule. There was a prehistoric quality to its narrow head and incredibly long, pointed teeth.

The dog turned its odd head as if it were scanning its surroundings. Before it took in the window, Mace ducked down, his pulse racing. *What the fuck kind of dog was this?* Nothing he wanted any part of.

He began backtracking, eager to get away from whatever was going on inside the beach house. The unmistakable sound of a gunshot forced him to freeze in the shadows. From that relatively hidden position, he studied the building, hoping for some clue, however subtle, that would suggest his next move.

What happened next was far from subtle.

The front door to the beach house flew open and one of the gate guards staggered out. He'd lost his green helmet, but he was holding a shotgun with both hands.

Mace hoped he was deep enough in shadow to remain unseen.

The guard stepped into moonlight and Mace saw that blood was pouring from his neck, darkening his brown shirt. *Had the goddamn dog ripped out the guy's throat?*

The guard headed for his scooter but he didn't make it. Both he and the shotgun hit the brick walkway. The shotgun made more noise.

Mace felt a need for the shotgun. He swallowed hard and went for it.

As he bent to reach for the weapon, the guard surprised him. He wasn't quite finished. He looked up at Mace, eyebrows raised in what might have been wonder. 'All dead inside . . . dog . . .' he gasped.

'Yeah, dog,' Mace said. 'I saw it.'

'No . . . dog . . . it's a whole . . .' He was done.

Mace realized that the blood was coming from a gunshot wound in the man's neck. Not a dog bite.

He stood and broke the shotgun. Fully loaded. He checked the man's leather holster. Empty.

He wondered if the shotgun would be of any use against

the massive dog. Doubtful. And there was a homicidal human inside the house with a gun. He knew he should get the hell away from there. But he was drawn to the open front door. At that moment he wasn't sure why. Thinking about it later he would realize it probably had been his concern for Angela Lowell.

The other guard lay just past the door on the tile floor of the reception area, a small room that smelled of gunsmoke and furniture wax. It had white walls filled with framed artwork that, in the dim light of the moon, could have been masterpieces or boardwalk paint blotches. The second guard had been shot in the chest. He, too, was dead. He had no holster or gun.

Mace moved past him and paused, shotgun raised, at the entrance to the room where he had seen the dog. Or had he seen it? There were no flesh and blood dogs like that. He'd laughed at the old veterans of the bayou who claimed to have come upon all manner of haunts and voodoos. Those apparitions had been the result of something real; home brew, perhaps, or marsh gas. Common sense told him there were no shimmering ghost dogs.

There was no dog of any kind in the room.

Maybe the bang-up in the limo had shaken something loose in his head. But the dying guard had mentioned a dog . . .

In any case, the room was now lifeless and silent, a large, dark area with an unusually high slanted ceiling. A skylight let a square of moonglow fall against the tallest wall, the one he faced. It was literally filled with paintings from floor to ceiling.

Once he'd taken in the moonlit display of art, he scanned the rest of the room. It was furnished with oddly delicate-looking tables and chairs. Antiques probably, though he had little knowledge of or interest in such things. An Oriental rug covered the center of the flagstone floor.

And . . . there were two more corpses in the shadowy room. Evidently he'd missed quite an execution by only minutes.

The body nearest the entry was a male in his early twenties lying face up, a Hollywood-hip stereotype in silk dinner jacket, black shirt, black pants. Chiseled features. Two- or three-day growth of beard on his unwrinkled, almost pretty face. Marring the total effect was a blackened hole where his left eye should have been. An impressive shot. A small line of blood ran down the side of his head to the rug where it almost blended in.

The dead man's hand was tucked inside his coat. Mace used the barrel of the shotgun to lift the jacket. The hand clutched a gun still partially holstered.

Mace had to break the man's index finger to pry the weapon free. He checked the clip. Nearly full up. Feeling a little less vulnerable, he wiped the shotgun clean and rested it beside the corpse. Then he moved on to the second figure, nearly tripping on an electric cord attached to a small black box lying on the flagstone floor.

This male was grossly fat, seated on a massive stuffed chair. He wore a dark velvet dinner jacket, a pleated white shirt open at his thick folded neck, black or midnight blue tux pants. The pockets of his pants and his jacket had been pulled out. His little feet were bare. Regardless, he still looked like a three hundred and fifty pound penguin.

Mace knew him. His and Paulie's former associate, Tiny Daniels. *A poster boy for morbid obesity.*

One patent-leather shoe rested on its side near two twisted, black stockings and a wine glass with a snapped stem. The other shoe seemed to be missing, maybe dragged away by the ghost dog.

Mace moved closer to the fat man. His pale blue eyes, though filmy, stared at him in what seemed to be mild bemusement.

There was a small hole in his black satin lapel. Mace was convinced he was looking at a dead man, but pressed a finger into the still-warm bulging neck to make sure. The huge body had evidently been doing a balancing act on the chair and it tumbled forward and sprawled on to the floor.

Mace caught sight of something protruding from the corner of Tiny's mouth.

He hunkered beside the mound of dead flesh and yanked the display handkerchief from Tiny's jacket pocket. He wrapped it around his hand and separated the dead man's rubbery lips. Tiny's teeth were clamped on an object smooth and dull.

Mace pried it out . . . A coin the size of a quarter. But not a quarter. Some kind of counterfeit. Or maybe a specialty item. On one side was a man's face and chest in bas-relief. Something was engraved on the reverse side, but he couldn't begin to make it out without light.

He might have studied it longer, but a door slammed.

Shoving the coin and handkerchief into his coat pocket, Mace followed the sound to a kitchen. The back door was open. It was a screen door that had slammed shut. As Mace exited through it, a section of its wooden frame splintered near his hand just as he heard the shot.

Ducking, he raised his gun. Too late. A thin man wearing an off-white suit slid over a cement wind wall separating the house from the sandy beach. Mace was surprised that Thomas could move so gracefully. Like a gymnast or a dancer.

He did not even consider pursuit. Judging by the house full of dead men, Thomas knew how to use his gun. And there was always Timmie. The cowboy Elvis and the limo had to be hiding somewhere nearby.

Mace had been wondering why they'd picked him up. He'd assumed it was because he'd been tailing Angela Lowell. But the murders suggested a more likely motive. Thomas had everything nailed down for his killing spree and suddenly Mace had appeared, an unexpected hindrance.

Or maybe they thought he might be of help. Assuming the chauffeur, Sweets, had identified him as the man who broke his wrist in the park, they'd known he and Paulie were tight. Since there was animosity between Paulie and Tiny Daniels, Mace was very suitable for framing. Had the drive up the country road merely been Thomas vamping, waiting for the approval of his employer?

In any case, he was definitely in the wrong place at the wrong time. The police would be arriving at any moment. He got out Tiny's handkerchief and wiped the screen-door handle. He'd been careful coming in, had done as much as he could to smear his prints on the shotgun.

He was making a swift exit when he heard a distinctive female voice call out from the floor above. 'What's . . . going on?'

He moved back through the house to a stairwell and raced up to a hall and four closed doors. He hesitated before opening the one nearest him, thinking about the giant dog. And the giant Timmie.

'Someone there?' the female voice asked from behind a different door.

Mace didn't want to touch the knob. He raised a foot, kicked in the door and ran past it, gun held high.

The room was dark, but not so dark he couldn't see more art on the walls. Or the woman in the bed.

Angela Lowell lay in a rumpled queen-size. The sheet that had been covering her had fallen to her waist. She was naked. Caution had to force him to look away and make sure they were alone in the room.

That accomplished, he turned back to her.

She was staring at him, her lovely patrician face showing no emotion whatsoever. 'Carlos?' she asked.

'No. Not Carlos.'

'I . . . see that now.' She smiled at him. 'I'm . . . awake.'

'Good,' Mace said. 'Put on your clothes.'

'Why?'

'We have to leave.'

'Why?'

Instead of answering, he gathered a black dress from the floor and a pair of white silk panties with ribbons worked into their fabric. The warmth of the panties gave him an erotic jolt. He ignored it and tossed the clothes beside her on the bed.

'Put 'em on now,' he said.

'I don't think . . . I . . . ca . . .' She slumped back on to the bed, eyes closed, breathing softly through open lips. He raised his arm but couldn't bring himself to slap her awake.

'Damn it,' he grumbled and stuck the gun in his belt. He jammed the panties in his pocket and began to struggle the dress over her rubbery body.

He found her shoes and purse, but there were probably other things of hers he was leaving behind. Her purchases of the day, perhaps. The clothes she'd been wearing earlier. Fingerprints, if nothing else. None of that would matter if, as he suspected, she'd been a frequent guest at the house.

He hoisted her over his shoulder. She was substantial, fuller-bodied than she'd looked from a distance. Now she was just a heavy burden. Under other circumstances though . . .

THIRTEEN

To Mace's annoyance, there were two cars lined up at the untended security gate.

They'd apparently just arrived. Or at least, the driver of the first – in a Rolls – had just decided to do something about raising the gate. Caught in her own headlights, she was a snake-thin, wild-haired woman in artificially faded denim, wrists weighed down with turquoise bracelets. She staggered drunkenly to the bar and began struggling ineffectually to lift it by hand. She screamed curses at the absent security guards.

She was going to make sure they were fired for 'deri-fucking-lection of duty.'

Mace did not think she had seen them in the yellow Mustang before he'd turned off the lights. He eased the car back to the nearest residence, parking in front of an Accura SUV before killing the engine.

From there he could observe the tableaux at the security gate.

A man in the second vehicle, a tomato-red Tesla electric sports car, shouted to the woman to use the switch in the guardhouse that controlled the bar.

She turned and gave him the finger.

The man got out of his car. He was wearing a khaki safari outfit, looking to Mace like a real dick in his short pants and belted shirt. The wild-haired woman thought he was a dick, too. She told him to go fuck himself.

Neighbors.

Ignoring her, the man stormed to the gatehouse and, in the dark, found the button. Definitely the great white hunter of Point Dume Estates, Mace thought.

The bar rose up suddenly, almost taking the skinny woman's arms with it.

'What the fuck are you trying to do . . . kill me, you bastard?' she shouted at the man.

'Move your goddamn gas guzzler, Leslie,' he replied. 'Or I'll move it for you.'

She was vibrating like a tuning fork, staring at him as he got into his car and slammed the door. 'Faggot,' she screamed.

Mace had used the Mustang's seat belt to secure the unconscious Angela in an upright position. He unlocked the belt and eased her down lower than the windshield.

He saw the skinny woman get back into the Rolls. He heard the grinding noise made when an ignition key is turned on an already active engine.

The Rolls bucked forward.

He'd slid down in the Mustang beside Angela, waiting for the Rolls to glide past, followed by the Tesla. When he was sure he'd heard the last of them, he rose up, lifted Angela into a sitting position and readjusted the seat belt across her chest. He wondered what she'd taken that had put her out so completely.

He looked at her, sleeping peacefully. Heartbreaking in moonlight. He had no problem understanding why even a street-smart guy like Paulie Lacotta had fallen for her. He had even less a problem understanding why she would have fucked Paulie over. He'd known women who were intelligent, educated, beautiful, probably well-born who had been intrigued by bad boys. But Paulie wasn't really a bad boy, just a guy with a soft conscience. Soft all over. Unlike the dead pretty-boy in Tiny's living room. Carlos. That was the name she'd mentioned when he surprised her in the bedroom.

Carlos. No longer in the game, whatever the game was.

He started up the Mustang and drove away, using the entrance that the dick in safari garb had thoughtfully left open for other inhabitants of Point Dume Estates. Or, as it would be referred to after the discovery of the bodies, Point Doom Estates.

FOURTEEN

Before the trek back to the Florian, Mace drove the Mustang to the mall where he'd purchased his pricey lunch. The dinner crowd was keeping the restaurants and fast food chains busy. He parked in the moderately full lot, turned off the engine and leaned back in the seat, gathering his thoughts.

He didn't spend too much time on it.

He picked up Angela's purse. It was small, made of some soft material, silk or satin, all the same to him. When he'd taken the car keys from it, he'd noticed . . . yes, a plastic prescription medicine bottle.

He held it up to where a mall light sent its glow through the windshield. The label on the bottle read: 'Honeymoon Drugs, Prescription #: 31124. Dr Bolitho. For: Monte, Jerold. Demerol. Take one (1) capsule as needed. Four (4) refills.'

Jerry Monte? Mace looked at the sleeping woman, whose appeal had waned slightly.

He shook the bottle. Nearly empty. He wondered how many pills she'd swallowed.

He returned the bottle to the purse, noticed her cellular and, on a whim, withdrew it.

He got out of the car and shut the door quietly. He found a bench out of earshot to the Mustang, sat and dialed a number.

Paulie Lacotta's voice was a mixture of surprise and hope. 'Angie?'

'Guess again,' Mace said.

There was a beat or two of silence, then, 'That you, Mace?'

'None other.'

'What the hell you doing with her phone? She with you? You sell me out, you prick? You sell me out for a quick fuck?'

Mace was almost amused by the way Paulie's mind worked. Cockroach logic, his dad had called it. Based on the assumption that everybody was as crooked as you were.

'She's with me, but I'm not sure who's selling who,' Mace said.

There was squawking on the other end. Lacotta cursing him, Angie and himself. Mace cut that off with, 'Shut the fuck up, Paulie.'

A little surprised when Lacotta obeyed, he began recounting the events of the day, from following Angela Lowell to Point Dume, through the episode with the limo crew – Sweets, whom he hoped Paulie remembered, and the Brit brothers, Thomas and Timmie the cowboy Elvis – to the murders at Tiny Daniels' that he presumed Thomas had committed. He neglected to mention the ghost dog, which would have made Paulie assume he'd lost it and discredit everything else he'd said.

'I don't get it,' Lacotta said. 'The spook – what'd you call him, Sweets? – said Tiny had sent him to kill me. Why would he be crewing with the guy who took Tiny out?'

'I don't know,' Mace said. 'But, assuming Tiny wasn't just blowing smoke about carrying life insurance, Montdrago had better call his lawyer or think twice before returning to the States.'

Paulie was silent for a beat, then said, 'You're positive the fat man's dead?'

Mace closed his eyes and took a deep breath. 'I'm positive.'

'Did it look like this guy Thomas had searched the place?'

'He'd gone through Tiny's pockets, but I think I spooked him before he did much else.'

'I don't suppose *you* found . . . anything?' Paulie said.

'Like what?' Mace asked, reaching into his pocket, fingering the coin to be sure it was still there.

'Never mind. Just a dumb thought,' Paulie said.

Mace wrinkled his nose in annoyance. 'You sure you don't know the hitman, Thomas?'

'A Limey with a brain-dead brother who looks like Elvis? I think I might have remembered.'

'What's going on, Paulie?'

'I swear to God, I told you all I know.'

Mace doubted that. But he didn't think he could get much more over the phone. Face to face would be different.

'You alone?' Mace asked.

'Why?' Lacotta asked defensively.

'You and Tiny weren't exactly close. You may need an alibi for the last hour or so.'

'Got that covered,' Lacotta said. 'You oughta see her, Mace. One of Abe's genuine specials.'

'She right there, listening to this conversation?' Mace asked.

''Course not. She's in the bedroom, watchin' a porno. What's the sitch with Angie?'

'Taking a Demerol nap,' Mace said. 'I'm gonna drive her to the Florian in her car. Get somebody to pick up mine, a dark gray Camry Hybrid parked on Wilderness Road. I don't think it's close enough for the cops to get too curious about it, but let's not press our luck.'

'You leave the electronic gizmo that starts the engine?'

'I've been a little busy. Christ, Paulie. Can't your guys handle a hot-wire job?'

Paulie was starting to babble about the new technology when Mace snapped the cellular shut. He returned to the Mustang. Before getting in, he remembered the gun he was carrying. A murdered man's gun. Something that could tie him to four homicides. He got out Tiny's hanky for the last time and used it to wipe the gun. Then he tossed both items into a trash bin resting inside a smooth cement shell that the mall's architect had created to make even the garbage look Malibu-pretty.

They were zooming past the Santa Monica beach club when Mace realized the atmosphere in the car had changed. He glanced at Angela Lowell. She was awake and staring at him. Not with warmth.

'Who the devil are you?' she demanded, slurring a little.

Instead of replying he returned his attention to the highway.

'Do you work for Tiny?' she asked.

'Nobody works for Tiny anymore,' Mace said, steering them on to the Santa Monica Freeway. 'Not even Tiny.'

'What do you mean? Why are you driving my car?'

'I'm getting you away from a bad situation,' he said. 'We left four dead men back there at Point Dume. Five, if you count Tiny as two.'

'My God. Who . . . ? *You* killed them?'

He smiled at that. 'No, ma'am. I don't kill people. Unless I have to.'

'Then who . . . ?'

'A tall thin guy who's either British or affected. His first name is Thomas. I don't suppose you've heard of him?'

'Of course not. But you evidently have.'

'Yes, ma'am.'

'Did you and he have a fight?'

'Come again?'

'Your clothes,' she said. 'You look like you've been fighting.'

'It's been a rough day.'

'Who *are* you?'

'A guy who found a beautiful woman unconscious in a house full of dead men,' he said. 'I thought it best to get you dressed and out of there before the cops showed.'

She looked down at her gown. If he expected her to blush, he was disappointed.

He reached into his coat pocket and pulled out her panties. 'I think these are yours.'

She took them from him. Without hesitation, hiked up her skirt and slid them on.

She leaned back against the headrest and closed her eyes. 'I . . . took something. To relax. I shouldn't drink when I do that, but . . .' She made a helpless shrug.

'Your timing couldn't have been better,' he said. 'It probably saved your life.'

She stared at him. 'My God!'

'Tell me what went on at Tiny's earlier, before you faded.'

'We were about to leave for dinner,' she said. 'Then Tiny got one of his phone calls, and that meant dinner would be postponed for a few hours.'

'Explain.'

'I'm not sure why I should be talking to you about this,' she said.

'Just trying to make some sense out of what happened back there.'

She studied him, obviously wondering if she should trust him. That done, she said, 'Well, with Tiny business always comes . . . came first. The caller said he had something to discuss and Tiny suggested he come to the beach house. He told us we could eat later. That's when I poured myself a glass of wine even though I'd taken a pill and knew better.'

'Who was the caller?' Mace asked.

She shook her head. 'Tiny didn't say and I didn't ask. He said I should go to my room, that Carlos would come tell me when the meeting was over and we could go to dinner.'

'When you were . . . sleeping, you didn't hear anything? Gunshots? Shouts? Anything?'

'No,' she said.

'Did Tiny have a giant . . . have any animals? Pets?'

She shook her head. 'The beach house is full of very valuable art. Not a place for pets.'

She was silent for a minute or two, then asked, 'You sure they're both dead? Tiny and Carlos?'

'Carlos a pretty boy who only uses a razor on odd days?'

She nodded.

'Dead,' Mace said, flatly.

'He . . . worked for Tiny.'

'If he was a bodyguard, he was a piss-poor one.'

Mace moved the Mustang around a creeper hogging the fast lane.

'You live at the beach house?' he asked, as if he didn't know the answer.

'I have my own apartment. But I . . . go there sometimes because the art makes me happy. It helps me to . . . unwind. That guest room is rarely used, except by me.'

'What was he to you? Lover? Friend?'

'Tiny is . . . was gay. He was a client. My profession is appraising works of art. I helped Tiny with his collection. He was also a friend. A very sweet man. Always concerned about me. Like an uncle.

'What about you?' she asked. 'Were you a friend of Tiny's?'

'Do I look like a friend of Tiny's?' Mace asked.

She shrugged.

'We used to work together.'

'In investments?'

He smiled. 'Yes. Investments.'

She was staring at him. 'Is that why you were at the beach house tonight?

'You got it,' he said. 'Where are we headed, by the way?'

She hesitated, then said, 'I live at the Florian. Above Sunset. You know the place?'

'I've driven by it,' he said.

FIFTEEN

As he remembered the nighttime Sunset Strip of the Nineties, it had not been a particularly wholesome venue. But that had been like Disneyland compared to the present streetscape. Garish. Ugly. Young Latinos bouncing up and down in their hot paint low-riders.

Paused at a red light, Mace watched male and female hookers hungrily work their way through the stalled traffic. The light changed and he started forward, almost hitting a huge man on Rollerblades. He was wearing a pink Mohawk, matching pink short shorts and tube top, gliding across the boulevard with a boom box under one heavily-muscled arm and a pink poodle under the other.

'What do you think?' Mace asked. 'Too much?'

She smiled. A first for the night.

Passing Honest Abe's Coffee Empourium, he indicated the crowd waiting to get in. 'Popular place, huh?'

'I suppose.'

'Ever been there?'

She gave him a curious look. 'I don't like coffee,' she said.

He turned left and headed up to the Florian, nosing the car on to the circular drive. 'Where do I put this?'

She directed him to the parking area she'd been assigned.

'What now?' Angela asked when he turned off the ignition and handed her the key.

'You go inside and get on with your life and I walk down to Sunset to catch a cab.'

He got out of the car and circled it, intending to open her door. She didn't wait, her expression indicating she considered such courtesy to be old fashioned and foolish.

Or maybe she was just eager to be free of him.

He stood near the car, letting her initiate the goodbye.

'Why don't I give you a lift to wherever you're headed?' she said.

'Better for you to go inside and get some sleep,' he said, leading her to the Florian's front door. 'The police will be calling on you sooner or later. You want to be fresh for that.'

'What do I tell them?' she asked.

'You've visited Tiny's often, but you weren't anywhere near there tonight.'

'Where was I?'

Mace smiled. 'I'll leave that up to you.'

At the door, he said, 'Be sure to lock yourself in.'

'Why not come up?' she said. 'Wait there for a cab. If that's what you want.'

A cab was not at all what he wanted. He was tempted, but he said, 'Rain check.'

He tried to read her reaction. Surprise. Disappointment. Maybe a hint of pique.

'This is it, then?' she said.

'I hope not.'

She started to say something, thought better of it. She nodded, turned and entered the Florian.

Mace didn't think she'd look back, but he waited to make sure. Then he circled the building.

SIXTEEN

'What the fuck happened to you?' Wylie asked as Mace let himself into the apartment. He'd been sitting at the window, chair leaning back, feet up on the table. He swung his legs to the floor and popped the electronic buds from his ears.

'I went for a drive in the country,' Mace said, removing his torn and muddied jacket.

'The cu . . . the subject's been gone the whole . . . Shit. Somebody work you over?' He was pointing at Mace's shirt which was ripped and crusted with dirt.

Mace took off the shirt, balled it up and threw it into the wastebasket near his bed. He moved to the bathroom, Wylie following.

'Your neck's scratched,' Wylie said. 'What the fuck?'

'Give me a few minutes, OK?' Mace said, and turned on the washbasin faucet.

Reluctantly, Wylie obeyed the request, fading into the bedroom.

Mace washed his hands, then his face. He dried off and opened a leather kit that was resting on a shelf over the toilet. He removed a bandage strip that he placed on a dry corner of the basin. He examined the inch-long scratch on his neck that he hadn't even noticed before. It seemed to be strictly surface, but he'd seen tiny wounds blossom into problems.

'Put a couple shots of Jack in a glass for me,' he called out to Wylie, who responded eagerly.

Mace drank two-thirds of the whiskey, then poured the rest on a rolled-up ball of toilet paper that he used to sterilize the cut.

'Ugly bruise starting on your shoulder,' Wylie said.

'I got kicked by Elvis,' Mace said.

'Huh?'

'Don't mind me,' Mace said, applying the adhesive strip to the scratch. 'What's Lacotta been up to lately?'

The question clearly discomforted Wylie. 'I . . . who knows? I don't get invited to the fucking board meetings.'

Mace zipped the leather bag, clicked off the bathroom light and went past Wylie into the bedroom, carrying the whiskey glass.

'A smart guy like you picks things up,' he said. 'This would be something a little different from the daily routine.'

Wylie was flattered but still wary. 'Mr Lacotta took a couple trips for this deal that didn't happen. That what you mean?'

'Maybe,' Mace said, pouring a drink for himself and one for Wylie. He handed Wylie the tumbler.

'Much as I know, it was some kind of thing with the government.'

Mace sipped the bourbon. 'When was this?'

'Maybe a month and a half ago, Mr Lacotta flew to Frisco. Day or two later, he took off for DC. Came back totally stoked, said he'd been wining and dining with a bunch of the big dogs at the White House. He was soaring. Never saw him so up. But that mood sure didn't last long. I think the whole thing tanked.'

Mace moved to the windows and picked up one of the binoculars. He looked out at Angela Lowell's apartment. The drapes were drawn, but a light was on in her living room. A shadow flitted across the drapes.

'No hint what the deal involved?' he asked.

'Hell, nobody tells me about the deals that go through, much less the ones that don't.'

Mace traded the binoculars for the booze bottle, poured Wylie another shot. He wondered how close that DC visit was to Lacotta sending Wylie to clock the visitors to Commingore Industries. But he couldn't bring up Commingore again at that moment. If there was a time link, he didn't want Wylie to be thinking about it.

'Speaking of people who don't tell me stuff,' Wylie said, 'if it was followin' the bi-atch got you bounced around, don't you owe me a fill-in? I follow her, too.'

So Wylie was not a total asshole after all and maybe he did deserve a heads-up.

'I was on the job, parked, waiting for Lowell to emerge from . . . a building when this oddball crew surprised me,' Mace said. 'Thomas has a little moustache, dresses like David Niven used to. Suit. Ascot. He's a shooter.'

'What kinda weapon?'

'I'm not exactly sure, but I'm guessing a Spitfire. Because it's British. He's very handy with it. His younger brother Timmie had his brain fried when he was a baby. Acts like a five year old. Looks a hell of a lot like Elvis, blown up to about six-five or -six. Got wrists as big as my thighs. He likes to dress up. He was wearing a cowboy outfit today.'

'Gee-zus. Never even heard of any dudes like that. Sure they weren't yankin' your chain?'

'I'm pretty sure it was no joke,' Mace said, thinking of the bodies at the beach house. 'They were using a mustard-colored limo.'

'Yuck. You get the plate number?'

'No,' Mace said. Why hadn't he? He closed his eyes, trying to recall. When Thomas had marched him to the vehicle, he hadn't had a clear view of either its front or rear. On the country road, the license plate had been obscured by a trail of dust. He wasn't even sure if it was a California plate.

'The driver was a guy they called Sweets. Black dude, maybe six-one. Tried to shoot Lacotta yesterday and I had to break his wrist.'

'Holy crap. When were you gonna tell me about *that*?'

'I should have. Sorry. You know the guy?'

Wylie shook his head.

'He told Lacotta he worked for Tiny Daniels.'

'Black?' Wylie frowned. 'The only guys I see with Tiny are slick-looking white butt-boys.'

A sudden surge of music came from Wylie's pocket. A TV series theme, Mace thought, though there was no way he could name the show.

Wylie got out his cellular and put it to his ear. 'Wylie.'

He listened a beat, said, 'Right here,' and tossed the phone to Mace.

Mace had to study it a bit before putting it to his ear. 'Yeah?'

'Cops got a lot of the area roped off,' Lacotta said. 'You were lucky you left when you did.'

'What about the rental?' Mace asked, getting to his feet. He headed toward the bathroom.

'Taken care of. Relax. Get some sleep.'

Mace closed the bathroom door and lowered his voice. 'How much do you want Wylie to know about the murders?'

'Whatever he reads in the papers tomorrow. Unless you feel he should know you're part of that sad tragedy.'

'He should be clued in on just how deadly these guys are.'

'You've had a rough day. Get some sleep. You worry too much.'

'Maybe,' Mace said and terminated the call.

He returned to the table by the window and gave Wylie his phone back.

'What's up?' Wylie asked.

Mace felt Wylie deserved a little more information. 'These guys, Sweets and the Brit brothers, you don't want to screw around with this crew,' he said. 'If they show, head the other way. Once you're clear, give me a call. Understand?'

'No. I don't. Sweets is a pussy. And from what you say, the Limeys don't sound like much. A skinny fag with an ascot and his brain-dead brother. No big threat.'

'I thought you didn't know Sweets,' Mace said. 'What makes you think he's a pussy?'

Wylie frowned, then said, 'You told me you broke his wrist. Anyway . . .'

When Wylie did not finish that thought, Mace said, 'Anyway what?'

Wylie shook his head. 'Nothing,' he said. 'I got nothing.'

Mace stared at the punk and wondered what he was holding back. He could probably get it out of him with three or four more shots of whiskey. But he didn't have the time or the patience.

He pulled his two-suiter from under his bed and opened it. He removed a fresh shirt from his still-unpacked clothes, shook it out and put it on.

He looked down at his dusty trousers. The left knee, scraped in the leap from the limo, was a shade lighter than the rest. He didn't care. He tried to beat some of the dust out, but the material had been damaged. Too bad. He undid the belt, button and zipper and tucked in his shirt before reversing the process.

'That the gizmo to start your rental?' he asked, picking up a small black device from the table beside Wylie's bed.

'My smart key, yeah. Why . . . ?'

Mace headed for the door.

'Whoa,' Wylie said. 'Time for *you* to house-sit. I'm gettin' hungry.'

'I'll bring something back,' Mace said. 'Cheeseburger OK?'

Wylie stared at him. 'Yeah. That's fine.' He turned, picked

up the binoculars and trained them on the opposite wing of the building. 'What if she goes out?'

'I don't see that happening,' Mace said. 'Oh, and I wouldn't be lingering at the window with the spyglasses. She may be visited by the cops tonight and I hear they're on the lookout for stalkers these days.'

'Cops coming here? Why?'

'It's what they do. So just take a quick check from time to time without the binocs. Make sure she's still there.'

'Wait a minute . . .!' Wylie yelled.

But he was alone in the apartment.

SEVENTEEN

Mace stood on the sidewalk in front of a run-down stucco duplex on Orange Avenue. He didn't see Simon S. Symon's broken-down grape Cherokee parked anywhere, but it could have been tucked away in a garage. The duplex's front door was open and a rectangle of light from its hallway spilled out over cracked and peeling white wooden steps and a section of sun-scorched yellow lawn.

An overweight woman stood in the doorway, cradling a crying baby in one fleshy arm, while she used the other to bring a cigarette to her pouty lips. Pink shorts cut into bulging thighs. She was wearing a tight, faded green T-shirt with a bib that rested on her jutting breasts like a doily on an over-stuffed chair. Mace figured she wore the bib in case the baby got so irritated by the cigarette smoke it had to throw up.

The woman stared at him with mild curiosity.

He checked the address on the business card.

'Lookin' for the little ho-ers?' she asked, not unkindly.

'Shoot On Site Photography,' Mace said.

'Yeah. Like I said. Aroun' back. One flight up. Don't do nothing I wouldn't do.'

At the rear of the apartment house, Mace found a wooden stairwell so old it had turned gray. It led up to a closed screen and wooden door combination above which a flickering bulb provided only very dim light.

If his climb up the squeaking, wobbling stairwell alerted anyone in the apartment, there was no outward sign. Someone was home. He heard sounds. A cough. A throat being cleared.

He applied his knuckles to the wooden frame of the screen door.

No response.

It was unlocked. The door past it was flimsy and paint-cracked. He used the side of his fist to hammer against it, shaking it mightily. This resulted in the sound of bare feet padding toward him.

The door opened as far as a brass chain allowed. A teenage girl peered out. Her round face had the potential for pretty, once it lost the baby fat and the chalky make-up. And the assortment of metal items piercing the flesh of her ears and nose, including, Mace noted, both a tiny mezuzah and a silver pork chop. She was wrapped in a ratty pink bathrobe.

'Yea-uh?' she asked.

'I'm looking for Symon.'

'Got no Symon. No Siegfried. No Seinfeld. We ain't got no esses, Esse.'

Mace tried to look past the girl, where a shaft of light caused shadows to dance around the darkened room. 'Tell Symon it's the guy with fifty bucks for him,' he said.

'Don't you listen, handsome? No Symon here.' She slammed the door.

There was muffled conversation in the room. Mace was about to knock again, when the door opened. This time the female behind the chain was taller, bigger boned, and about a decade past the teen years. Blonde, sunburned. No hardware dangling from her face. Had that post-starlet look of disillusioned, fading beauty. She was wearing bikini panties and a push-up bra, smiling placidly, as if greeting a stranger at the door in her underwear were her thing.

She gave Mace a head-to-toe appraisal and said, 'You look like fun. I vote we let you in.'

She shut the door long enough to slip the chain, then opened it all the way. He stepped into a small, sparsely furnished room.

A video projector rested on a footstool casting silent, moving images on a wall to the right. In the ambient light, Mace observed a rescue-mission brown couch, three chairs, two of them matching the couch, the third a yellow beanbag, the kind he hadn't seen since he was a kid.

The girl with the embedded face jewelry was drifting toward a couple lounging on colorful pillows on the bare wooden floor, watching the wall. The prone girl had brown hair worn long over a flimsy caftan. She drank from a Coke can and passed the can to the boy beside her, a muscular teen who looked like he belonged on a surfer poster, except for the tattoo of Botticelli's Venus on his cut, hairless chest. He was wearing ragged denim cut-offs, unbuttoned and unzipped as if he'd put them on and forgotten to finish the process.

'Our pierced princess is named Liz,' the undressed blonde said. 'Short for lizard. I'm B.J. Short for . . . well, maybe you'll find out. That's Pippa on the floor and Keith, a.k.a Beaver, as in "Leave it to . . ." They're in luuuv. And don't care who's watching.'

The tattooed Beaver glanced at Mace and lifted his chin an inch. Pippa was too entranced by the movie on the wall to pause for even that minimal a welcome. Her vapid face showed a brief annoyance as Liz stepped over her legs, blocked the projected image for a beat and plopped down beside Beaver.

Liz's bathrobe opened exposing a plump, naked body that was about as appealing to Mace as an open wound. Not that she cared. Staring at the wall movie, she casually began to caress the boy's bare chest. She seemed to be stroking the Venus tattoo.

'Where's Symon?' Mace asked the blonde.

'He doesn't live here, honey,' she said. 'Just uses this place for . . . business transactions.'

'Where can I find him?'

'Not here. Not now.'

'Where does he live?'

'Like I'd know?' B.J. said. 'He pays me to do things. I'm not his wrap. He's too old and too ugly.'

She moved closer, pressing against him. 'Relax, honey. Lose some of that tension.'

She lowered a graceful hand.

He grabbed her wrist before it reached his groin. 'What the hell is this?' he said.

'Let go,' B.J. whined, dropping the seduction act. 'You're hurting me.'

Mace released her wrist. She swung at him with her other hand, but he stepped away from it.

The swing carried her against the open door and she made a yelp and sent a few curses into the air. Then she settled down a little and began to rub her wrist. 'Jesus, you almost broke it,' she said. 'What the fuck, asshole?'

He hadn't meant to be that rough, but she'd surprised him. He wasn't about to apologize.

'Out of the way, Jack,' Beaver yelled.

Mace realized he was blocking the projected images. He stepped out of the bright light and, for the first time, noticed the images on the wall. A hardcore threesome; two guys and a gal.

What the hell was he doing there?

He headed for the door, but B.J. blocked his way. 'I . . . look, I'm sorry. I was just fucking with you. Your name's Mason, right?'

He glared at her.

'Gotta be. Simon said you looked like the guy plays the lead on *Mad Men*. Hang on a sec'. He left something for you.'

B.J. crossed the room and disappeared down a hall.

The three people on the floor were now fondling each other, seemingly enraptured by the erotic images on the wall.

B.J. crossed through the stream of light carrying a Manila envelope. She handed it to Mace.

He took it and started to go.

'Hold on,' B.J. said, all business now. 'Fifty bucks.'

Mace fumbled out his wallet, peeled off two twenties and a ten and made his exit.

'If you do get lonely, you know where to find me,' B.J. said, before she closed the door.

He was halfway to the Florian before he realized the blonde had used his name. He hadn't mentioned it to Symon.

EIGHTEEN

Mace was surprised that Paulie had actually done something right; the leased Camry was parked where it belonged in the Florian lot. He drove past it and put Wylie's vehicle into its allocated space.

With a white bag in hand and the envelope with Angela Lowell's photos under his arm, he walked to her yellow Mustang. Its hood was cool to the touch. The tracking device was still attached to the rear of the license plate. He next went to the Camry, got in and pressed the button. It started right up.

Everything was as it should be. Would wonders never cease?

He got out of the car with bag and envelope and locked the Camry, then headed to the stairwell and up to the apartment.

The room was in darkness. In the moonglow, he saw Wylie, slumped over the table near the window. Asleep. He smelled of booze.

Across the way, a light was on in Angela Lowell's bedroom.

Mace switched on their ceiling light. He stood near the table watching Wylie wake up by degrees. First came the frown. Then a clearing of the throat. Squinting, followed by a full scowl.

Wylie sat up, yawned and said, finally, 'Shit. I was asleep.'

You live asleep, Mace thought but refrained from saying it. Instead, he put the bag on the table in front of Wylie. 'Dinner,' he said.

Wylie removed the bag's contents, three quarter-pounder cheeseburgers and a waxed cardboard drink container. He pointed at the drink. 'I hope that's a Coke. I fuckin' hate Pepsi.'

'Milkshake.'

'No shit? For me? That's fuckin' def, Mace. I love 'shakes.'

Mace sat across from him. He slid the photos out of the envelope and spread them on the table. He reached over them, grabbed one of the three burgers, unwrapped it and begin eating it while studying the eight-by-ten glossies of Angela Lowell getting into her car and driving away from the Florian lot.

'Where'd you get those?' Wylie asked.

'Guy with a camera.'

'Duh. I didn't think they came with the burgers. What guy?'

'You been asleep long?' Mace asked.

Wylie had been sucking the viscous drink through a straw. The question threw him and he swallowed too fast. He squinted his eyes and groaned. 'Brain freeze,' he said, pushing the heel of his hand against his forehead. 'Man, that was intense. How long was I . . . ? Half-hour, tops. Look, I been sittin' in this fuckin' room all fuckin'—'

'Take it easy,' Mace said. 'It was a question, not a criticism.'

'Oh. About thirty minutes. Nothin' was going on over there. No cops. Nothin'.' Wylie went back to his shake. He sucked, grinned. 'Micky D makes a badass fucking 'shake, dude. Truth.'

Mace stacked the photos, put them back in the envelope and looked out of the window at the light in the Lowell apartment. He wondered why the cops hadn't visited her. He supposed they could have without Wylie noticing.

He assumed that the media was busily parsing details on the murders. There was a TV resting on top of a chest of drawers, but they hadn't turned it on yet and he didn't want to establish a precedence that could wind up with Wylie watching Sponge Bob Squarepants while Angela Lowell went into the wind. For a minute, he considered asking Wylie to light up his laptop. But only for a minute. He could wait for the morning paper to tell him what he needed to know, assuming the paper still had crime reporters.

He shrugged, picked up what was left of his burger and polished it off. He stood, yawned. 'OK with you I turn the light off and get some sleep?' he said. 'She's probably in for the night.'

'Crash,' Wylie said. 'I'm awake now. Good for a couple hours at least. I, ah, appreciate the 'shake and the QPs.'

Mace turned out the overhead. He walked across the dark room to his bed, sat down and began to undress. He watched Wylie put his music earplugs in place, take a suck of milkshake and peel the wrapper from the second burger. He wondered just how much Wylie knew about the limo chauffeur. He also wondered if he'd have to seriously hurt the kid to find out.

Ah, well, he'd worry about that tomorrow.

NINETEEN

The Killer Cafe was located a block west of the Coffee Empourium on Sunset. In the days when Mace had been a local resident its name had been The Edible Egg and its fame had been the result of a twenty-four-hour breakfast menu. The pale off-white interior still resembled the Egg's, Mace saw, as he moved past the morning diners.

The main change was the choice of framed photographs that adorned the Killer Café's walls. The Egg's publicity shots of celebrities enjoying the most important meal of the day had been replaced by stark black and white photos of famous murderers of recent vintage: David Berkowiz, the Son of Sam; Ted Bundy; John Wayne Gacy; Dennis Rader, the serial strangler known as BTK; Gary Leon Ridgway, also known as The Green River Killer.

Several were tagged by Day-Glo yellow stickers marked 'Local Slayers'. Mace recognized the now-infamous record producer Phil Spector. The Menendez Brothers. Juan Corona. Richard Ramierez, the Night Stalker. Sirhan Sirhan. Charles Manson, of course. And, yes, the ever-popular O.J. Simpson, though, as his sticker noted, 'he beat the law.' At least on the big one.

These sinister visages, many of them grinning as if they believed that sooner or later they'd be back walking the streets, did not seem to affect the appetites of the morning diners any more than the cholesterol count of the industrial-sized omelets they were consuming. Nor did the current hot topic of conversation: the media-tagged 'Point Dume bloodbath'.

Mace moved past the carbo-pounders to a side exit leading to an outdoor patio behind the main building. It had once been

the Egg's busiest spot, but the bravery that allowed The Killer
Cafe's patrons to ignore the mug shots of murderers evidently
did not extend to a more mundane threat like skin cancer.
Most of the tables were unoccupied, even those under the
protective cover of faded red umbrellas.

Only one patron seemed to be not only tolerating the rays of
the late-morning sun but embracing them. Honest Abe sat next
to an umbrella-less table on which rested a half-full cup of black
coffee, a neatly folded napkin and a plate, fork and knife,
smeared with the remains of egg yolk. He was dressed in khaki
cut-offs and a vivid red and orange colored Hawaiian shirt. He
was leaning back in his chair, wearing little plastic eye protectors with an aluminum sun reflector tucked under his chin.

Mace pulled back a chair from the table and sat.

'Who's there?' Abe asked, responding to the scrape of the
chair. 'Sylvia?'

'Morning, Abe,' Mace said.

Startled, Abe jerked upright, the reflector sliding down on
to his lap. He removed the eye protectors and squinted at
Mace. He seemed discomforted.

'Uh, Mace . . .'

'They told me at your place where to find you. I'm surprised.
I thought you liked it cold.'

'I do. It's just kinda hard to get a tan in the cold. And they
still do a bang-up breakfast here.'

'You ought to be more careful. Somebody could have walked
right up and –' Mace made a gun with his thumb and forefinger
and pointed it at Abe – 'Bingo! You'd be playing Lincoln for
real.'

'That'd be carrying an impersonation a mite too far,' Abe
said with a nervous giggle. 'Why would anybody—'

'You told Paulie Lacotta I'd been in to see you.'

Abe seemed surprised and maybe even relieved. Momentarily.
He lowered his eyes in a show of embarrassment. 'I . . . kinda
had to, Mace. I got my debts, you know. I'm sorry. It wasn't
personal. You understand that, right?'

Mace didn't bother to reply. He took a folded glossy photo
of Angela from the inside pocket of his jacket and held it up
in front of Abe.

'Tell me about her,' he said.

'Why are you—'

'Look at the goddamned picture, Abe.'

Abe gave the photo a quick scan and said, 'Never seen the lady before.'

Mace rose suddenly, his chair tipping over behind him. He grabbed the front of Abe's hula shirt and dragged him up from his chair. Then, aware of the silence, the sudden stillness in the air, he looked around the patio and saw that the few diners were staring at him. He was getting a lot of that lately. He managed to contain his anger enough to let go of the shirt.

Abe fell back on to his chair, blinking nervously.

Mace folded the glossy and slid it into his pocket. Then he leaned in on the lanky man, grabbing the armrests of Abe's chair. 'You tell me what you know about this woman, or I beat the crap out of you right here in front of these citizens.'

Abe licked his lips. He wasn't anxious to call Mace's bluff. 'It's the dame you mentioned before, Angela Lowell,' he said. 'She's come into my place once or twice.'

'With . . . ?' Mace asked. He moved back out of Abe's personal space.

'Lacotta,' Abe said. 'Didn't look like anything hot and heavy. You know Lacotta. His taste runs to, ah, earth mamas with big tatas. You must remember that from the old days?'

Mace did. But tastes changed.

He righted his chair and sat down again. 'Who else does she hang with, Abe?'

'You're tapping the wrong source,' Abe said, as if he meant it. 'Power on my computer, you will not even find the lady's name. I've seen her. I remember her because it's my business to remember pretty women. But that's it.'

Mace gave him the hard eye.

'Swear to God. Either she's what we used to call a square, a straight, or she's got the discretion thing down cold.'

'No connection to Tiny Daniels?'

'Jeeze, Mace,' Abe lowered his voice, looking around the sun deck to see if anyone had an ear out. 'You don't want to be dropping that name today above a whisper.'

'Why not? Everybody else in town is talking about the murders. We'll get to them in a minute.' Mace noted Abe's wince. 'Right now, I want you to tell me about Angela Lowell and Tiny.'

'Tiny was never into the ladies, figuratively or literally,' Abe said in a rough whisper. 'But he liked to be seen with pretty woman. I suppose I may have spotted a picture of them in Los Angeles magazine or one of those Beverly Hills back-pat journals, at a gallery opening or charity soirée. Tiny played that part, you know. Businessman contributor to good causes and culture. He was a big art collector. The paper this morning said there might have been twenty million dollars' worth of paint hanging on the walls of the murder house.'

Mace frowned, struck by a thought he should have had earlier. 'Who gets it?' he asked.

'Say again?'

'Who gets the art? All of Tiny's estate?'

'The paper didn't say,' Abe replied. 'Not me, surely. You're thinking Angela?'

'No,' Mace said, but he wasn't sure that was the truth. 'What've you heard about the murders?'

'Not even rumors. Still too soon. By afternoon, everybody will have a theory. Even Charlie Manson will offer his thoughts.'

'Are you familiar with an old-school Brit named Thomas who carries a gun and knows how to use it.'

Abe's face showed nothing. 'Not on my playlist. Is he the one –' Abe lowered his voice until Mace could barely hear him – 'took out Tiny and the others?'

'How would I know that?' Mace asked, annoyed.

'Of course you wouldn't,' Abe said. 'I didn't realize we'd changed the subject.'

'I had a run-in with Thomas and his brother Timmie, a big boy who looks like Elvis and acts and talks like he's in kindergarten. They were in a mustard-colored limo with a black driver named Sweets.'

Abe grinned. 'Not exactly sneaking around, are they? I can say without equivocation I have neither seen nor heard of such apparitions. What sort of run-in did you have?'

'Nothing fatal,' Mace said.

'You might ask your paparazzo about them,' Abe said.

'My paparazzo?'

'Symon,' Abe said. 'I saw his name on your picture of Lowell.'

Mace took the photo from his pocket. Simon S. Symon's name was stamped on the back.

'Colorful odd characters in a yellow limo? Symon lives for that kind of photo op. He's the west coast Diane Arbus.'

'He's a scumbag.'

Abe shrugged. He settled down in his chair and began to readjust his reflector. 'These days, who isn't?' he said.

TWENTY

At the stucco duplex on Orange Avenue, there was no sign of the fat woman with the baby. She'd probably already had her morning tobacco fix. Mace moved quickly to the rear of the building where he took the wooden stairs two at a time, not giving a damn how much noise he was making.

Past the screen door, the door to the apartment stood open. There was no sign of life.

He opened the screen door and stepped in.

The worn couch and chairs were still there. The people, the projector and even the yellow beanbag chair weren't.

He moved through the small apartment. The bedroom was in semi-darkness, old-fashioned paper shades blocking the sun, except for a torn edge that let in a shaft of light. A stripped, stained mattress rested on a metal frame. There was sand or grime on the floor that crunched when he walked.

The single bathroom was damp and smelled of soap perfume. There were no towels, nothing in the medicine cabinet, not even a roll of toilet paper.

Nothing in the apartment for him.

As he headed for the front door, he felt something under

his shoe that was neither sand nor grit. A couple of coins; a quarter and a nickel. He guessed they'd fallen out of The Beaver's pants while he was lying on the pillows.

Thirty cents didn't buy much. The departing tenants hadn't felt the coins worth the bending over.

Mace left them, too. But they reminded him of something.

He reached into his pocket and looked at the strange coin he'd taken from a dead man's mouth. He decided it was time for a visit to old friends.

TWENTY-ONE

There was a sign indicating that the Santa Monica Pier was celebrating its hundredth year of operation, which explained why it had had at least one makeover since Mace had last visited. The Merry-Go-Round in the old Hippodrome building, which was providing music and entertainment for a group of gleeful children, had been recently painted. The restaurants and shops looked much less seedy. There even seemed to be more tourists than homeless people, though Mace had to admit the distinction was not always apparent.

He paused in front of a brightly colored electric blue storefront displaying the drawing of a human hand. An unlit neon sign read 'MADAME SUZY' and in smaller letters, 'By Appointment Only.'

He tried the bright blue door and found it open.

A bell tinkled as he entered a small room with indirect lighting. As was the case with the rest of the pier, obvious improvements had been made. The walls had been painted aqua and the room refurnished with retro 1950s' couch and chairs, chrome based with aqua-colored, vinyl-covered seats. They surrounded a coffee table with a laminate top on which were artfully scattered books and pamphlets with titles like, *The Key to Your Sixth Sense* and *The You Beyond the You*.

Mace remembered a door in the wall directly across from the entrance, but it seemed to have disappeared with the remodel. He was searching for some way to move on into the rest of the house when he heard a familiar voice exclaim, 'Well, I be goddams.'

A section of the wall opened and an elderly woman entered the room smiling at him. She was dressed in blue denim trousers and a paler denim shirt. Though she had to be in her seventies, her hair was jet black, piled up on her head with what looked like a fresh magnolia pinned to it.

Before he could say a word she rushed across the floor and began hugging him.

'Hey, you goddamn galoots, you,' she said against his chest.

'Hi, Suzy.'

She pulled back and stared at him, putting on a fake pout. 'Hi Suzy. Hi Suzy. Nine years and it's "Hi Suzy", huh?' She patted her hair. 'Drop in like this, no warning. No time to fix myself up.'

'You look great,' he said.

She grinned. 'I look like what I am, an old voodoo. But you, David . . . you some hunk of man, sugar. Damn, it's good to see you.'

'You, too, Suzy,' he said. 'The Marquis around?'

'Whea else he be?' she replied. 'We was so sad to hear about yo' daddy. It didn't sound like he suffered, no?'

'No. He just got beat down by the hurricanes and tough times.'

'Oh, God, yeah. The hurricanes, the oil spill and the floods. And that po' goddamn city o' New Ah-leens. So *tragique*. Ah always figgered we'd go back some day, the Marquis an' me. But no more. We got this place fixed up nice, no?'

He looked around the room. 'Yeah,' he said. 'Looks great.'

'I see you on the spy cam,' she said, pointing at the flat lighting fixture in the center of the ceiling. 'We hi-tech, no?' Mace could see a tiny object, like the tip of a pen, pointed directly at him.

Suddenly, she was hugging him again. 'It's been so long. Damn, but I miss you Masons.' She took his hand and stepped back. 'It don't seem that long ago yo' gran'daddy and Hildy

and the Marquis and me were playing a club on the Gulf
Coast and this big son-bitch shrimper come in . . .'

'And accused granddad of cheating at poker?' Mace said.

'Aww, I tole you that story, huh?'

'Not more than fifteen or twenty times,' he said, smiling.
'Honey, I have to see the Marquis.'

'Oh, sure, Davey,' she said. 'I get too sentimental.'

'I love your stories about the old days. But I'm a little
pressed for time right now.'

'You got trouble?'

'Trying to avoid it.'

'OK,' she said. 'But –' lowering her voice to a whisper –
'the Marquis ain't the same, you unnerstand. Not since the
. . . sickness. Come.'

She lead him through a small dining room with peach-
colored walls, a polished oak table and six chairs, to a short
hall and, finally, to a small, dimly lit room at the rear of the
building where an old man sat in a wheelchair before a large
flat-screen TV, watching a game show in which the contest-
ants were given the answer and had to provide the
question.

The Marquis continued his concentration on the monitor,
apparently oblivious to their arrival. On the wall were posters
featuring him and Suzy in their salad days. The billing read:
'The Marquis, The Man Who Knows Everything. With the
Beauteous Suzy.'

'Hey, look who dropped out of the sky,' Suzy almost yelled
at the old man.

The Marquis spun his chair around and stared at Mace. His
face, which Mace remembered as strikingly handsome, was
narrow and deeply lined. And old. His intelligent eyes were
almost comedic, magnified by thick glasses.

A wide grin of recognition erased some of the years. He
tried to stand, pushing himself up, then remembered he was
in a wheel chair for a reason and slumped back down.

'Sorry, David, but you catch me at a disadvantage,' he said,
his voice still deep and rich.

'You look fine to me, Marquis,' Mace said.

'I look like George Burns a year after they put him under

the sod. Please sit. Don't make me strain my neck. It is the one part of my body that hasn't failed.'

Mace dragged a chair near him and sat.

The old man used his chin to indicate the TV. It was a game show Mace knew: *Jeopardy*. 'Television should be the last great art form of a civilization teetering on the brink of extinction,' the Marquis said. 'But of all its vast resources and possibilities, we get only five brief half-hours a week that ask us to use our memory.'

'I'm sorry if I'm interrupting . . .' Mace said.

'Not at all. It's being recorded. I can watch it anytime I care to. Ah, technology. We are your slaves.'

'I think Davey needs yo' help, Marquis,' Suzy said.

The old man nodded and smiled at Mace. 'You were never one for small talk. Business over badinage, just like your grandmother, God rest her soul.'

Mace reached into his pocket and took out the coin he had pried from Tiny Daniels' mouth. The old man raised his right hand to receive it, then winced in pain, and lowered his arm with a grimace of self-disgust. 'What fun,' he said.

Using his thumb and forefinger, Mace held the coin up for the Marquis to observe through his thick glasses. The old man gave it a curious glance and, continuing to rest his arm on the chair, turned his hand palm up. His long fingers resembled a spider's legs as he wiggled them impatiently. 'Let me feel it.'

Mace placed the coin on his palm.

'Light weight, eh? Odd material. Not metal. Not plastic. But what?'

'Any idea who's picture it is?'

'That's easy,' the Marquis said. 'Basil Zaharoff.'

'What team did he pitch for?' Mace asked.

'Google him and you'll get the full story.'

'As long as I'm here . . .' Mace said.

The Marquis grinned. He closed his eyes and began speaking as if he were reading from a text. 'Basil Zaharoff. A Turkish-born Frenchman who, in the early nineteen-hundreds, became a leading dealer in guns and armament for Great Britain's Vickers Co. A liar, a cheat, a schemer who bartered fluently in at least eight languages. He supplied weapons to both sides in the Boer War, the Balkan conflicts and the First World War. Became one of the wealthiest men in Europe and bestowed upon himself the title of Sir Basil Zaharoff. But he was more widely known by his nickname, The Merchant of Death.'

He opened his eyes and grinned.

'Bravo!' Suzy shouted and clapped her hands. 'You still got it up here, ba-bee.'

'Zaharoff couldn't still be alive?' Mace asked.

'He was born in eighteen forty-nine. You do the math, Davey.'

Mace smiled and took back the object 'Any idea why some-body would put his face on a fake coin?'

'I suppose it must have something to do with weaponry. You might want to put the coin under a microscope, see if it has any tales to tell.'

'I'll do that, Marquis,' Mace said, standing. 'Thanks for your help.'

Suzy looked disappointed. 'You not stayin' for coffee? I use chicory. Taste like home.'

'I'm sorry, but I've got to go. Thanks again, Marquis.'

'A breeze. Come back soon and I'll give you my theory about this so-called age of information and our obsession with the life and times of such crucial figures as Kim Kardashian and Charlie Sheen.'

The old man spun around and returned his attention to the television monitor.

Suzy took Mace's arm and led him back through the building.

'Is it cancer?' Mace asked.

'No, hon. The MS,' she said softly. 'Started slow, but it's got the upper han' now. You come back soon, before it takes him away.'

Mace promised he would.

TWENTY-TWO

Mace spent the next hour or so at a public library in West LA, using the computers to Google everything he could about Basil Zaharoff. There was an abundance of material, but nothing to suggest why his countenance might have been engraved on a coin.

Annoyed and frustrated, he returned to the Florian where he angled the Camry into its slot. Angela Lowell's Mustang was not in its space. But, he discovered with both alarm and anger, Wylie's car was still parked.

Fast-walking past the pool, he looked up to see that their apartment curtains were drawn.

He took the stairs two at a time, then paused at their door.

He heard bedsprings and a moan.

Furious now, he unlocked the door, rushed in and closed the door behind him.

He crossed the dark apartment to stand beside Wylie's bed. It was occupied. More moaning. Mace reached for the bedside lamp and turned it on.

There was only one person in the bed, covered by the spread. Mace pulled it back. Wylie lay in a fetal position, his face battered and bleeding, shivering in a combination of sickness and fright.

He looked up at Mace, as spooked as a horse facing fire.

'I . . . I . . . oh, Mace. Thank you, Jesus,' Wylie said.

'Keep still. I'll get a doc.'

'No!' Wylie forced himself into a sitting position, moaning in pain. 'I . . . left word with Mr Lacotta. Gotta wait . . . for his OK.'

'Screw that,' Mace said. 'You're hurt bad. You need help now.'

Wylie swung his legs around and sat on the edge of the bed. 'Not . . . so bad.'

He coughed. There was blood on his lips. 'I was . . . on

the bitch, Mace . . . truth. They caught me downstairs . . . in garage . . . big fucking bastard . . . Elvis, jus' like you said . . . Bear hug . . . broke inside.'

'Sit down, man. Stay still.'

'They wanted . . . you. Bullshit about . . . a coin. I didn't know . . . what the fuck?'

The quarter-sized counterfeit in Mace's pocket seemed to be getting heavier.

'I've seen . . . the big bastard . . . before . . . *King C-hole* . . . *Kid Gal-I-Had* . . . *Roust-a-butt.*'

Mace thought Wylie was hallucinating. Spouting nonsense. He saw the kid's cellular on the bedside table and picked it up.

'Yeah. Call Mr Lacotta,' Wylie yelled, more blood spilling over his lips. 'Tell him . . . not my fault.'

'You got internal bleeding, son,' Mace said. 'No time for Lacotta. You need a doc.'

'No.' Wylie pushed off the bed and staggered to the door. 'Can take care of . . . myself.'

He opened the door and stumbled out.

'Shit,' Mace said and tossed the phone aside. He ran after the kid.

By some magic or adrenaline surge Wylie had already cleared the stairs.

Arriving at the patio, Mace saw him weaving toward the garage. The last two sunbathers, men in thongs, had just left their poolside chairs and were walking toward the main building carrying lotions and iPhones and rolled scripts.

Mace was distracted by them, watching to see if they noticed Wylie. They were too absorbed in their conversation to notice anything but themselves. Once they'd entered the building, Mace shifted his attention to Wylie, saw him stumble forward and fall face down on to the pool deck. By the time he arrived, blood was forming what looked like a large, dark-red jigsaw piece under the kid's head.

Mace searched for a pulse and discovered Wylie was beyond his help.

It was time to help himself.

TWENTY-THREE

Mace tossed his gear into his canvas bag. He searched the room, stuck Wylie's cell phone and car keys into his jacket pocket and grabbed the bottle of bourbon, adding that to the bag, along with the two sets of binoculars. He went over the apartment, more carefully this time. When he was convinced that he'd left nothing obvious, he zipped the bag shut.

He was not unmindful of the fingerprints and DNA samples he'd left behind. There just wasn't anything he could do about them.

He stood at the window, pulled the curtain back and looked down on Wylie's body. As best he could tell, it hadn't attracted any attention, but it wouldn't be long before somebody started screaming. He didn't want to be around for that.

He raised his eyes for one last look at Angela Lowell's draped windows.

He left the apartment and moved quickly to the Lexus Wylie had been using. He unlocked the door and gave the interior a quick search. Satisfied that the laptop that Wylie had been using to track the Mustang was the only thing worth taking, he grabbed it. He was backing out of the vehicle when he saw an odd-looking black box, the size of a thin cigarette pack. Curious, he studied it for a beat, discovered it was nothing more than smartly packaged chewing gum and slipped it into his now bulging jacket pocket.

Then he got the hell away from the Florian.

A block down Sunset, he pulled over to the curb and used Wylie's phone to put in a call to Paulie. After a couple of rings, voice mail kicked in. Mace broke the connection and tried the office.

'Mr Lacotta is unavailable,' a pleasant female voice informed him, 'but if you'd just give me your—'

'Tell him it's Mace and it's important.'

'I'll be happy to give him the message, Mr Mace. If you'd—'

'No message. I need to talk to him now.'

'I'm sorry, but Mr Lacotta is in a meet—'

Mace hung up on her.

He tossed Wylie's cellular and computer on the passenger seat, put the car in drive and, forcing himself to stick to the pace the traffic was setting, headed west. Twelve minutes later, he was descending into the sub-basement parking facilities beneath a building on the eastern edge of the Century City complex of business offices and high-end retail stores.

Four minutes after that, he joined the throng of mainly smartly dressed young men and women who seemed happy to be returning to work after lunch at a time of more than ten percent unemployment.

Mace ignored them as he pushed through the revolving doors and entered the astringent-scented, chilly lobby. Two security officers, manning a desk as long as a wild west saloon bar, seemed to be performing the useful service of mentally undressing the continuous parade of attractive females. He strolled past them to join a crowd waiting at a bank of elevators.

In front of him, a thin young man wearing a two thousand dollar suit and a Dodgers cap backward on his head was regaling a similarly garbed but capless corporate turk with a tale of the marketplace. 'So I told the towel-head to take a hike and he says, "Why get upset? This is business." And I say, "'Cause the B'nai B'rith wouldn't understand, you Arab bastard."'

'Holy shit! Then what?'

'The son of a bitch has the brass to raise the ante to eighty thou.'

'Damn. Hard to turn down.'

One set of elevator doors opened and Mace was swept in along with a dozen others, including the two young conversationalists.

'Turn down?' the Dodgers cap said, as he pressed the '24' button. 'He goes up to a hundred and ten thou.'

Mace was too far away from the buttons to press his floor, so he called out, 'Could someone please hit twenty seven?'

No one responded.

Maybe they were too intrigued by Dodger cap's tale. 'So I got him up to one hundred and twenty thou. And he's telling me he respects my faith and he really wants to make this deal which has nothing to do with our religious beliefs. Yadda, yadda, yadda. And he throws out one hundred and twelve.'

'No shit?'

'We close at one hundred and fourteen.'

The door opened on the twenty-fourth floor. As the two men exited, Mace heard Dodgers cap say, 'And, bottom line, I'm not even Jewish.'

The doors closed on his self-satisfied chuckle.

Mace had already been on edge. And he didn't appreciate the self-involved passengers ignoring his request a second time. He pushed a man out of his way and reached over a plump woman just in time to stop the elevator on the twenty-seventh floor.

He squeezed out of the sardine can to a spotless off-white hall. To his right, the hall led to an exit stairwell. To his left, restrooms. Directly in front of him was a polished wooden door that read 'Mount Olympus Industries' in shiny brass letters. It was the only door on that side of the building, which meant that Mount Olympus occupied the complete floor. Definitely a step up from the company's old offices, which had been in a bungalow in the Studio City Business Park.

The reception area was designed to resemble an exotic port of call. Softly lit. The walls were a pale, pastel violet. Air circulated, as cool as an ocean breeze. It carried a hint of perfume and possibly suntan lotion, though Mace wouldn't swear to that. Stunted potted palm trees were placed at various key points in the room. The furnishings, comfortable looking chairs and sofas, were constructed of faded rattan and leather, with cushions covered in bright island prints.

There was a wall that curved inward on an entryway to what Mace assumed was the working office. Just to the right of the wall, a receptionist was seated behind a kidney-shaped rattan desk. She was a beautiful, very black woman with an orchid in her hair. She was wearing a pearl-gray suit over a blouse that picked up the color of the walls. Mace was a little let down that she hadn't gotten into the spirit of things with a sarong. But she did compliment the decor. Which was more than he could say about the big, raw-boned dude with a crew cut giving him the stink-eye from a chair to his left.

The receptionist was observing Mace, too, but in a much friendlier manner.

'Good afternoon, sir,' she said. 'May I help you?'

She sounded a little like she might have been the woman who'd answered the phone. 'I'd like to see Mr Lacotta.'

'Ah. And you have an appointment, Mr . . . ?'

Mace walked past her through the entry to a room where half a dozen employees sat in cubicles, busy with tasks that he could not begin to imagine.

'*Sir*!' the receptionist called behind him.

He double-timed it past the cubicles and faced four closed doors. He figured Paulie would want windows and a nice big corner space.

'Really, sir . . .' The receptionist's heels were clicking nearer on the floor tiles.

He headed for the corner door and had it open before she could stop him.

It was a Paulie-type office. Dark leather, smoked glass. Drapes covering the windows. A rich, thick carpet. An absolutely pristine desktop. Signed portraits of the Lakers and the Dodgers on one wall. A shelf with uniform, buckram-bound books. The only thing that surprised Mace was Paulie's absence.

'What the hell do you think you're doing?' the receptionist said, anger removing a thin veneer of practiced cordiality.

'This is Lacotta's office, right?' he asked.

'It is.'

'He's not here,' Mace said stupidly.

'No he isn't. Now leave these premises or I call security.'

Mace stepped back out of the office and without pause headed for the next door.

'Damn you,' the receptionist said, and rushed after him.

He opened the door to a conference room. Lacotta and three guys in suits sat at a long table. Two had notepads in front of them. All had coffee cups.

They turned to stare at him.

Paulie didn't seem too disturbed. 'Mace?'

'It's important,' Mace said.

'So's this. Gimme a couple minutes.' Paulie looked past him to the receptionist. 'Teddi, get Mr Mason some juice or something.'

'Yes, sir,' she said though clenched teeth. She reached past Mace to pull the door shut in his face.

'What kind of juice would you like?' she asked flatly as they returned to the reception area.

'Any beer?'

'I'm afraid not.'

'Then forget it.'

He moved to a chair. The raw-boned man gave him a lazy glance, then shifted his interest to the copy of Forbes open on his lap.

Eighteen minutes later, by Mace's watch, the conference room door opened and the four men exited. Paulie led his guests to the elevator, where they shook hands. Mace judged the mood to be more strained than cordial.

The raw-boned man got to his feet and sauntered to the others. He paused beside a thickset man in a tailored blue pinstripe suit. A banker, maybe. Or a politician. The occupations seemed interchangeable. The raw-boned man whispered something in the other's ear and they both stared openly at Mace.

He gave them a wink and a friendly wave.

They did not seem amused.

The elevator arrived and they and the other two men departed.

Paulie walked toward him, his face unreadable. Mace stood and followed him into his private office.

As soon as he'd closed the door, Paulie wheeled on him. 'This is a goddamned place of business, not a barroom. You used to have some control, some class. What the fuck's the matter with you?'

'We have to talk.'

Lacotta checked his watch. It was big and gold-rimmed. 'OK. Come. I wanna show you something.'

He headed for a door to the left of his desk, leading Mace

to a small windowless room that seemed to be a mini-gym. Black pads on the carpet. A couple of campaign chairs, several pairs of bright red dumb-bells and an exercycle. The only unusual element was some kind of space age fixture in the center of the ceiling, a shiny black box with black metal tubes telescoping from it, aimed at three of the room's four walls.

Paulie removed his coat and placed it on an empty chair.

Mace said, 'It's important. It's about Wylie.'

'Cool your jets,' Lacotta said. 'Check this out.'

He moved to the exercycle, straddled it and pressed a button on its dashboard. The room was thrown into darkness. Within seconds, lights streamed from the metal tubes and the three blank walls were turned into a 270-degree cyclorama of a beautiful rural bike path. Birds were singing. Clouds floated by.

Mace was not impressed. His patience had worn through. He stepped forward to drag Lacotta off the exercycle. And a remarkable thing happened. A fully dimensional but oddly transparent young woman in shorts and a halter appeared at the left of the room and walked to the right. She blew Mace a kiss.

'What the hell . . . ?' Mace said, momentarily stymied. There was something about the semi-transparent woman that reminded him of the giant dog he'd seen at Tiny's.

'It's a prototype of a system called Simureal,' Lacotta said. 'Something, huh?'

A male jogger appeared from nowhere. His image pixilated a little before he disappeared. *Holograms!* Mace remembered the dying security officer. He'd thought the man's last words had been 'dog' and 'whole'. He'd been trying to say that Tiny's big white dog was a hologram.

Intriguing, but not why Mace had come to Lacotta's office.

'Paulie . . .' he began.

'Wait. Watch this,' Lacotta said, his feet turning the pedals.

The scene changed. It was as if the room were zooming forward along the path, keeping pace with Lacotta's pedaling. Dimensional images of fellow cyclists and joggers appeared and disappeared.

This may have been entertaining to someone sitting on a cycle, pedaling, but for Mace, standing still in the room, it was annoying and disorienting. 'Listen to me, you son of a bitch.' he shouted. 'Stop this goddamn thing.'

'Can't stop the future,' Paulie said. 'You got any idea the kind of money people spend on exer—'

'Wylie's dead,' Mace said.

It took a few seconds for the words to work their way past Paulie's exuberance.

Then he stopped pedaling. He pressed the machine's off button and the holographic image froze and disappeared. The ceiling lights went back on. He sat on the machine, frowning for a beat.

'Dead,' he said. 'How?'

'The group who picked me up near Tiny's grabbed him in the garage at the Florian. The big guy, the one with the mentality of a kid, got him in a bear hug. When I found him he needed a doctor. But he didn't want one, because he thought you wouldn't like it.'

'A good kid.'

'Was,' Mace said. 'He got out of bed and ran out of the door to prove he didn't need a doctor. He made it as far as the pool.'

'Jesus! How . . . ? Why didn't you . . . ?

'Why didn't I *what*, Paulie? What more could I have done? I left him dead in his own blood beside the Florian's swimming pool and got the hell out of there. You might want to phone your buddy the manager with instructions. While you're at it, make damn sure he forgets I was ever there.'

Paulie slipped off the exercycle, dazed.

'Yeah,' he said. 'Better phone.'

TWENTY-FOUR

Uniformed cops had been at the Florian for about half an hour Henry Sussman, Paulie's buddy the building manager, informed him. They'd thrown a tarp over the dead man and taped off that section of the deck. They'd closed the pool. Like them, Sussman was waiting for the homicide detectives and the forensics people. He wanted to know what he should say to them.

'Keep it simple,' Paulie told him. He was seated at the desk in his office, using the speakerphone so that Mace, perched on a corner of the desk, could hear. 'Tell 'em the truth, Henry. Wylie checked in a week ago on a week-to-week basis. He was quiet, kept to himself.'

Sussman seemed to need guidance. He mumbled something about shredding Wylie's registration card.

'No, don't do that,' Paulie replied. 'Show it to the cops when they ask for it. Jesus, Henry, don't fall apart on me. No problem with them knowing where the kid worked. They come here and I talk to 'em. No big deal.

'Here's the thing to remember. The kid was staying there by himself . . .'

'Should I tell them he rented the apartment for business?'

'No. No. No. You don't know why he checked in or how long he was planning to stay. He was using his credit card to pay the bill, right? Good. That's what the cops are gonna want and you give it to 'em.'

'What about his car? What do I do with it?'

Mace shook his head in dismay.

'It's a rental, Henry,' Paulie said, his face reddening. 'The cops'll probably impound it. If not, Avis will send somebody to retrieve it. It's not your problem, OK?'

'I guess.'

'Good. OK,' Paulie said. 'Give Lois and the kids my love.'

'Sure . . .'

Paulie clicked his phone shut and stood up.

'Excuse me if I'm not placing a lot of confidence in Henry,' Mace said.

'I don't even think he knows your name,' Paulie said, pacing back and forth.

'I sure as hell didn't give it to him.'

'You think I did?' Paulie's face was crimson now.

'I think you're spending too much time in your virtual world and not enough in the real one. What happens when the detectives working the Point Dume murders decide to check out your ex-girlfriend and tie that in with Wylie's murder?'

'You're a goddamned doomster, Mace. You're lovin' this, aren't you? My life gets any more fucked up, you'll be in paradise.'

'You going to cry?'

Paulie took a swing at him. Slow enough for Mace to slide off the desk, move under the punch and hit him once in the stomach.

With a painful grunt, Paulie folded and fell to the carpet. Wheezing, holding his stomach, he looked up at Mace through tears of pain and said, 'Bastard . . . Call yourself a friend . . . Hate my guts, don't you?'

Mace extended a hand to him. 'Sure. That's why I came back to LA. Why I've been dodging bullets and risking a return trip to Pel Bay.'

Paulie took the offered hand and got to his feet. 'My head's all screwed up,' he said, his mood shifting into maudlin. 'I know you're my buddy, Mace. My only trustworthy amigo.'

'Tell me what you're into.'

Paulie merely sighed and shook his head.

'Weapons deal?' Mace prompted.

Paulie narrowed his eyes. 'Where'd that come from?'

'Wiley told me about Commingore Industries,' Mace said. And your trip to DC.'

Paulie sighed again. 'I might as well level with you. Sit, for Christ's sake. You make me nervous.'

Mace took a chair and watched Paulie move to a cabinet that contained a small compact refrigerator. 'Water?' he asked. When Mace shook his head, he removed a bottle of Perrier for himself, popped the cap and took a long swig.

He carried what was left of the water back to his desk chair and sat. 'It was a gold mine,' he said.

Mace stared at him, waiting for more.

Paulie reached under his desk and, behind him, the row of what had appeared to be Morocco-bound books turned out to be leather book spines attached to a wooden panel that swung out on hinges. Exposing a wall safe.

Mace watched, bemused, as Paulie hopped to his feet, punched a few numbers on the safe's lock and pressed his thumb against a small glowing green square that appeared.

The door to the safe clicked open. Paulie reached in and removed what looked like a Colt Double Eagle pistol.

Mace tensed.

Paulie tossed the weapon to him. He'd expected it to be much heavier and he almost fumbled it. He hefted it, puzzled. He pressed a catch behind the trigger and released the magazine. He tapped the magazine against the gun butt. 'It's not real,' he said. 'It's a prop.'

'You musta seen *The Graduate,* huh,' Paulie said. 'Dustin Hoffman is this kid who doesn't know what the fuck to do with his life after college. And this asshole tells him he's got one word that's gonna make Dustin's future. The word is: "Plastics".'

'OK,' Mace said. 'So this is plastic and it looks real enough, but it's still a prop.'

'It's real, Mace. It kills just like a gun made of metal. The plastic is so fucking hard you can make a missile out of it. A warhead. An airplane, if you want. It's as strong as steel.'

Mace cocked a skeptical eyebrow. He worked one of the bullets from the magazine. 'This isn't fake,' he said.

'Neither is the gun. I ran out of the plastic bullets doing the tests.'

'Plastic gun, plastic bullets,' Mace said.

'There's never a depression where weapons are concerned, and right now there's maybe four companies in the US draggin' down nearly forty billion a year selling arms overseas. Wasn't long ago, everybody was going nuts over the new Howitzer because the manufacturer was able to bring the weight down to nine thousand eight hundred pounds. That's because it was made of high-tensile titanium. This plastic could cut that weight by two-thirds, Mace. It'll make titanium all but fucking obsolete. Not only that, it's cheap to manufacture. And the beauty part is that it can't be detected by any existing defense gear.

'Before I could board a plane two weeks ago, they made me take my shoes off. And my car keys set off a buzz, but they still don't know I walked through their metal detector with that weapon, armed and ready, in an ankle holster.'

Mace placed the gun on Lacotta's desk.

'And it's all legit. This is gonna help us kick Al-Qaeda's butt. Or anybody else's.'

'So what's the problem?'

Paulie gave him a wry smile. 'You know me, Mace. If there's a way to miss a slam dunk, I'll find it.'

Mace wasn't sure he wanted to hear Paulie's tale of woe. Billion-dollar deals. Plastic guns. It meant about as much to him as a Hollywood starlet's cocaine habit. But there was one point of interest. 'Where does Angela Lowell fit in?' he asked.

Paulie blinked as if the question caught him off-guard. 'Angie?' he said. 'That's a long story.'

'Highlight it for me,' Mace said.

TWENTY-FIVE

'Angie's story is another example of me reverting to form,' Paulie said. 'One of the guys who was just here – the one in the tailor-made suit . . . '

Mace frowned.

'Blue pinstripe. Gabardine. Nipped in the waist. High armholes.'

'Yeah,' Mace said. 'The first thing I notice about a guy is the way his clothes fit.'

'Sorry,' Paulie said. 'So I started out in the shmata business . . .'

'Stealing shmata,' Mace said. 'But I know the guy you mean. Gray hair. Stone face. Had a bodyguard waiting in reception.'

'His name's Corrigan. Ex-CIA. He set up the auction for the formula a while back. Mount Olympus was the high bidder. We wired the loot to his offshore account. The transfer of the formula was a little trickier. Corrigan brokers his deals from an art gallery in Paris. It's a front, but he knows one painting from another. Does a lot of legit business in Europe and here in the States. So I get this idea.'

'Angela Lowell is an art appraiser,' Mace said.

'Bingo!' Paulie said. 'She's gone over there on buying trips before. I figure I'll send her to Corrigan's to pick out some art for my place. Corrigan can put the formula in with the canvasses for Angie to mule here.'

Mace casually slid his hand into his pocket and touched the coin. He was surprised that it comforted him, like a talisman. 'Why so complicated?' he asked. 'The deal was all above board, right?'

'It was and it wasn't. See, the CEO of Commingore started hemming and hawing, so we had to find another partner. I can't get into the specifics, but our new associate is . . . well, the government has used him to supply weapons and armament in Iraq and Afghanistan, but . . .'

'But it's been on the QT, because he's not a good guy,' Mace said, 'and the public probably would not approve this country being in bed with him.'

'Right. The idea was to keep the whole thing on the down low. At least until we get into production.'

'OK, you wired the money to Corrigan. Why didn't he just wire the formula to you?'

'Well, in the first place, the genius who came up with the formula used it to make a coin and then engraved the formula on it. Not so easy to wire.'

Mace shook his head. 'This genius sounds like he's on the weed. The world isn't fucked up enough, he's got to make it even more complicated? And Corrigan. Why didn't he just copy the formula off the coin and wire that to you?'

Paulie looked uncomfortable. 'He says it's too easy to compromise digital formats. He's old school. Like you, Mace. He still uses couriers, for Christ's sake.'

'Why didn't he use one of his couriers?'

Paulie winced in embarrassment. 'He wanted to. That's where I screwed the pooch. I . . . thought Angie might like a couple days in Paris.'

Mace stared at him. If Paulie was being straight, which was always doubtful, he'd put an incredibly valuable item at risk just to send his girlfriend on a trip. This was business in America? No wonder the economy was in such fucking bad shape.

'Did she know the real reason for her trip?' he asked.

'Not from me.'

'What went wrong?'

Lacotta shrugged and showed Mace his palms. 'I sent a limo to LAX for Angie and a truck for the crates. She got back to her place OK, but the truck just disappeared. The coin. The paintings. My three guys. All gone. Never to be heard from again.'

'What did she have to say about it?'

'She made sure the crates got through customs. Waited till my guys rolled 'em into their truck. Then she took the limo home.'

'But you don't quite trust her.'

'I put one of my guys on her,' Paulie said. 'That's how I found out she was spending time at Tiny's beach house. She said it was business. He hired her to appraise his art collection.'

Mace remembered the paintings, worth twenty million. He also remembered a dead pretty boy whom Lowell had called Carlos and wondered if she might have been appraising more than the art.

'Before you ask,' Paulie said, 'she claimed she didn't see any of the missing paintings out there.'

'Who knew the formula – the coin – was coming in with the paintings?'

'Just me.'

'And Corrigan,' Mace said.

'He's straight.'

'He's a former spook who sells weapons,' Mace said. 'Not exactly a candidate for sainthood.'

'Maybe not. But he's solid.'

'Why doesn't he get the inventor to scribble out the formula again?'

'Well, that's the thing,' Paulie said. 'Corrigan says the inventor isn't around anymore. He's pretty pissed about the whole thing. That's why he and his leg-breaker are here.'

'Why should he care? He got paid.'

'I . . . to make sure that the auction went our way, I cut him in for profit points. And he's on the warpath.' He shook his head. 'I'm so fucked.'

'Why'd you drag me into this mess?' Mace asked.

'I was hoping you'd be able to figure out if Angie set me up. Then maybe I could get her to tell me what happened to the coin. As soon as Uncle Sal comes back from his business trip down south, he's gonna want a report. His first move will be to drag Angie in and start cutting her fingers off until she talks. I'd sincerely like to avoid that.'

'You in love with her, or what?'

'I don't know. Maybe. Probably not.'

'You're hopeless,' Mace said.

'Tell me something new.'

'OK. Since nobody sends a hit man to steal a coin, I think we can assume that whoever sent the Brit wasn't just after the formula; he wanted Tiny dead.'

'So?'

'So Thomas's employer was miffed with Tiny. Sound like anyone we know?'

'You think it's me? Christ! I don't do murder. And the first I heard of this guy Thomas was when you mentioned him. You said he was with the guy who tried to kill *me*.'

Mace nodded. 'Who else might have had it in for Tiny?'

'You knew him. The guy was a sewer rat. Nobody likes sewer rats.' He leaned his head back in his chair. 'I put Angie in the sewer with him.'

'How do you figure?'

'If I hadn't been hot for her, Tiny wouldn't have gone after her.'

Mace wasn't sure if it had been the nuns who'd done a state-of-the-art guilt trip on Paulie or if it was middle-age paranoia, the belief that the whole world revolved around him. 'You ought to be more concerned about yourself,' Mace said. 'Montdrago might figure *you* for the sell-out.'

'Thanks for keeping it optimistic,' Paulie said. 'Maybe we grab this Thomas, we get the coin.'

'I don't think he had time to find it,' Mace said. 'The shooting couldn't have taken place too long before I got there. The bodies were still warm. Tiny's socks were off, which suggests Thomas might have been getting ready for a little torture to find the coin. But something happened and he wound up shooting everybody instead. Something – probably the arrival of the security guards – distracted him. And when he'd finished with them, I showed up. And he ran.'

'Then where's the fucking coin?' Paulie asked. 'I need the damn thing. I paid for it.'

'Have your toy gun analyzed,' Mace said.

'I tried. They can break down the elements, but not the process.'

Mace looked at his old pal slumped in the chair and thought about reaching into his pocket and handing Paulie the precious coin. But that was always an option. There was too much Paulie wasn't telling him. The more pressure, the more truth.

'Who were the other two buttoned-down types in your meeting with Corrigan?'

'They're, ah, with Tideland Security.'

Mace shook his head. 'Mercs? The same Special Forces dropouts who were paid a fortune to fuck up in Iraq?'

'They're working for our other business partner—'

'The one you won't name.'

'Yeah. It's better you don't know. He hired Tideland to check *me* out, for Christ's sake.'

'When exactly did Corrigan blow into town?' Mace asked.

'A couple hours ago. He and his shadow came to the meeting directly from the airport.'

'What does that tell you, Paulie?'

Lacotta looked at him blankly.

'He's not here because you were ripped off,' Mace explained. 'That happened weeks ago. He's here because Tiny was killed and the coin's gone south.'

'You could be right,' Paulie said. 'But that still leaves us with the question of who sent the hitman to kill Tiny and get the coin?'

A name suddenly popped into Mace's head. He'd been hearing it ever since he arrived and it had been on the pill bottle in Angela Lowell's bag. 'What do you know about a Jerry Monte?' he asked Paulie.

'A Jerry Monte? Like he's not the current king of show biz and if not king maybe a crown prince on Wall Street. I love you, Mace.'

'Other than the hype what do you know about him?'

'A Jersey guy. Everybody likes him. Women love him. A real talent and he's smart as hell. A genius, really. Computers. Electronics. He's into all that shit. Why do you ask?'

'He was at Abe's. They were lined up around the block to see him. Olympus own a piece of him?'

In spite of his mood, Lacotta smiled. 'He could own a piece of us,' he said. 'You don't get it, do you? This guy is big. He's up there with Oprah and Spielberg. But, as a matter of fact, we are investors in that exercise environment thing I showed you. Simureal. That's his company.'

'Would Angela Lowell know him?' Mace asked.

'I don't know. Maybe. A lot of people do. The guy's pretty accessible. Throws these weekend parties at his place in Cabrillo Canyon. My uncle's been to a couple.'

'You know the address?'

'Not offhand. You're not thinking Monte is mixed—'

He was interrupted by a buzzing sound. His desk phone. He picked up the receiver. 'Yeah?'

He listened for a beat and said, 'Shit. Keep her on hold for a minute.' To Mace, he said, 'It's Wylie's mother and she's all fucked up. I gotta take it.'

Mace stood. 'Good luck with that. When you're finished, maybe you can get somebody to book me a hotel room. Any place but the Florian.'

'Stay at my place,' Paulie said.

'Sure. Why not?'

'You think Jerry Monte's fucking around with my deal?' Paulie asked.

'I'll let you know,' Mace said.

TWENTY-SIX

Mace decided the best way of getting a fix on Jerry Monte was through Angela Lowell. At least that's the rationale that found him parking down the road a bit past the Florian. He got out of the car and walked back to the apartment hotel, probably the last place in the LA area where he'd want the police to find him. Well, maybe the second to last place, next to Tiny Daniels' bloodstained beach house.

He walked only as far as the garage. If Angela Lowell's yellow Mustang was there, he'd hang out parked on the street, keeping his eye on the driveway from a safe distance until she left the hot area.

But the Mustang was gone.

He was annoyed with himself for not having bothered to figure out how to use the tracking device that had been planted in the Mustang. Maybe he could get Paulie . . . no, bad idea. Paulie would pimp him about being too old school to use a computer. And then he'd start quizzing him about the Angela-Monte connection.

There was an easier way to locate Monte. And probably Angela Lowell.

As he walked back to his Camry, a black van zoomed past him and screeched to a stop, parking across the street from the Florian. The guy behind the wheel had shoulders like a line-backer. He was wearing a black T-shirt, Ray-Bans and a blinking blue beetle in his ear. The name on the van was Beverlywood Cleaners.

Mace figured Lowell was lucky to be gone. Otherwise she'd be entertaining Tideland Security. In lieu of interrogating her, they'd probably clean her apartment, but not in a way that would leave it nice and tidy.

He got into the Camry, started it up and made a U-turn to head back to Sunset.

Passing the van, he saw that the driver had exited and was waiting for another buffed up guy who was leaving the vehicle via its back door. The last Mace saw of them in his rear-view mirror, they were strolling casually toward the entrance to the Florian.

TWENTY-SEVEN

Honest Abe groaned when Mace's image appeared on his security camera, stopping to talk to the idiot who was setting up the tables and chairs. The idiot pointed up toward Abe's office.

Abe looked around the room, saw nothing that needed to be put away and settled back behind his desk. At the knock, he said, 'Come on in, Mace.'

The big man entered, scanning the office. 'Nice,' he said. 'And it definitely smells better than your old one.'

'Take a chair. Coffee?'

Mace accepted the chair and refused the coffee.

'You're getting to be a regular,' Abe said. 'I may have to put you on my speed-dial.'

'Tell me about your pal the poet,' Mace said. 'Jerry Monte.'

'What do you want to know?'

'What's he into besides poetry?'

Abe laughed. 'Anything and anyone.'

'A little more specific.'

Abe sighed. 'He makes movies. He sings. He dances. All of which gives him a fortune in entertainment buckos. And he's the brains behind an electronics company that'll probably make Sony look like dog shit one of these days.'

'What about off camera and out of the spotlight?' Mace asked. 'Perv? Goofy religion? Drugs?'

'I gather he covers the waterfront when it comes to sex. Religion, not so much.'

'Drugs?'

'This is Hollywood, Mace. You musta heard the joke. "I don't like cocaine. I just like the smell." Jerry doesn't overdo, but he's an excellent host. By that I mean he and some other heavy-hitters own a drug store.'

'Honeymoon Drugs?' Mace asked.

Abe nodded before remembering that Mace previously had

asked him about the Honeymoon. In connection with what
. . . ? *Aw, shit. Angela Lowell.*

'I hear Monte throws parties at his place in Cabrillo Canyon,'
Mace said.

'He's a party animal, for sure.'

'Got one tonight?'

'The usual. Hot cooze and cold vodka.'

'Where in Cabrillo Canyon, exactly?' Mace asked.

Abe wondered if he should bullshit or play it straight. The
scowl on Mace's face made up his mind for him. He mentioned
an address on Cabrillo Canyon Road.

'Can you get me an invitation to the party?'

Abe shook his big head, his features showing sincere regret.
'We're friends, Mace. And we go back a ways. But, frankly,
you're a little . . . unpredictable? I can't afford to have Jerry
pissed at me because somebody I recommended started slug-
ging his party guests. Or him.'

'I've mellowed, Abe.'

'So you won't manhandle anyone. You'll just piss in the
punchbowl. You're gonna have to find another way in.'

'You're more afraid of Monte than you are of me?' Mace
said. 'Good to know.'

Abe felt a chill, but he said, 'I respect you more. But he's
got money in this place.'

Mace smiled. A rare thing. 'You're OK, Abe. Thanks for
the address. I'll work something out.'

He stood and lost the smile. 'But if I hear that you tipped
Monte to be watching out for me, it'll be the end of our beautiful relationship.'

Abe followed Mace's departure on his security monitor. It
wasn't until the big man had cleared the front door that he
remembered to exhale. He reached out a hand to the phone,
then thought better of it. *Let Jerry fucking Monte handle his
own problems.*

TWENTY-EIGHT

M ace had driven just a few blocks west on Sunset when he spotted a black Bentley sedan several cars back that seemed to be pacing him. He speeded up and so did the Bentley. He slowed and the Bentley fell back, too.

He continued along Sunset until Charing Cross Road where he took a sharp left. Then a right on Hilgard, which he followed to Westholme where he drove on to the UCLA campus. Not for the first time, he wondered what the designer of the campus had been smoking when he laid out the streets. He took rights and lefts as if he had some destination in mind. Eventually he had to stop a jogger to find out how to get to Sunset. Then another student.

Rejoining Sunset Boulevard at Westwood Plaza, he checked his rear-view mirror and saw that the Bentley was no longer following. Of course, the tail could have been passed to any of the other vehicles lined up behind him.

There were only two cars trailing him when he turned right off Sunset on to Cabrillo Canyon Road. According to the address Abe had provided, Jerry Monte's party central was way the hell up Cabrillo. A tenth of a mile before he got there, Mace took a road to the left that doglegged up the canyon.

His Camry was the only car on that narrow road.

He kept driving until he arrived at a lip that provided a nice view of the lower Canyon. He parked the Camry as close to the protected side of the road as he could. There was barely enough space for another car to pass, but he didn't think that would be a problem unless a driver came barreling up or down and was surprised. The odds of that were slim. People using that road had to be careful drivers or they wouldn't still be alive.

He opened the trunk, unzipped his bag and pulled out a pair of binoculars. He took them to the edge of the road and scanned the area below. Some of the homes beneath the steep cliff were big enough to pass as principalities, but there was no problem spotting Jerry Monte's. It wasn't just because his estate was at least three times the size of his neighbors'. His face was on a large flag that snapped in the breeze beside a huge man-made lagoon, complete with waterfall. It fed several other smaller faux ponds and pools. All that in a city whose mortal inhabitants often suffered the depravations of drought conditions.

The estate's main building was huge, a sandstone, three-story, castle-like affair. It was separated from the Canyon Road by a high stone wall bordering a bright green rolling lawn that could have served as an eighteen-hole golf course. A metal gate – presumably operated from the house – allowed approved vehicles entry to a wide flagstone driveway that traveled the hundred or so yards to the main building. There was a second gate and drive, further up Cabrillo Canyon Road at the far edge of the property. For the help to use, probably.

A matching flagstone walkway surrounded the house and branched off through a series of landscaped, verdant terraces, past fountains, redwood decks and a cabana, near the fake lagoon, from which two naked young women emerged, towels wrapped around their hair, drinks in their hands.

They were both Hollywood pretty, Mace thought, as he focused the binoculars. Very comfortable in their surgically enhanced and bikini-waxed skin. They blissfully strolled along the brick road, much to the amusement of workers who were putting together a white tent that was large enough for a two-if not three-ring circus just below the mini castle.

The naked ladies entered the castle and the workmen went back to their tenting.

Mace turned his magnified attention on the rest of the property, including a double tennis court beyond the lagoon area where two mullet-haired guys in muscle shirts and baggy shorts listlessly whacked a ball back and forth.

Past the courts was a garage large enough to handle at least six vehicles, above which was what appeared to be living quarters for a chauffeur. It would have been too much to ask for the chauffeur to be the black man known as Sweets. More likely, it was the blond shirtless guy in jodhpurs and boots, for Christ's sake, posing in front of the garage as he hosed off an electric-blue Rolls.

Next in line for a washing was a yellow Mustang convertible.

Mace lowered the binoculars.

He'd seen enough to convince him that Jerry Monte's party would be worth crashing, if only to become reacquainted with Angela Lowell. He was convinced she was the key to getting Paulie out of the soup. But he was self-aware enough to realize there may have been another reason he wanted to see her again.

He was turning to walk back to the Camry when the sound of a car horn echoed upward. A white panel truck had braked near Monte's servants' gate. Mildly curious, he picked up the truck with his binoculars just as the gate swung inward in response to the horn. The vehicle entered the property and headed directly to the garage area.

There was a drawing of a mortar and pestle on the door below the name 'Honeymoon Drugs'. It braked behind the Mustang. A tanned surfer boy who may still have been in his late teens, with sun- or chemical-bleached, near-white hair, hopped out of the truck. He was wearing khaki shorts, flip-flops and a pale green T-shirt with the mortar and pestle logo on its front. Mace thought he may have seen the boy during his brief visit to the drug store.

The chauffeur said something that sounded like, 'Hi, sweet-heart,' and the surfer boy shot him the finger. Then he opened the truck's rear door, reached in and withdrew what appeared to be a heavy two-suiter. He struggled it to the rear door of the castle where he placed it on the bricks.

He pressed a door button and Mace could hear the resulting gong.

The rear door was opened by a big black guy who'd been with Monte at Abe's coffeehouse. He took the suitcase from the surfer boy and carried it back into the house.

The surfer boy remained at the door until the black guy returned and tossed the suitcase to him. It floated like a feather.

The surfer boy, whistling now, got back into the white panel truck and left the way he'd come.

The good stuff had arrived. The party was on.

TWENTY-NINE

Paulie lived off Mulholland Drive in a treeless and consequently sun-baked, ranch-style house with pale, adobe plaster walls and a dark shake roof. There was a narrow lawn, freshly mowed but with yellow patches, in front of the house and a garden colored by white and pink hydrangeas. But for the most part that portion of the property was taken up by a vehicle gate and concrete slabs on which Paulie parked his Mercedes sedan and a Range Rover which, judging by a thick coating of dust, had fallen victim to the escalation in the price of gas.

Inside, the place reminded Mace of a bachelor pad, circa 1980. Or maybe earlier. Dark hardwood floor, heavy beamed ceiling. Casual, leather furniture. He had to smother a laugh when Paulie proudly showed him the living room with its giant Hi-Def, microthin TV screen and a goddamned bearskin rug in front of a massive fireplace.

Sliding glass doors led to what looked like a junior-size version of the lagoon at Jerry Monte's. Mace wondered if they had come from the same pool company and, it being the movie capitol, if its designer had taken his cues from the old Tarzan flicks. This one included a fake-rock grotto and a black sand bottom that served, Paulie claimed, as an organic filter.

But with all those wonderful things, including a big, round bed in the master suite and a Wi-Fi set-up that allowed him to access the Internet from anywhere on the property, what really sold Paulie on the place was, 'It's just a block away from where Nicholson lives. And Brando used to live.'

'It kinda reminds me of our digs at Manhattan Beach,' Mace said.

Paulie's face reddened. He was about to protest when he realized Mace was goofing. 'Yeah,' he said, 'except the ceiling doesn't leak, the toilets work and we don't have hot and cold runnin' hookers living next door. But, you know, those weren't bad times.'

'If you don't mind having to bathe in the ocean in March,' Mace said.

'C'mon, you son of a bitch. We had a blast.'

Mace didn't disagree.

It had been nearly twenty years ago. They'd met a couple of years before that in Italy, where he'd been sent by the Army; a new Warrant Officer assigned to Second Lieutenant Lacotta in the Quartermaster Corps. By then, Paulie had an arrangement going with the local representative of Mafia boss 'Toto' Riina. It consisted of a simple transfer of Army supplies – cigarettes and whiskey in the main – for cash.

At first, Paulie had been suspicious of the big, too-intelligent non-com. But those suspicions dissolved one drunken night when the normally taciturn Warrant Officer Mason had explained how his temper had gotten him tossed out of Louisiana State University in his sophomore year when he'd nearly killed a frat boy who had allegedly raped a young Baton Rouge girl of his acquaintance.

She later admitted that the sex had been consensual, but by then Mace's formal education had been cut short. He'd escaped arrest only because the battered boy's father, a state senator, had preferred to avoid the publicity of a trial.

Mace's father, however, was not as willing to forgive and forget. He gave his son two options. He would arrange for young David to go to work with a cousin who trapped muskrat and nutria in the bayou, a hard, heading-nowhere job that paid just enough to live on. Or he could serve a stint in the Army, learn a little about life and then go back to college and make something of himself.

'Your dad sounds like he's got his head on straight,' Lieutenant Lacotta had told him. 'He saw you were a green kid who got fucked up trying to be a hero. He figured the Army would smarten you up. So are you ready for a life lesson that'll put some coin in your khakis?'

He and Paulie amassed a comfortable amount over the next few years providing goods for the local black market. They were conservative, limiting their theft to products and quantities that were neither essential nor easily missed. They would have re-upped had Rome not dispatched seven thousand troops into Sicily to bust up the Mafia. Then the Carabinieri collared Riina, after nearly three decades of ignoring his fugitive status. Reform was definitely in the Italian air.

When members of the Christian Democratic Party began being accused of having Mafia connections, Paulie, suspecting that the scandal might eventually trickle down to his politician pals near the base in Pisa and Livorno, took his discharge before it turned dishonorable.

Four months later, as soon as his enlistment was up, Mace mustered out. Intrigued by Paulie's tales of Hollywoodland, he eagerly accepted his service buddy's offer of a place to crash in Manhattan Beach. His timing couldn't have been better. Or worse, as it turned out. By then Lacotta had used family ties to secure a position as an executive with Mount Olympus Industries, a company that had been created primarily as a money laundering facility for the family back East.

Its president and Paulie's uncle, Salvatore Montdrago, who'd graduated near the top of his class at the Stanford Business School, had not been satisfied with merely legalizing hot cash. He'd sought out ways of using it to turn a healthy profit and transformed the company into a nearly above-board major player in the California real estate boom. Then, using the company's increasing wealth he expanded its goals and its assets by investing in various enterprises, from fast-food chains to mall construction.

He had immediately displayed a fondness for Paulie, whom he thought of not as a nephew but a younger brother, and Paulie had wisely played that part to the hilt, going to 'Sal' for advice on clothes and women and making sure the boss's every request, business or personal, was met one hundred percent. With the company experiencing a growth spurt, Montdrago had promoted him from the junior executive ranks to a place at his right hand.

The promotion had not gone over well with the other two junior execs who'd been with Montdrago from the start. One, Rudy Bertoni, quit and began working for a record company, where he was eventually shot to death by a rapper in a contract dispute. The other, Tiny Daniels, decided to stay on for as

long as it would take for him to be in a position to start his
own operation modeled on everything he'd learned from
Montdrago.

When Paulie convinced his uncle to hire Mace to replace
Bertoni, Tiny had shown no animosity toward the new boy.
He had become, in fact, a frequent guest at the elaborate
parties Mace and Paulie had thrown at their Manhattan Beach
place and, later, at the beach house they'd shared in Santa
Monica.

Those had been heady days and nights. Beautiful women.
Booze. Recreational drugs. The best of LA. The work had not
been demanding. It had been, as Paulie noted, 'a blast'.

And then Mace was arrested.

The original warrant had stemmed from his involvement in
a dispute at a mixer bar-restaurant in Marina del Rey that
Mount Olympus had just acquired. When Paulie pink-slipped
the employees of the Tail Fin Inn, a laid-off doorman-bouncer
went after him with a bar stool. Mace had stepped in and
handled the situation, breaking the man's jaw and leaving him
in a concussed state.

The bouncer later claimed it had been an unprovoked attack
and several other fired employees sided with him. Mace's
arrest for assault and battery caught the attention of a US
Attorney named Fonseca who'd been trying to build a case
against Mount Olympus and Montdrago. He threw in a few
other crimes, the most notable being insider trading, something
in which Mace had participated, though not nearly to the extent
of either Paulie or his uncle. Fonseca used the crimes to build
a racketeering case against Mace, one that carried a life impris-
onment tag.

Fonseca had explained that he could, of course, go for a
much lesser charge if Mace would assist in his investigation
of Mount Olympus Industries.

That was when Tiny Daniels had shown his true colors. He
pressed Montdrago to have Mace silenced. But Paulie still had
his uncle's ear and convinced him that his friend would not
turn state's evidence. Montdrago's lawyer had no trouble
getting the insider trading case dismissed, along with most of
the other charges.

Fonseca's racketeering case dissolved. But the assault charge made by the fired club bouncer suddenly was raised to attempted murder. Witnesses lied under oath. The judge admitted evidence concerning the earlier fight that had caused Mace's expulsion from LSU. And he was on his way to Pelican Bay Prison for a term not to exceed ten years.

He was out in six because of good behavior. Even though he'd killed a man during his first week of incarceration. The man, a member in good standing of the Aryan Brotherhood, had been annoyed by Mace's rejection of his philosophic and physical advances and had tried to rape him in the shower stalls.

Mace had banged the guy's head against the tile until six other inmates were able to drag him away. By then the would-be rapist's skull was cracked and his neck broken.

Mace thought the guards knew who'd killed the man, but they did nothing about it. Either they felt he was justified or Montdrago had paid them to ignore the whole thing. He knew definitely that Paulie's uncle had arranged for his safety behind bars. Shortly after the death, when the deceased's fellow brotherhood thugs confronted him, a half-dozen hard cases he didn't know stepped in to inform the Brothers that Mace was 'protected'.

For the next six years, no one bothered him. He kept to himself, eventually being assigned to the library, where he established a system of self-education that he thought, probably erroneously, to be the equivalent of earning a college degree. In any case, it, and the hours he spent in the weight room, kept him reasonably sane.

Upon his release, he went home to Louisiana and an ailing father.

Paulie had provided care for the old man, as he'd promised. Mace took over that responsibility until his father's death. By then he'd sold off most of his family's holdings along the bayou – primarily a cannery that had been built by his great-grandfather. Though the proceeds had not added up to a fortune, he'd had enough return on his investments to live in a modest sort of early retirement. Eventually, he'd grown tired of doing nothing, so he went to work a few days each week with his cousins, crabbing and fishing in the bayous.

That's when Paulie called.

Paulie was standing in the doorway of the guest bedroom, watching Mace as he finished unpacking. 'You chewing gum?' he asked.

'Isn't that allowed here?'

'Sure. I just . . . I don't remember you ever . . .'

'I found a pack in Wylie's car,' Mace said. 'Thought it might help me cut down on the smokes. Tastes pretty good.'

'Got any more?'

'Yeah.' Mace put his now empty bag in a closet and closed the door. He handed the black gum pack to Paulie as he exited the room.

They headed into the living room where two welterweight boxers were going at it on the big screen. The high definition caught the scars and scrapes and droplets of sweat and blood in almost three-dimensional clarity.

'This does taste good,' Paulie said, handing the gum pack back to Mace. 'Not as good as a smoke, as I remember, but good.'

He saw Mace looking at the big screen, nestled in its huge cabinet. 'Fifty-three inches,' he said proudly.

Mace walked to the cabinet, reached up and grabbed the top of the screen. 'Thin, too,' he said. 'I may have to get one of these for my place at Bayou Royal.'

'Remind me,' Paulie said. 'I got a guy who'll deliver it at fifty off. Swear to God, a full fifty.'

'Good to have friends,' Mace said.

'Tell you what,' Paulie said, 'let's go have dinner at Chow's. Like an anniversary.'

'Have to make it tomorrow,' Mace said. 'I've got something on tonight.'

'Yeah? Do I know her?'

'I'm working here, Paulie. Remember?'

'Right. What's your plan?'

'As soon as I have one,' Mace said, 'I'll let you know.'

THIRTY

It had been a slight untruth.

Mace did have a vague plan, which was why he was driving down Sunset that night at a little before eleven. He could probably have had dinner at Mr Chow's with Paulie, but there would have been drinks and more drinks. Better that Paulie had made other arrangements, while he had settled for a couple of chili dogs at Pink's.

He turned off Sunset and drove past the old brick building that housed the gun shop and Honeymoon Drugs. There was a light on inside the drug store even though a sign in its window said that it was closed.

Mace circled the block until he found the alley behind the drug store. The white panel truck was parked near the rear door. He stopped the Camry and turned off its headlights. The car beeped when he opened the door, so he killed the engine.

The beeping stopped.

He got out and walked to the barred window of the drug store's rear door. He stared in at the surfer boy who was busily filling his suitcase with pills and powders. Interesting. Mace had decided that the truck would be his ticket to the party. He'd hoped to find it parked near the drug store where he could jack it and drive it into the Monte compound, pretending to have a delivery for the party.

This was even better. He'd actually have a delivery.

He moved the Camry to the street, nearly half a block away, in a slot where meter use ended at six p.m. Then he doubled back to the alley where he waited for the surfer boy.

It was a short wait. Maybe fifteen minutes.

The boy let himself out the back way. He bent to pick up the suitcase and Mace rabbit-punched him once behind the ear. He caught the boy before he crashed and dragged him back inside the store where he lowered him to the tile floor.

He picked up the suitcase. It was as heavy as it had looked.

The party had been going for a while and a second phase of invited guests was arriving, causing a traffic jam along Cabrillo Canyon Road that was enough to piss off even the non-millionaires. Polished and gleaming vehicles – Mercedes, Range Rovers, Jeeps, Alfas, Jags – were lined up, bumper to bumper, for nearly a quarter of a mile, inching their way toward the main entry to the Jerry Monte estate.

There, the funseekers, who seemed to be very casually dressed, deserted their cars to be met by security guards, some with guest lists, others with metal detectors that they wielded with practiced, non-threatening dexterity.

The vehicles, meanwhile, were placed in the care of The Parkettes, a cadre of young woman in starched white shirts and black trousers, many of them starlet-wannabees, who drove them way up the canyon where roadside parking was still available.

A Parkette with a headset, stationed at the entrance to Cabrillo Canyon on Sunset, was instructing arriving guests to stay to the left of the road, allowing all other vehicles a small sliver of space to come and go. Mace drove the white-panel truck up that sliver. He had to pause only once to accommodate a descending car by partially entering an estate to the right of the road.

When he reached the main gate, he had to deal with Parkettes who were driving vehicles up the canyon to his left, aggressively refusing to let him turn into the estate's service entrance. Finally, he matched their aggression and made his turn, causing a Parkette to test the on-a-dime braking facility of a new Porsche Carrera.

Mace sat with the truck's front bumper about a foot from the closed gate and tried not to look at the tiny camera that he was sure was trained on his window.

'Where Chas?' an electronic voice asked.

'He had to go home,' Mace said. 'Threw his shoulder out lifting the suitcase.'

There was a quick chuckle, then, 'What they call you?'

'Leander.' The name had popped into his head, no doubt a reference to the despised racist political boss of the Delta, Leander Perez. 'Well, Lee Ander. Come on in.'

The gate swung open and Mace entered the brightly lit flagstone path to the garage, which was now closed. The two cars that had been there earlier in the day were both missing. He hoped the Mustang was in the garage.

He got out of the truck and removed the suitcase.

As he carried it to the castle, he was aware of the thump-thump-thump sounds of synthesized rock-rap. Guests seemed to be enjoying themselves, wandering in and out of the tent, splashing in the lagoon. He had no idea what passed for fashion on the coast, but these people were wearing clothes that looked suspiciously like outfits designed for the bedroom, not a party. The men were in pajamas and robes, the women in frilly peignoirs or less. They were young, mainly. Glitter people. Tattooed, pierced. Stoned. Poor Wylie would have loved the place.

Even before Mace pressed the buzzer beside the back door it was opened by the same black bodybuilder, only now dressed in baggy tiger-striped pajamas. 'Took yo' time, Lee Ander,' he said. 'Got folks in here in need.' He took the suitcase from Mace. 'Be right back,' he said, and closed the door.

Mace realized that, at a party where bedroom dress was in vogue, his sport shirt and slacks stood out like, well, an uninvited guest. He walked quickly to the one place where he thought he could find some camouflage – the lagoon where nudity seemed to be encouraged.

There was enough mist rising from the water to indicate that a heavy-duty heating system was keeping the naked bodies splashing around in it safe from the goose bumps of a typical chilly Southern California midnight. Exotic birds in golden cages chirped their alarms as Mace moved swiftly through the cabana, trying not to disturb the fornicating couples as he searched for nightwear that would fit his frame.

He settled on a pair of black silk pajamas that smelled of some musky cologne, which he hoped would dissipate as the night wore on. He removed his pants and shirt, folded them and placed them beneath a pile of colorful cushions on the straw mat floor. He wore the borrowed pajamas over his boxers and did not bother to replace his shoes and socks. He emerged from the lagoon area feeling foolish and oddly vulnerable but less noticeable.

The first thing he saw was the black man in tiger striped pajamas searching the crowd.

Mace ducked back into the lagoon area and watched as the big man stormed toward the tent. Less than a minute later, he emerged and, running now, headed for the castle.

Mace made his way to the tent.

This was the party's main dining area, judging by the food counters along one wall, staffed by sleepy men in rumpled white coats and sagging toques, and the tables and chairs being bussed by a team of servants in livery. Fewer than a quarter of the tables were still in use. The trays of food were down to the dregs. A tiny hamburger here, a boiled shrimp on a toothpick there.

The ice sculpture, which Mace suspected had been designed in the image of their illustrious host, was now barely the size of a snow cone resting in a puddle of water. The most active display table currently was at the rear of the tent filled with desserts, including a chocolate fountain and fresh strawberries.

Some sixth sense told Mace to take a seat at the nearest table. It was occupied by a couple nibbling on brownies and one another. They pulled apart when he joined them. The male was Mace's age at least, paunchy and balding in what looked suspiciously like a toga. The female was barely in her twenties, a full-bodied platinum blonde wearing a black see-through bra and silk panties. They didn't seem to mind the interruption. They grinned at him, obviously somewhere in the outer zone.

The male squinted his eyes and said, 'I know you.'

Mace was sure he'd never seen the guy before in his life.

'You're the dude on *Mad Men*. Dude fucks anything that walks. What's your name?'

When Mace didn't reply, the balding man turned to the girl. 'What's his name, Trink, the dude on *Mad Men*?'

Trink was squinting at Mace, too. 'I don't know,' she said. 'What's *Mad Men*?'

From the corner of his eye, Mace spotted tiger-striped pajamas standing at the entrance to the tent with two guys in a different sort of costume. Security guards.

'Some goddamn great party, huh?' Mace said, moving closer to the couple, turning his back on the hunting crew.

'You got that right,' the balding man said. 'So, wha' do ya think of my girl, Mad Man? Fuckable, right?'

'And then some,' Mace said.

The girl giggled, leaned forward and fell on to his lap, almost sending him and the chair over backwards. He managed to stay upright even when she pressed her lips against his. She tasted of gin and brownie and something mildly medicinal. It was a pretty good kiss, all things considered, and he let it continue while the hunting party moved slowly past their table.

'Hey,' the balding man complained, 'save some for Uncle Ralphie.'

Uncle Ralphie had to wait until Tiger Stripes and the security guards left the tent.

'Here she is,' Mace said. 'Good as new.'

'Not fair, dude,' Uncle Ralphie said. 'You got that beautiful blonde wife and you still screw around.'

Mace had no idea who the balding man thought he was. Nor did he care.

'You guys keep the party going,' he said, and left the table.

At the entrance to the tent he saw the hunting team heading toward the lagoon where a naked guy his size was waving his arms and yelling. Not good. On their next round, the hunting party would know which color pajamas to look for.

He crossed the lawn at a modest pace and strolled through the open doors of the mini-castle. What may have been a living room and dining room had been combined and transformed into one huge ballroom. Most of the furniture had been removed, except for a few suits of armor and some original art on the paneled walls.

Thankfully, the level of lighting was low enough that Tiger Stripes would have to be right on top of him to make an identification. Adding to the room's invisibility quotient was a round, disco ball spinning near the ceiling, its tiny mirrored surfaces reflecting little shards of light that were sent around the room in almost dizzying patterns.

A pop band, five musicians of undetermined gender, was playing discordant music at the far end of the room. They were dressed in black, men's pajamas, like Mace, but their faces had been painted white with black lips. Their name, if the logo on their drum skin was to be believed, was Dr Caligari.

Some of the ballroom crowd were trying to dance to music that was basically undanceable. Others merely groped one another. A few groped Mace as he looked for Angela Lowell among the dancers.

His attention was caught instead by a flash of light in the next room.

It was a smaller ballroom. Just as dark, and without a disco ball. As he entered, another flash brightened the room. Its source was Simon S. Symon gleefully aiming his camera at a buxom woman with wild red hair who was standing at the edge of a spotlight trained on a huge fishbowl full of rainbow-colored pills.

She was an actress, popular enough that even Mace recognized her. She had evidently consumed a fair amount of Jerry Monte's mind-altering answer to Skittles. That face that looked so stunning, was now splotched and sagging. Her eyes were glassy.

A male guest laughed and yanked down the top of her peignoir and her large breasts bounced free. 'No,' she screamed and tried to cover herself, but not before Symon had captured the moment.

Mace moved toward the photographer. But the ever-watchful Symon spotted him and backed away, bumping against guests in his hurry. Mace closed the gap.

At arm's distance, he reached out to grab the little man. But Symon brought up his camera and Mace was blinded by the flash. In the moments it took for him to regain his sight, he lost track of the photographer.

He took the nearest door and entered a vestibule where three men in business suits were entering an elevator. He blinked away the effects of Symon's flash just as the elevator's door was sliding shut. He recognized the trio. The tall, brown-skinned man with the goatee, he'd only seen in newspaper photos. The other two had been in Paulie's office. Corrigan and his stooge.

Just before the elevator door slid shut, the stooge smiled and raised a hand to point a thumb-and-forefinger gun at him.

THIRTY-ONE

Mace moved back into the room where he'd lost Symon. The dynamic seemed to have shifted and he quickly realized why. Tiger Stripes and the security guards were going through the crowd with penlights, checking faces.

Mace departed the room through yet another door, this one placing him in a short corridor. To his right was a walk-in closet housing two vacuum cleaners, a floor waxer, and an assortment of soaps, clean rags and liquid wax. To his left was a closet with linens and towels. That narrowed his path of escape to a pebble-grained glass door at the end of the corridor.

Taking it, he stepped into a puddle of water and an atmosphere so humid you could almost drink it. The water and the humidity were caused by an open sauna door. The sauna was large with more than enough space to handle the two young men and three young women who were obviously planning on using it.

The women and one of the men had removed their clothes, which they'd draped on wooden benches. They were waiting for the other man to remove his shoes. They seemed to be body-proud, with figures that were too perfectly sculpted to have occurred in nature. Two of the women and the male who was finally shoeless displayed body art – blue and red and green swirls and curlicues, some covering a shoulder, some forming a 'V' on the lower back.

They welcomed him with nods and smiles. 'Room for one more.' The invitation came from a brunette whose perfect figure nearly convinced Mace to go off game. But whatever parts of his body were saying, his mind was dealing with the reality of his present situation. He'd allowed his infatuation for a woman he barely knew to put him in jeopardy. True, when he made up his mind to crash the party, he'd thought he'd be dealing with your typical celebrity, admittedly one with considerable clout.

He'd assumed the worst that would happen if he was caught would be a beating, maybe, or a couple of days jail-time. But the presence of Corrigan and his sidekick, not to mention the man with the goatee, meant that he'd underestimated the danger. Ergo, his capture could have consequences much too serious to risk by having a fling with a brunette. Even one with the body of a goddess.

'I may join you in a minute,' he said. He pointed to the only other exit. 'Any idea where that goes?'

'We just came from there,' one of the men said. 'It's a tunnel. Goes to the pool.'

'The lagoon,' one of the women corrected.

'The lagoon,' the guy repeated, sarcastically as he playfully slapped the woman on her naked rear.

'Later,' Mace said and moved slowly toward the tunnel door. But he didn't use it. Instead, he waited for the quintet to enter the sauna and close the door behind them.

He moved back to the bench and picked up a pair of pale blue pajamas one of the men had been wearing. He left the dark pajamas in exchange.

He followed the brightly lit tunnel to its end and emerged maybe ten feet from the lagoon. A security guard stood sentry duty there with a communication device stuck in his ear.

Mace joined a group of partygoers who were walking in the direction of the tennis courts. As they neared the garage area, he saw that more guards had been stationed at the servant's gate. The Honeymoon Drugs van was no longer in view. Had it been put in the garage? Had someone driven it back to the store? Not that it mattered. He'd be leaving on foot. If he got the chance.

The apparent leader of his new-found group, a man in his fifties with a sharp profile and half-lidded eyes, was regaling his mainly youthful admirers with stories about someone named

Charles who'd taught him everything he knew about acting. 'We're talking television acting, of course,' he qualified. 'Theater is something else entirely. The broad gesture. Acting for the camera, TV or film, is . . . subtle. The flicker of an eye. The faint hint of a smile.'

Mace was trying to place the man. He looked familiar. Had he seen him in something?

'Are you an Elgin Blake fan, Mr Mason?' someone whispered behind him.

He turned to find Angela Lowell.

She was wearing a thin, tight halter of some metallic silver substance that barely covered her breasts and gauzy pantaloons that looked like those worn by a pasha's concubine. 'I gather he was a secret agent on TV in the sixties,' she said, 'before my time.'

'How do you know my name?' Mace asked.

'It's the talk of the party.'

'Hard to believe,' he said. A man in a suit and tie emerged from the castle, not playing the pajama game. Corrigan's thug. He scanned the area and zoned right in on Mace.

'You know this place pretty well?' Mace asked Angela.

'Pretty well.'

The raw-boned thug was heading their way.

'Can you get me away from here?' Mace asked.

'I think some people want to talk to you,' she said.

'I don't want to talk to them.'

She turned, saw Corrigan's man, saw the look on his face. She took Mace's hand and said, 'Why don't we talk first?'

He let her take him in the direction of the lagoon.

THIRTY-TWO

Angela's destination was the cabana.

They moved through it quickly, then entered what appeared to be a changing area, done up in Hawaiian tiki style. Lots of bamboo and carved wood and exotic plants.

At a far wall, Angela unhooked a bamboo panel and moved past it. He followed and she closed the panel behind them.

They were in a small chamber lit by a recessed halogen bulb. The walls and ceiling were painted a flat black.

'Come on,' she said, heading toward what looked like a wall. It was, but angled so that it allowed entry to a tunnel that joined the one Mace had used to leave the castle. Now, it took them back, past the sauna and then up three flights of stairs to a hall with a thick Oriental runner.

'Where are we headed?' he asked.

'To a safe harbor.' Angela approached a door that had a combination lock. He watched her punch the numbers 2-4-4-5-7-9 and the door clicked open an inch.

They entered a brightly lit windowless room that belonged in some other building. Perhaps some other universe. It reminded Mace of the decks of spaceships in science fiction movies. It was all white. White ceiling. White walls. White tile floor, a portion of which was covered by a white rubberized pad.

To their right was a sort of space age workstation. Two ultra-modern white, molded plastic chairs faced an assortment of instruments with glowing dials that rested on top of a white metal counter that ran the length of one wall. Above the counter and instruments was a long wide-screen monitor on which the phrase, 'This is Jerry's Room' appeared in 3-D, disappeared and was replaced by another comment, 'Jerry is a genius.'

Several feet from them, a white leather sofa and two matching chairs faced a wall filled with nine flat screens, which, though dark, reflected the bright glow of the overhead halogen lights.

'What the hell is this?' Mace asked.

'Jerry's retreat,' she said. 'The game room. Let me show you.'

Angela moved to the sofa where she found a white plastic remote. She pressed a button on it and one of the nine screens came to life with a view of the main party room below. 'The film director who built this monstrous castle in the thirties had secret peepholes drilled into the floor so he could secretly watch his guests,' she said. 'The more things change . . .'

She pressed another button and a second screen was filled with a rear-of-the-house panorama.

It wasn't until she'd turned on the fifth screen that she got what she was after. The scene was a comfortable room with dark wooden bookshelves lining walls of a flat ivy green color. It was decorated with heavy, masculine furniture constructed of oak and soft leather and brass fittings. The floor was covered by Persian rugs of subdued hues. It was a Hollywood set designer's idea of an Edwardian men's club. But, instead of British actors sunk down in plump chairs discussing wagers or time travel, Jerry Monte, wearing a black silk dressing gown over his flame red pajamas, Corrigan and the brown-skinned man with the goatee sat at a green, felt-topped, octagon-shaped card table.

They were not playing cards. Nor were they paying attention to the giant snifters of some sort of liqueur, probably cognac, resting before them.

'Rub-a-dub-dub,' Mace said.

'Shhh,' she said and turned up the volume. There was the hiss of white noise but no conversation. 'Damn,' she said. 'I was hoping we could hear if they were still talking about you. Jerry must've turned off the sound. He does that sometimes.'

'When?' Mace asked.

'What?'

'When does Jerry turn off the sound?'

'Oh. When he's into something that he doesn't want people to hear, I guess. Usually, he makes video and audio copies of everything he does.'

The conversation in the Edwardian room seemed to be growing heated.

'What were they saying about me?' Mace asked.

'The stocky man . . .'

'Corrigan.'

'Yes, Mr Corrigan. You know him?'

'We didn't actually meet,' Mace said. 'But I know him.'

'He asked Jerry why he'd invited you to his party. And Jerry seemed surprised and said, "People get invited," or something equally vague. Then he asked Mr Corrigan to describe you, which he did, only neglecting to mention how handsome you were. And Jerry said that sounded like the guy Rufe told him had crashed the party.'

'Rufe being a big black man wearing tiger stripes?'

She smiled and tapped her nose. 'Then Mr Corrigan told his associate – I believe his name is Drier – to assist the people who were looking for you. And Jerry suggested I go have fun while they discussed business. So I came up here and used the wonder wall to find you.'

'Why didn't Rufe use the wall?' Mace asked.

'Because this room is off limits to Rufe.'

'But not to you?'

She shrugged.

On the screen, the man with the goatee stood suddenly. He looked angry.

'You know who the beard is?' Mace asked.

'Acosta, I think Jerry said.'

'Enrico Acosta,' Mace said. It was not a name immediately recognizable by the general public, but a former felon, even one who had retreated from the world for the past few years, knew about Enrico Acosta, the world's most notorious arms dealer. He sold to anyone. Some say he pocketed a billion dollars ferrying supplies to American soldiers in Iraq and Afghanistan. He was the modern day equivalent of the guy on the coin. The new merchant of death.

And, evidently, a player in their game.

On the screen, Jerry Monte had risen and was attempting to placate Acosta, whom he convinced to return to the card table.

'What's the deal with Monte?' Mace asked.

'What do you mean?'

'Where's his clout come from?'

'From here,' she said, tapping her head. 'He's a genius.'

'That's what everybody tells me. A genius and a poet, huh?'

'The poetry thing is silly,' she said. 'It's . . . just a phase. But . . . here's how his mind works. He hears this poem for the first time. A famous poem. William Blake's Tyger! You know, "Tyger!, tyger!, burning bright . . ."'

Mace shrugged.

'Well, Jerry heard it and loved it. So he had his composers put it to music. It'll be on the new album and, at the same time, he's got screenwriters working on a script in which the poem will play a key role. Synchronicity.'

'And this makes him the new king of pop?'

'Some kind of king,' she said. She moved across the room to the instrument panel with the glowing dials and picked up an object that looked like a six-inch silver triangle. She held it in a two-hand grip, her thumbs poised over buttons on its flat surface.

The screen above the panel, on which Jerry Monte comments had been dissolving and reappearing, went suddenly bright red. Then it seemed to shatter with a loud bang and out of the destruction floated a new name in letters resembling a battered brick wall: Captain Combat.

Angela worked the buttons and the screen filled with the figure of the captain, rock-jawed, helmeted, khaki shirtsleeves rolled to display muscled arms.

Mace recognized the figure. He'd seen it on the machines kids played in Bayou Royal.

'That's the key to his kingdom?' Mace asked derisively.

'Did you know he created the Captain Combat computer game?'

'Must have been a slow day,' Mace said. 'Compared to his other conquests.'

Angela looked at him and laughed. 'You're priceless,' she said. 'Computer games rule the entertainment field. It's the biggest paycheck of them all. And it's made Jerry the top show biz figure in the Forbes Four Hundred.'

Mace found that hard to believe. But he knew nothing about such things.

'Maybe, but he didn't create Captain Combat,' he said. 'That character's been around for a long time.'

'Not in a game format.'

'Meaning what? That Monte just ripped off the guy who really thought up the character?'

'As far as I know, it's Jerry's creation,' she said. 'And if it isn't, I haven't heard of any lawsuits.'

'What's the real story on Monte?'

'Pretty much what's in his press bio. Only a while ago, he was just a singer from Jersey. Popular, but no more so than the average *American Idol* runner up. He could have settled for a couple of years cutting albums and playing Vegas. Maybe doing some acting in movies or TV. But, then what?

'He read the trades, saw the trends. Realized that songs, singers, actors, records, movies went in and out of style. In show business, nothing remains constant. Vaudeville was replaced by movies and radio was replaced by television. And now, TV and movies were being replaced by the Internet. The goal was not merely to rise to the top, but to stay there. And that meant staying ahead of the curve.

'He spent several years learning as much as he could about computers. Then, with the help of a quartet of what he says were then "pimple-face geek teenagers", he created his first game, *Captain Combat: Worlds at War*. It made him a fortune. He used most of it to buy back the shares he had to sell to launch the game.'

'And what happened to the geeks?' Mace asked.

'They're multimillionaire executives in Palo Alto, in charge of MonteVision Games. But they're running out of space and soon they'll be alternating between studios there and here. Jerry's purchased a B-movie factory in Hollywood that's been on the market for years. His plan is to create a state of the art facility. It'll be used mainly for a new branch of the company that nobody knows about yet called Simureal.'

'The fake exercise environment?' Mace said, trying to impress her. 'I've seen it.'

'Really? There are only three in existence. The official unveiling at Wonderworld in Las Vegas isn't set for another two months. Where'd you see it?'

'I get around,' he said.

She gave him a crooked smile, as if she suspected he was joking and hadn't really seen Simureal.

'Tell me more about what makes Jerry Jerry,' he said.

She seemed to be trying to decide if he really wanted to hear more about Monte or was goofing on her. She must have settled on the former. 'Well, he says there are four rules for success: maintain control, diversify, synchronize and stay ahead.'

'Let me guess: control is the biggie.'

'Maybe.' She clicked off the game and the screen reverted to repeats of the Jerry phrases.

Mace walked back to the flat screen focused on the meeting. It looked like the main discussion was over. Monte was showing a leather-bound book to the new merchant of death. Corrigan was sampling his liqueur.

'Why'd you come here tonight?' Angela asked.

'To see you.'

'How did you know I'd be here?'

'I took a chance.'

On the screen offering a view of the tent and the lagoon, Mace saw Corrigan's thug – what had Angela called him? Drier – standing on the grass making a slow scan of the area.

Angela must have seen him, too. 'Why are they trying so hard to find you?' she asked. 'Not just because you crashed a party.'

'They want to kill me. Or maybe just hurt me a little.'

'Don't be such a fool. These people aren't murderers.'

'Tell that to Tiny Daniels,' he said.

She reacted as if he'd slapped her. She blinked and backed away. 'Tiny . . . you've no reason to think . . . Jerry didn't even know him.'

'What about the hologram of the big white dog at Tiny's? Isn't that one of Jerry's creations?'

She was staring at him now. 'How did you . . . I gave Tiny the dog. It was just a prototype that Jerry was going to toss. Tiny liked big dogs, but he had such expensive items in the house. Not only the art, but pottery and exquisite small, glass creations. Anyway, Jerry said I could have the hologram and I gave it to Tiny. Who loved it, by the way.'

'Any idea why it would have been turned on the night he was murdered?'

'He'd put it on when he was going out. I suppose he thought it might chase away thieves. He didn't think the guards at the entrance to the Estates were enough security. He felt it was too easy for thieves to come in off the beach.'

'He was right,' Mace said. 'Not that being right helped. Somebody paid the guy who shot Tiny and the others. Maybe

Corrigan. Or the charming guy with the goatee. These people wanted something Tiny had. I think your brilliant boyfriend Jerry wanted it, too. Maybe part of his diversification plan.'

'You're being ridiculous.'

'The guy I saw running away from Tiny's after the murders is named Thomas. He and his brother killed a kid I was working with. Crushed the life out of him. So, until I find out who hired them, excuse me if I'm a little nervous about Monte and his pals.'

'Monte has nothing to do with killers,' she said, shaking her head. 'You're wrong. You have to be.'

She turned and he realized he'd pushed her too hard too quickly. He reached out to stop her, but his hand closed on air. She threw open the door and raced out and away.

Mace turned to the screens and studied the one covering the rear of the castle. Drier had moved on. Where?

Better question: where can I make a safe exit out of here?

It wouldn't be at the rear of the property. That backed up to the side of the canyon. The sheer side of the canyon.

He grabbed the white remote. Maybe he could bring up a view of the front of the house. Find a break in the security set up. If he could just get to the canyon road . . .

He was fiddling with the buttons when his attention was drawn to the screen covering the study. Angela had just entered. She was saying something to Jerry Monte. Whatever it was caused Corrigan to put down his snifter and get to his feet. He shouted something. Monte shouted something back.

They all turned to look directly into the camera. It was as if they were staring at Mace.

Corrigan headed for the door with Monte following.

Mace understood it was time for him to leave the party. One way or another.

THIRTY-THREE

Heading down the rear stairwell, he made it only as far as the first landing when he heard people coming up. '. . . don't see the danger, Corrigan. What can he know that would hurt us?'

'Let's make sure, shall we?'

Moving as silently as he could, Mace turned and went back up the stairs.

On the third floor, he passed the game room. That was obviously where the men were headed, where Angela had sent them. The hall was long. There were several closed doors. But they all seemed to be locked.

The men on the stairwell were approaching quickly.

Mace moved past an alcove that housed an elevator door. It sounded as if the elevator was arriving. He knew it wouldn't be empty.

Only a few doors left.

One was unlocked.

He slipped into a room that, at first, seemed pitch black. He leaned against the door and tried to catch his breath. That's when he saw the thin red beam of light that he'd broken when he stepped through the door.

A security device of some kind. A signal that would tell them immediately where he was.

He pressed his ear to the door. He could hear the rumble of voices at the other end of the hall. Then a door slamming.

If he was going to get off the damn floor, now would be the time.

But the door wouldn't open. He was locked in.

Maybe a window!

He began feeling his way through the blackness.

Suddenly a light filled the room, so bright it sent an arrow of pain into his skull. He staggered backward.

'You there. Freeze,' a gruff voice commanded.

The bright light had subsided, but the room had not reverted to total darkness. Blinking to clear his sight, Mace became aware of a huge man standing in the center of the room. Another blink and he saw that the man was in combat gear. He was slightly taller than Mace's six-two, thicker and heavier-muscled. He was pointing a gun at Mace.

Mace's eyes were watery and stinging. He rubbed them with the knuckles of his right hand and took another look. The man's weapon was a Hammerli 280, a high-tech pistol.

'Identify yourself,' the soldier demanded.

'Get fucked,' Mace replied.

'Do not move, Get Fucked,' the soldier said without a hint of sarcasm.

Mace studied the figure more carefully. He took a step forward. There was definitely something weird going on. He wondered if he could have suffered a stroke. Or was in the middle of a too vivid dream. If only he could—

'Stop. Another step and I will be forced to shoot.'

Mace stopped. His eyes and his brain were both returning to form.

A second blast of light blinded him again.

When the flash dissipated to a dim glow, he saw that the room had a new occupant. This one was an impossibly voluptuous woman almost as tall as the soldier. And almost as muscular. She was wearing a tight black leather halter that barely held in her huge jutting breasts and matching leather short shorts that fit her rounded hips like Spandex. Thigh-high black leather boots completed the fanboy's fantasy outfit.

She, too, was pointing a Hammerli 280 at Mace.

'Get Fucked giving you trouble, Jerseyboy?'

'I've got him covered, Morgana,' the soldier said. 'We'll just keep him here until—

The door to the room opened and Jerry Monte entered, followed by Corrigan and Drier.

'What the hell . . . ?' Drier said, gawking at the two images as they shifted their attention from Mace to them. He drew his gun and aimed it at the soldier.

'Put it away, Drier,' Monte said. 'They're not real.'

'No shit?' Drier said. He kept the gun in his hand.

'Identify yourselves,' the soldier said.

'I'm Captain Combat, Jerseyboy,' Monte said. 'At ease.'

The two figures lowered their weapons. The male was grinning, the woman smiling seductively. 'I've been waiting for you, Captain,' she said, thrusting out her breasts.

'Uh, this is creeping me out,' Drier said.

'Turn the bullshit off, Jerry,' Corrigan said. 'It's a distraction we don't need right now.'

Monte shot him an angry look. 'That "bullshit distraction" is my future, asshole.'

'I'm sorry,' Corrigan said, backing down. 'I didn't mean—'

'Lemme tell you a little story, Corrigan,' Monte said, taking an odd-looking cellular device from his pocket. 'A few years ago, when I was trying to launch MonteMagic, the precursor to MonteVision, the Chinks came sniffing around. A dude named Zhang and some skinny bitch who thought she was the goddamned Dragon Lady.'

He tapped his device twice with his thumb and the two armed holograms vanished. 'They figured they were dealing with some supernerd dickhead. The bitch giving me the fuck-eye, like I'd touch her skanky bod without hermetically-sealed gloves.'

Mace had been busily searching the room for some way out. But the shaded windows were too narrow for a dive-through, even if he had been inclined to try a three-story leap. There was only one exit and the men were in the way.

'This Zhang dude was playing the war lord, tossing the infidel a few coins from his treasure chest,' Monte continued. 'He offered me five point five mil for MonteMagic. And when I took it, he and his bitch laughed like the goddamned jackals they were.'

Corrigan, ostensibly doting on Monte's every word, gave a subtle eye-shift command to Drier that started him moving slowly toward Mace.

'But I laughed harder,' Monte was saying, 'because all their fucking millions bought 'em was a worthless name, a bunch of computer games that had lost their cache two gens ago. And a set of eyeglasses with prisms that had no practical use.

Now the fuckers are wasting their time and coin with *virtual reality*, while I'm gearing up for the next generation in computer gameware: interactive holograms.'

'Brilliant,' Corrigan said.

He turned to Mace. 'OK, brother, it's come-to-Jesus time. What's your story?'

'It's not as interesting as Mr Monte's,' Mace said.

'I'll be the judge of that,' Corrigan said. 'I saw you at Mount Olympus. Did Lacotta send you here?'

'Why would he?' Mace asked.

'That's what I'm wondering. He had his shot. He fucked up. What's he want now?'

Mace was puzzled. 'What's he want? What he paid you for.'

'I thought I'd explained our position to him,' Corrigan said. 'I handled my end of the deal. He was the one let it unravel.'

'How exactly did it unravel, Corrigan?' Mace asked. 'Who knew when the shipment was coming in besides you? Your pal Drier?'

Corrigan frowned. He turned to his host. 'I don't want to keep you from your party, Jerry.'

'Don't worry about it,' Monte replied. 'This is more interesting than the party.'

'Yeah, but I'd like a couple minutes alone with Mr Mason.'

'Oh. Sure. Enjoy. I've got the hologram boxes turned off, so you won't be bothered.'

He hesitated a few seconds before leaving the room.

Corrigan waited for the door to click shut before asking, 'How much did Lacotta tell you about our arrangement?'

'Basically, that something went missing,' Mace said.

'And you know what that is?'

'Is it bigger than a dime but smaller than a half dollar?' Mace asked.

Corrigan and Drier exchanged looks.

'You know why the coin's so valuable?' Corrigan asked Mace.

Mace nodded. He said, 'I'm a little surprised you didn't make a copy of the formula.'

'Maybe you need that AND an analysis of the goddamn coin to complete the package.'

'That does increase its value.'

'So here's the thing,' Corrigan said. 'I love the green and I'm certainly not a saint. But this is my country. My beloved mother's in a home here, and I'm not about to put something like this in the hands of a bunch of gibbering third-world maniacs, regardless of the money. So I limited the auction to the US and its so-called allies. It got down to five serious bidders. One each from Japan, Germany and India and two from the US.'

'The locals being Lacotta and the new King of Pop?' Mace asked.

'No. Jerry . . . I hadn't been thinking that far outside the box,' Corrigan said. 'Tiny Daniels was my other bidder. And, in point of fact, he became the high bidder. It surprised me because the final offer from Lacotta and his people was an eye-opener and I didn't think Daniels was that heavy a hitter. Then I discovered he wasn't. He had a backer: Maxil Brox. You may have heard of him. Russian Mafia boss and now Putin's best buddy. Fuck him. I threw the deal to Lacotta and Lacotta let me down.'

'Did you happen to mention to Tiny how you'd be transferring the formula?' Mace asked.

'Do I look like I'm simple?' Corrigan said.

'You have him killed?'

'Not me, brother. I don't kill US citizens. Even ex-cons.' He grinned. 'Speaking of ex-cons, what about you, Mason?'

'I didn't kill him,' Mace said.

'I guess we're just a couple of guys who didn't kill a fat man,' Corrigan said. 'Too bad, because I figure whoever killed him has the coin. And if you don't have the coin, then what the fuck are you doing here?'

'If I'd come to sell a coin engraved with a nearly priceless formula to the host I don't think I'd have had to crash the party,' Mace said.

'Then why are you here?'

Mace wondered if he might have given Corrigan too much credit for corruption. Maybe he wasn't a master criminal, just another hustler trying to hold a deal together. That's why he was huddling with Monte and Enrico Acosta. To lay the ground rules for a business arrangement that was missing a key part.

'I asked you a question, champ,' Corrigan said.

'I came to see a lady,' Mace said. Half-truths were always better than lies.

'Don't yank my chain, Mason.'

'Some women are worth risking your life for,' Mace said.

'Uh, I did see him cozying with the Lowell broad, Cap,' Drier said.

Corrigan frowned. He stared at Mace, thinking it over. Then he leaned in closer and said, 'I kinda go for that ice-queen type myself. But, she just fingered you.'

'Little lover's spat. A misunderstanding,' Mace said.

'For Christ's sake,' Corrigan said, 'don't tell me we've wasted all this time and tension just because you've got a woodie for Jerry's piece of ass.'

Mace swung at his head. The stocky man was faster than he'd suspected and the blow only brushed an ear. But Mace's other fist connected with Corrigan's gut, sending him back into Drier.

Drier was a pro. He sidestepped, keeping his gun on Mace while his boss hit the carpet with a thud. 'God Dammit,' Corrigan yelled, wheezing and gasping for breath.

'Sorry, Cap,' Drier said, his hand steady.

Mace, breathing hard, pretended to be having a difficult time getting himself under control. 'You don't talk about her like that,' he said to Corrigan.

'Awww shit,' Corrigan said, grunting as he pushed himself off the floor. 'I'm too fucking old for this kind of crap. Getting drawn into some asshole's dream of romance.'

'What do you want me to do with him, Cap?' Drier asked.

'Christ, I don't care. Feed him to Monte's dogs.'

Drier gave him a patient look and kept his gun trained on Mace.

'Let him go,' Corrigan said. 'A low-rent Lochinvar. I got no use for him.'

Drier returned his gun to its holster, but he wasn't happy about it.

Mace didn't wait for Corrigan to change his mind. He headed toward the door.

It opened before he got there.

Jerry Monte entered, followed by two security guards and the muscled Rufe, looking angry as a tiger in his striped pajamas. 'You finished with Mason?' Monte said to Corrigan.

'Had your ear to the door, Jerry?' Corrigan asked. When Monte replied with only a bored look, he added, 'He's all yours. We're out of here.'

Monte said to the security guards, 'Will you escort Mr Corrigan and Mr Drier to their car?'

Corrigan frowned and seemed about to respond. Instead, he shook his head and left the room, hand pressed against his abdomen where Mace had punched him. Drier paused at the door and, grinning, asked Monte, 'Sure you and tiger man can handle him?'

'We'll chance it,' Monte replied.

As soon as the guards led the two men out of earshot, he added, 'Fucking losers.'

He turned his attention to Mace. 'So what do I do with you, Mason?'

Mace assumed that Monte had overheard the reason he'd given for crashing the party and that he now was dealing with a jealous lover. 'Wish me well?' he said.

Monte smiled. 'I'm inclined to go the opposite. Unless you change my mind.'

'How do I do that?'

'Where are you carrying your valuables?' the pop star asked.

Puzzled, Mace raised the right pajama pants leg, exposing the bulge under his sock.

'See what he's got for us, Rufe.'

The black man bent down and removed Mace's wallet and the device that started the Camry. He handed them to Monte, who opened the wallet and ran a finger around its various compartments. He handed the two items back to Mace.

'I didn't really expect you to be carrying the coin,' Monte said. 'How much do you want for it?'

'Like I told Corrigan, I don't have it.'

'He believed you, like the asshole he is,' Monte said. 'You either have the coin or you know where it is.'

'Why would you think that?'

'Because you're here, dude.'

'You know why I'm here,' Mace said.

Monte smiled. 'I heard what you told the gray man. Angie's top-drawer material, but, if that's what rocks your boat, you'd be better off hopping the wall at Hefner's. So stop fucking around. Name your price.'

'I don't have the coin. I don't give a shit about the coin.'

Monte moved closer until he was barely a foot away from Mace. He stared into his eyes, as if he were looking for something that puzzled him. Finally, he stepped back and began to sing. 'Did he smile his work to see? Did he who made the Lamb make thee?'

Mace understood the questions did not require answers, even Karaoke-style. He also understood that the man who sang them was clearly shy a few keys on his piano. He looked at Rufe, who was staring at the floor, trying to keep what he was thinking off his face.

'The melody work for you?' Monte asked. 'The words are brilliant, of course, but I'm not sure about the melody.'

'I'd have to hear more,' Mace said.

Monte's face broke into a wide smile. 'Straight talk. You listening, Rufe? That's what I've been telling you. When I ask for an opinion, that's what I want. Not a kiss on the ass.'

Rufe nodded, then glared at Mace.

'You leveling about not having the coin, Mason? It's worth a lot to me. I might even be willing to add a certain beautiful blonde to the deal, if that's what it takes.'

Most of Mace's anger at Corrigan's demeaning of Angela had been manufactured, but this was different. He felt the fury building inside him and knew it could erupt into something beyond his control. Before that happened, he said, 'It's impossible to make a deal for something I don't own.'

'OK. You say you don't have the coin, I've gotta believe you, because you strike me as a guy traveling the straight-talk express. So, here's some straight talk from me to you. For a reasonably smart guy, Mason, you evidently don't know the first thing about bitches. Put 'em up on a pedestal, they'll piss on you every time. They don't want you to do stuff for 'em, they want you to do stuff to 'em. That's a lesson in love from the new King of Pop.'

'Thanks for the lesson,' Mace said. 'I'd better be going.'

'We're not quite finished,' Monte said.

Mace stared at him.

'You busted up an employee of mine at the drug store. You crashed my party and you tried to make time with my main bitch. I'm not gonna let you just stroll out of here. Now I'm going back to my party and Rufe's gonna let loose on you a little. Nothing hardcore. A broken jaw tops. You hear me, Rufe?'

Rufe nodded.

'Just to clarify,' Mace said, 'you don't want Rufe to kill me, right?'

'Not this time,' Monte said with a chuckle and made his exit.

When the door closed, Rufe smiled and took a step toward Mace. He had the advantage of two inches and maybe forty pounds. And, judging by the way he moved, he'd spent some time in a ring.

He was expecting Mace to do something. At the very least to assume a fighting position. Mace merely stood there, staring at the bigger man.

'Take a good look at me, Rufe,' Mace said. 'What do you see?'

'A guy gonna get his jawbone broke.'

'Maybe. But that won't be the end of it.'

Rufe paused. 'What you sayin'?'

'Your boss wants me alive.'

'So?' Rufe was frowning, confused now.

'You take the first swing and it'll come down to this: you kill me or I kill you. Either way you lose.'

'Fuck you. You messing with me.'

'Look at me, Rufe. Do I strike you as a guy who gives a shit whether he lives or dies? Lay a hand on me and I will kill you unless you kill me first.'

'Bullshit. Ah'm gonna break yo' jaw, then toss you out.'

'Either kill me or I kill you.'

Rufe stared at him, a big man looking foolish in his tiger pajamas. But not foolish enough to doubt what Mace had just said.

'You a crazy muthafucka. That fo' sure.'

'Kill me or I kill you.'

'Go on, get the fuck out of here, then,' he said. 'And don't let Mr Monte see you go.'

Mace was willing to let him have the last word.

THIRTY-FOUR

Familiar now with the ways of the castle, Mace used the tunnel to return to the lagoon area in search of his clothes. The party was winding down, but it wasn't over. In the cabana, he found a naked couple sleeping on the cushions that were hiding his pants and shirt. He rolled them off on to the grass carpet and ignored their angry exit while he exchanged the powder-blue nightwear for his original outfit.

Walking to the castle at a leisurely pace, he observed maybe fifty stragglers in various stages of inebriation. Some were wired and angry, some lost in that near-unconscious state of chemical bliss. He was searching for Angela, though he wasn't sure if he wanted to find her.

In the castle, the sleepwalking band had departed to dreamland or points west, but the main rooms were still well populated by night owls using up the remains of Monte's hospitality. At that time of morning, it consisted of booze and platters of brownies and other pastries that rested on tables beside silver pots of hot black coffee, demitasse cups and trays of manually rolled cigarettes, rainbow-colored ecstasy pills and larger, pure white OxyContin pellets.

Some guests necked, some fondled, some used straws on lines of cocaine that were being quickly added to and replaced by a razor blade in the expert hand of a bored, pale young woman in an old-fashioned maid's outfit who occasionally applied a little-finger's worth to her own gums. Some of the faces were celebrated enough for Mace to recognize, though he would have been hard-pressed to come up with names.

The face he was looking for was not there.

Simon Symon entered the room, camera poised. When his eyes met Mace's he lost his smile and scurried away. Running to Monte, of course. Mace took that as the final reason for him to depart.

Just before he made it to the front door, he felt a hand on his shoulder. He turned to find his host standing at his side.

'How fucking rude, Mason,' Monte said, 'leaving without saying goodbye.'

Symon was hovering nearby with several security guards. Mace didn't care anymore. Nor did he care about Monte. He was experiencing an odd, totally unfamiliar sensation and was rather amazed to realize what it was. He felt invincible.

'You throw a pretty good party,' he said to Monte. 'For a supernerd dickhead.'

Before the new king of pop could reply, Mace turned and walked to the front door. He opened it and left.

No one tried to stop him. He'd have been surprised if they had.

THIRTY-FIVE

He walked past the security gate and headed down Cabrillo Canyon Road without thinking much about how he was going to get to his rental, parked near the Honeymoon Drugs. He could jack one of the guests' cars. Or he could walk. Hell, the way he felt, maybe he'd fly. He wondered if there was such a thing as a second-hand cocaine high.

When he saw the yellow Mustang double parked down the road he was not at all surprised. It seemed inevitable Angela would be there, waiting for him.

'You certainly took your time leaving,' she said when he slid on to the bucket seat beside her. She was about to say something else, but he didn't give her the chance, just drew her to him and kissed her. Made as much contact between their bodies as the car's gearshift would allow.

He was on an unbeatable lucky streak.

At any other time, he might think about heading for Vegas. At the moment, his feeling of elation was pushing him in another direction.

Angela made a moaning sound when he stopped the kiss. He was as erect as a stallion and the moan almost pushed him over the edge.

'God,' she said. 'My God.'

'Drive us away from here,' he said and she started up the engine and did just that.

'My apartment?' she asked.

He was not so far gone that he forgot the men in the van he'd seen heading into the Florian. He didn't want to be the subject of a hidden audio or video transmission. 'Make it a hotel, the bigger the better.'

She maneuvered the Mustang around a Parkette who was returning a shiny Ferrari to a departing guest. 'Why not a nice little intimate motel?' she said.

'The clerks in those places are too nosey.'

'Don't let paranoia blow the mood,' she said. 'I vote for intimate.'

She headed the car west to the ocean. At the Coast Highway, she turned north, then abruptly pulled over to the side of the road. 'I want the top down,' she said. 'You mind?'

He helped her unhook the frame.

There was hardly any traffic as they sped down the highway, waves breaking and rolling into the sand on their left. Feeling the cool wind in his hair, Mace leaned back against the head-rest and watched the lights of a plane that seemed to be dodging stars as it headed for LAX. 'We always had convertibles,' he said. 'My dad loved 'em, no matter how impractical they were.'

'Where was that?'

'On a planet far, far away,' he said.

When Angela turned into their destination, he was dismayed. Wally's Surf's Up Motel was exactly the kind of establishment he wanted to avoid, a collection of small, funky-looking ramshackle cabins circling a royal blue, neon detailed manager's shack.

'This place is an institution,' Angela said eagerly, oblivious to his reaction.

'Come here often?' he asked.

'Not since I was in my teens,' she said. 'Wally's used to be *the* hangout for weekend surfer dudes, which my first boyfriend was, no big surprise. It was the kind of place where you could do anything you wanted as long as it didn't close down the beach.'

'Maybe it's changed.'

'Oh, I hope not,' she said. 'I've driven by a hundred times or more since those days and it's always looked the same.'

He assumed some of those drive-bys had been on her way to and from Tiny Daniels' beach house which was only five or six miles away. He said, 'Sit here while I wake the manager.'

'Get cabin seven if you can,' she said.

The yawning man who unlocked the office door in answer to the night bell had the wrinkled face of a seventy year old and the body of a forty year old. He was wearing striped boxer shorts and a rumpled flannel shirt, unbuttoned, the better to display a deep-tanned, reasonably flat stomach and a wash-board chest decorated with several strands of long white hair. More there than could be found on his sun-spotted scalp.

Mace followed him into a small office space decorated with surfboard wall hangings and framed photos of healthy-looking young men and women engaged in the sport. A deep-sea mask and fins rested on the floor near a clerk's counter housing an ancient cash register.

The motel manager mumbled something.

'Say what?' Mace asked.

The manager didn't reply. Instead, he moved past a raised panel attached to the clerk's counter. He lowered the panel and continued on into a room directly behind the counter space. He reappeared a moment later and said, clearly, 'Had to put in my choppers.'

He did a show and tell, displaying a set of teeth that were all impossibly white save for one in front bearing the stars and stripes of the American flag. 'Ever read Tom Wolfe's *The Electric Cool-Aid Acid Test*?' he asked. 'No? Too bad. Brilliant piece of reportage that sums up the whole fucking sixties. Anyway, Kesey, the writer Ken Kesey, meets up with this guy operating a gas pump who has an American-flag tooth. I read that and told myself, "I got to get one of those."'

'Looks like your dentist did a good job,' Mace said. 'We—'

'Dentist? Hell. I did this myself. Years ago. Epoxy. No problema. You need a cabin, right?'

'Right,' Mace said.

The transaction didn't take much longer. The old guy was the owner as well as the motel manager, a second generation Wally. He was happy for the business, he told Mace. Surf was up at the Wedge at Newport Beach, which meant they literally had their choice of cabins. Number seven? *No problema.*

It was a bare bones cabin facing the ocean, smelling of disinfectant, brine and, thanks to a garden just below the window, night-blooming jasmine. Angela took a deep breath and threw her arms around Mace. 'You got my cabin and it's exactly the same, down to the jasmine perfume I remembered.'

'Glad you're happy,' he said and led her to the bed.

'They call jasmine the queen of the night,' she said as she helped him unsnap her shiny halter.

'Not with you around,' he said and kissed her.

There were any number of reasons why making love to her was a terrible idea, but none of them mattered.

He felt his heart flutter as she began to moan again, pressing against him, then shoving him away so that her shaking hands could work the buttons of his shirt.

Then it was on to his belt.

Her frenzy was contagious. It seemed to take less than a second for them to be naked together on the bed.

'Wait,' she said, breathlessly. 'Wait. We need something.'

'I don't—'

'Wait,' she said again and hopped from the bed.

He watched her, marveling at her body as she found her small purse and removed from it a small square packet. She joined him on the bed and tore open the packet, withdrawing a sheath thin as a membrane.

He watched her slide the sheath over his erection, giving the latter a loving tug.

Then it was just a matter of putting the final touch to Mace's extraordinary evening.

THIRTY-SIX

I f there was anything Paulie Lacotta disliked more than having his sleep interrupted, it was being awakened in his own bed by a couple of over-muscled assholes he'd never laid eyes on before.

'What the fuck?' were his first words.

'Get dressed,' the asshole nearest the bed ordered in an accent that sounded like a bad stand-up parody of the Austrian-born ex-governor's.

Paulie was too confused and exhausted to be angry; a good thing because either of the men could have killed him with one punch.

'Get dressed,' asshole number one repeated.

'OK,' Paulie said. 'What's the deal?'

'Mr Brox want you. Get dressed.'

Brox.

Lacotta knew the name. Maxil Brox, Russia's boss of bosses. Shit! What had he done now?

He dragged himself out of the bed and realized that he was wearing only a silk pajama top. There'd been a broad . . .

He looked around the bedroom.

'Your whore gone,' asshole number one said. 'She prob'ly go look for some man with bigger ding-dong, eh, Gulik.'

Gulik, the other asshole, nodded. 'That would be any man, Klebek.'

Both assholes laughed merrily.

'Fuck you guys,' Paulie said, picking up the silk underwear he'd dropped beside the bed a couple of hours ago. He was not as annoyed at them as he was at Mace, the reason he hadn't activated the security system. And the guy was still a no-show. 'Let's see how big you are after laying pipe for a couple hours,' Paulie said. 'And that's without fucking Cialis.'

The two Ruskies were not impressed. They continued to ridicule him as he finished dressing. Then they led him to a black Bentley parked in front of his home. The one called Klebek sat beside Lacotta on the rear seat. Gulik took the driver's seat.

'You guys know who used to live right there?' Paulie asked as they drove away on Mulholland. 'Marlon fucking Brando. And Jack Nicholson, there, behind that gate.'

The Russians didn't seem to care.

Paulie was surprised when the Bentley wound up on Sunset, even more so when it parked in front of Abe's Empourium, which was closed for the night. A minimal janitorial crew was readying the place for the day's business, using mops to splash some liquid cleanser on the tiles. As far as Paulie could tell, all they were accomplishing was to add a tear-inducing Clorox element to the stale booze and coffee odors.

His twin guides ushered him up the stairs to Abe's office where the club's cadaverous owner was waiting with a small, wiry man in a cheap black suit, bright red tie and white shirt. He was in his early forties. With his pinched, humorless pale face and poverty wardrobe he resembled an underpaid junior accountant. With one notable exception: his luxuriant brown hair which he kept long and lovingly tended.

'Welcome, Mr Lacotta,' he said. 'My name is Maxil Brox. Perhaps you have heard of me?'

Paulie nodded dumbly. Everybody had heard of Brox, but, because Brox managed to keep a shadowy distance from the public eye – no small feat in this era of photographic overload – few had had the dubious pleasure of seeing him, much less meeting him face to face.

'I regret having to disturb your slumber, sir,' Brox said, 'but I have several extremely important goals to accomplish and I'm already eleven hours behind the rest of Moscow.'

'Why don't I just go check up on my cleaning crew,' Abe said, moving toward the door, 'and let you gentlemen take care of business.'

'Please remain,' Brox said. 'I want all parties to be clear on where we stand in our little arrangement.'

'I got no arrangement with you,' Paulie said. 'And I don't plan on having any.'

Brox barely moved his eyes, but it was enough of a signal for Gulik to deliver a non-fatal but devastating fist to Paulie's right kidney, sending him to his knees.

Dizzy from the pain, he stared up at the Russian crime boss who was standing within an arm's distance. The cool bastard knew that even if Paulie could take a swing without one of the thugs intervening, he'd be too weak to do anything more than pat him.

'Let me explain myself, Mister La-ca-ta,' Brox said. 'I had an arrangement with one of your acquaintances, Mister Daniels. I paid him a great deal of money in return for a certain object. Due to Mister Daniels' untimely death, his obligation to me has transferred to you.'

Paulie didn't really get the drift of what Brox was saying. He was trying to catch his breath, but deep breathing resulted in a knife-like pain so overpowering he was too worried about suffocation for his mind to take in what his ears were hearing.

Brox shook his head and said to Gulik, 'Did you have to hit him that hard?'

'I thought I was supposed to,' Gulik said, then seemed to correct himself. 'I thought he could handle it.'

Annoyed, Brox waved the big man away. He bent over Paulie and placed a thin, pale hand on his shoulder. 'Can you hear me, sir? Nod, if you can hear me.'

Breathing heavily now, Paulie was thinking that he'd have to see his internist ASAP. Get that creeping Jesus out of bed. Even if he wasn't permanently damaged, he'd be pissing blood for weeks. Blood coming out of his wang, like he was on the rag. *Gee-zus.*

'Nod . . . if . . . you . . . can . . . hear . . . me,' Brox was articulating. In his face.

Paulie nodded.

'Since Mister Daniels is dead, you have inherited his obligation,' Brox said. 'We are now partners.'

'No. I work for . . . Sal Montdrago.'

'So?' Brox asked. 'I will . . . how did the *kumovstvo* – the godfather say it? I will make him an arrangement he cannot refuse.'

'An *offer*,' Paulie said. 'Not an arrangement. An *offer*.'

'Whatever.' Brox looked at his watch. A cheap Cartier Panther knock-off, Paulie was not too much in pain to notice. Was that the best the guy could do, a mob chief with a fist-hold on the Russian black market? The prick had no taste. No style.

'I must leave soon,' Brox said. 'I can trust you to turn over the coin to our friend Abraham?'

'I don't have the fucking coin,' Paulie said. 'What makes you think I do?'

'My associate Mr Daniels had the coin. You had him killed. Ergo . . .'

'I didn't have Tiny killed.' Paulie was shouting now, forgetting his pain.

Brox turned to Abe. 'Did you not assure me this was true?'

'Hey, look. I was just passing along the word on the street,' Abe said.

Brox frowned. 'I am faced with a dilemma,' he said. 'Either you are untrustworthy, Abraham, or Mr Lacotta is lying. I haven't the time to puzzle this out.' He sighed. 'Find out the answer for me, Gulik. Quickly.'

In less than a second, the big Russian had Paulie lying on the carpet, his giant foot pressing on the struggling man's chest. 'If he uses his full body weight,' Brox said, 'he will crush your rib cage, probably sending jagged sections of it into vital organs.'

Paulie had just started to breathe normally. Now fear and the pressure of Gulik's foot was causing him to gasp again.

'He cannot speak if he cannot breathe, Gulik,' Brox said.

The big man shifted his weight so that his foot barely grazed Paulie's chest.

Paulie responded with a deep intake of breath. He released it and said, in a voice so calm and certain it surprised even him, 'If I had taken the coin from the fat fuck, don't you think I would have put the formula to use by now?'

Brox barely considered the comment before turning to Abe. 'What does your *word on the street* have to say about that?'

Abe made a helpless gesture with his hands.

'Wasting time. It is where you Americans excel. I cannot afford it. And now, neither can you gentlemen. I give you twenty-four hours to find the coin. At midnight tomorrow, if it is not in my hand, I will have this establishment burned to the ground.' He headed for the door. 'And you both will be used for kindling.'

Abe waited until the Russian trio had left the room, then tried to help Paulie to his feet.

'Don't touch me, you fucker,' Paulie warned, using Abe's desk to pull himself upright. 'Putting me on the spot like that. I ought to burn you myself.'

'I didn't tell Brox anything he hadn't heard,' Abe said. 'And now I'm in this mess, too.'

'Boo hoo, prick,' Paulie said. He arched his back and moaned. The kidney pain began again, still strong and deep. 'Selling me out to that pasty-faced fuck.'

He headed for the door.

'Wait,' Abe called. 'What do we do about the coin?'

'You made the problem,' Paulie said. 'You solve it.'

'How?'

'See what the word is on the street.'

Paulie was moving through the building now, Abe running to keep up with him. 'What about Brox? He said he'd kill us.'

'He's gonna have to find me first,' Paulie said.

'Hold on, for Christ's sake.'

Paulie had never heard Abe whine before. It stopped him. 'What?'

'If you didn't kill Tiny, you must have some idea who did. I was thinking maybe it was Mace? Got that temper, you know.'

Paulie frowned. Could Mace have had a meltdown at Tiny's? Cleaned house? Then lied about the Brit gunman?

'If he killed the fat man, Paulie, you know damn well he's got the coin.'

'Naw,' Paulie said, shaking his head. 'Mace is not that guy.'

'You hesitated,' Abe said. 'You must have a doubt.'

'Mace is fucking not that guy,' Paulie said, disgusted with

himself for letting Abe see his momentary loss of faith in his friend.

Abe shrugged. 'Well, somebody shot up that place,' he said, 'and came away with the prize.'

A new possibility flashed in Paulie's mind. Could Angela have had four men killed for the coin? Hard to believe. And yet, she was there. And who else was left?

He hoped Mace had been able to get a fix on her whereabouts. Then, maybe together they could . . . force her to give up the coin. Not that he'd be turning the coin over to Brox. Screw the Russkie and the boat he sailed in on. The coin was his property.

If only Mace knows where the bitch is.

THIRTY-SEVEN

Mace stood beside the bed, looking down at Angela as she slept.

The last time he'd experienced the sight of her sleeping in just that same position it had been in a dream.

Was he dreaming now? Maybe.

She stirred, opened her eyes and looked up at him. Smiling. Holding out her arms. He offered no resistance when she drew him back into bed, back into a long kiss, and, eventually, back into another euphoric sexual climax.

They broke apart and he lay on his back, breathing heavily. Dreamily satisfied. But the satisfaction was short-lived. A darkness descended on the room. Suddenly fearful, he looked at her, eager for reassurance.

Angela was facing the open window where a thin curtain fluttered in the morning breeze off the ocean.

He touched her shoulder and she slowly turned toward him. She was wearing a sweet smile even though, like Tiny Daniels' worthless bodyguard Carlos, a bullet had removed her left eye.

He awoke with a start, his body covered in sweat.

'What?' she asked beside him.

It was still dark. She was frowning, not quite awake and preferring not to be. She opened her eyes and stared at him. 'What is it?'

When she saw the look on his face, her voice softened. 'What's the matter?'

'Just a bad dream,' he said, looking away.

'Want to talk about it?'

'No.'

He looked at his watch. Could it still be just two thirty?

He got out of bed and located his pants. He checked the pockets but knew he wouldn't find what he was looking for. 'Don't suppose you have cigarettes?' he asked.

She shook her head. 'Too unhealthy and too retro,' she said.

He moved to the window and watched the light traffic zoom by. Beyond the coast highway and the expanse of shadowy beach the nervous dark ocean seemed to blend into the waning night.

The sweet smell of mimosa was still in the air.

He looked at the Mustang, parked where they'd left it, alone and lonely at the manager's office.

He left the window and walked across the room for a wooden chair that he dragged to the door and jammed under the knob.

'What are you doing?' she asked.

'Something I forgot in the heat of the moment,' he said, returning to bed.

'Don't tell me you're worried about Jerry?'

'He's just the tip of the iceberg.' He slipped under the sheet, feeling electric shocks when his body touched hers. 'But I wouldn't mind knowing why you wanted this particular place and this particular cabin.'

'It's nothing for you to worry about,' she said.

'I worry about everything.'

'I guess you think I'm pretty naive,' she said.

'Why would I think that?'

'I really believed Corrigan was an art dealer.'

'He is,' Mace said. 'But it's just a sideline. He brokers weapons.'

'Guns?'

'Any kind of war toy. Missiles, tanks, WMDs probably.'

'What's he want with Jerry?'

'Corrigan's last deal went sour,' Mace said. 'The merchandise got lost.'

'The coin,' she said.

He stared at her.

'I was in the game room,' she said, 'eavesdropping on your conversation with Corrigan.'

'Then you know,' he said. 'Corrigan won't return to Europe until his deal is back on track. Jerry has the loot to make that happen, if the coin surfaces.'

'You've got it, haven't you?' she asked.

He frowned. 'Where's that coming from?'

'Why else would you be so certain the others don't have it?'

'I thought you said you were listening in. They sure as hell wouldn't be bothering with the likes of me if they had the coin. They're as desperate as Paulie Lacotta.'

'And you work for Paulie.'

'No, I don't. I've known him a long time. He told me he was in a mess and asked me to help.'

'By romancing me?' she asked.

He smiled. 'That wouldn't be number one on his to do list.'

'Why not? Everyone seems to believe Tiny had the coin intended for Paulie. It's logical Paulie would assume I knew something about it. He'd ask you to find out.'

'To question you, maybe,' Mace said. 'But not this. Jealousy is one of Paulie's many flaws.'

'Jealous?' she asked. 'He and I weren't . . . my God, he didn't tell you we . . . ? That's ridiculous . . . We went out a few times. He hired me to purchase paintings for his place on Mulholland Drive. I wouldn't call that a romance.'

'Paulie flaw number two: a rich imagination.'

Mace rolled on to his side, facing her, brushing a strand of blonde hair from her forehead.

She pushed his hand away. 'So *this* isn't about the coin?'

'Of course not.'

'Because you already have it.'

'Suppose I did. What do you think I should do with it?'

She shrugged. 'If it belongs to Paulie, give it to him.'

'Then what? Go back to my home and never think about how many poor sons of bitches would be on the receiving end of all the bullets and bombs and missiles?'

'If you feel that way,' she said, 'you might as well toss the bloody thing into the ocean.'

He smiled and kissed her, a tender kiss this time.

When it ended, she said, 'I picked this cabin because it's special,' she said. 'It's where I lost my virginity.'

There were tears in her eyes when she added, 'I wish I'd been with *you* then.'

'We'll just have to settle for now,' he replied, thinking how nice it would be if what she'd said was true. And if what he was feeling turned out to be real.

THIRTY-EIGHT

As the cab headed up Mulholland Drive to his residence, Paulie listened to his own voice suggesting he leave a message. He sounded like a punk. He was gonna have to redo the recording, put more man into it.

He'd called his house hoping that Mace would be there to pick up. If he was there and if he knew where they could find Angela, that was that. Even if Mace didn't know, then at the least he'd have company and protection until he was packed and on his way out of town. Maybe to one of the furnished properties Mount Olympus owned in Reno.

He wondered if he should call Jamey Scalise, tell him to send a couple of leg-breakers up to keep him company until Mace showed. The problem with that: Jamey was very loyal to his Uncle Sal and Paulie didn't want Sal calling to find out why he needed muscle.

The cab turned into his driveway.

He got out, shoving a twenty and a ten into the cabbie's hand. The meter registered only $19.80, but a fifty percent tip didn't seem to merit a thank you anymore. Wearing a disgusted scowl, he watched the vehicle depart. *Terrorist bastard,* he thought, mistaking his Korean driver for an Arab. *Probably sends his tips back to buy al-Zawahiri new turbans.*

His kidney was still tender. He paused to test it by taking a big, deep breath of cool but polluted Southern California night air. That's when he realized there was a black Cadillac convertible parked with its top up, partially hidden by the Range Rover he hadn't used in months.

And he heard the TV going inside the house.

He forgot the pain entirely.

He circled the black Caddy, wondering if Mace had gotten into a scrape where he'd had to jack the car. He tried the door. Locked. So much for the jack theory.

Inside the house a Limey announcer was doing rapid-fire color on a game while a crowd of spectators did a lot of screaming.

What the hell . . .

Paulie decided to call Jamey after all.

But before he could get out the smart phone, his front door opened. Drier was standing there. He gave Paulie a friendly grin and holstered the weapon. 'Welcome home,' he said. 'We were worried you might be on a sleepover.'

Corrigan was in the living room, sitting on Paulie's leather couch, drinking one of his special hefeweizens and watching his big flat fifty-three inch monitor. 'League One football all night long,' the weapons broker said with a grin. 'And in high-def. You gotta love this country.'

'Make yourself comfortable, why don't ya?' Paulie said. 'Beer OK?'

'Actually, it tastes like crap. Drier couldn't find any imports.'

'You're drinking an import. From Germany, where they know a little about making beer.'

'Yeah? Well they can put this one back in the horse.' Corrigan placed the bottle on the carpet, grabbed a remote and clicked off the TV before turning to Paulie. 'Sit down, brother Lacotta. You and I need to chat a bit about brother Mason.'

Paulie took a stuffed leather chair near the couch. 'What about him?' he asked.

'Exactly what team is he playing for?'

'What are you talking about?' Paulie asked, the question making him uneasy.

'I . . . bumped into him a few hours ago at Jerry Monte's little shindig,' Corrigan said. 'Know why he was there?'

'Sure,' Paulie lied. 'But I don't know why *you* were.'

Corrigan gave him a fake smile. 'Interestin' guy, Jerry. We all may be doing some business, down the line.'

'He got the coin?' Paulie asked, getting to the heart of the matter.

'Regrettably, no. But it's Mason I want to talk about. Why do you think he crashed the party?'

'Looking for the coin,' Paulie said.

'Hmmm. There may be some truth to that, but it's not what he told me. He said he was there because he'd fallen under the spell of the lovely Miss Lowell.'

'He conned you.'

'He's conning somebody,' Corrigan said.

'They looked pretty cozy at the party,' Drier said. 'And when we left, we passed the dame in her car, waiting for somebody. I don't think it was that putz Monte.'

'Let me get this straight,' Paulie said. 'You guys rush right over here and bust into my home? Watch my fucking television? Drink my fucking beer? All this just to let me know my best pal is slipping it to my old girlfriend?'

'Take it down a notch, Lacotta,' Corrigan said. 'The point is, I think they've got the coin and they're selling us out.'

'Always nice to hear what *you* think,' Paulie said. 'Here's what *I* know. Maxil Brox is in town and he says he's gonna burn me alive if he doesn't get the coin by midnight tomorrow.'

Corrigan's hooded eyes opened wide. 'Brox? Here? That's bullshit. He wouldn't risk it.'

'You're batting zero, Corrigan. Not half an hour ago, I was this close to the son of a bitch.'

Corrigan shrugged. 'Well, hell, all the more reason to reel in Mason and the broad right now, shake 'em upside down and see if the coin doesn't hit the carpet.'

'How would that solve my problem?' Paulie asked. 'Even if we get the coin, I'm not gonna turn it over to Brox. That still leaves me on the Russkie's list of things to light on fire.'

Corrigan opened his mouth to reply. But instead of speaking, he frowned. He turned toward Drier who drew his gun and started moving silently toward the kitchen area.

'What?' Paulie asked.

'You didn't hear it? A creak,' Corrigan said. 'Probably nothing, but, if not, Drier will handle it.'

Paulie saw the big man slip silently into the darkness of the hall leading to the kitchen. 'Getting back to Brox,' Corrigan said, 'you let us worry about him. You just concentrate on getting the coin. Why not give brother Mason a call? See what he's up to?'

Paulie took out his phone, turned it on, then shook his head. 'He's a throwback. Doesn't use a phone. But if he's with Angie, we got a tracker on her car.'

'Perf—' Corrigan began. Instead of completing the word, he paused to reach down and remove a small pistol from an ankle holster.

What happened next in the room was disturbing and potentially mind-blowing. Paulie saw Drier emerging from the shadowy hallway. But he wasn't using his legs. It was like this six-foot-two strongman was floating toward them, eyes closed, lifeless, his head twisted at a very unnatural angle, blood spilling over his lips on to his chin.

Then he was flying.

He collided against the couch, bouncing back against Corrigan just as the gray-haired man was starting to raise his gun.

The giant who had been carrying Drier, who had thrown him like a beach ball, stood in the middle of the living room, grinning at Paulie. Huge. Muscled. Wearing a Superman outfit complete with red cape. Looking like fucking Elvis Presley, pretending to be Superman.

Corrigan had lost the gun. With Drier's body pinning him, he moved his hand frantically trying to retrieve it. Before he could, a man wearing what Paulie thought to be a beautifully tailored Savile Row gray suit, almost danced across the room to pluck the gun from the carpet.

Paulie suddenly remembered the phone in his hand. As the giant advanced toward him, he turned and began walking away.

'That one's leaving,' he heard the giant announce.

'Stop him,' the other man ordered.

Paulie was blinking at the fucking phone, pressing the screen, trying to get it to start recording. It responded with a click, the loudest goddamn click he'd ever heard. He felt the big man getting closer. He saw that there wasn't much memory left, but anything was better than nothing. If he could find some place to put—.

He didn't get the chance. A hand the size of a honey-cured ham closed around the back of his neck. He thought the giant's fingers and thumb were actually touching under his chin.

'Don't kill him, Timmie,' the thin Limey commanded.

'Jesus, no. Don't,' Paulie croaked.

As the big man turned him around, Paulie let the phone slide down his leg to the carpet. He kicked it under a table before Timmie started dragging him to the center of the room.

But . . . what were the odds that it was recording? Or that Mace would show up? And find the phone? And be able to figure out how to operate it?

Still, a guy had to try.

The well-dressed Limey pointed Corrigan's gun at him as he grunted to his feet. 'If either of you gentlemen are in possession of the coin,' he said, 'now would be a propitious time to admit it.'

'Mason's got it,' Corrigan said. He was looking at Drier's twisted body and Paulie was surprised to see that the guy was tearing up.

'And where might Mr Mason be at this moment?'

Corrigan forced himself to look away. He sniffed and said, 'Somewhere with the dame.'

'Ah, *cherchez la femme.*' The well-dressed Limey kept the gun trained on Corrigan as he said, 'Mr Lacotta, did I hear you mention something about a tracking device?'

THIRTY-NINE

I t was a little before six a.m. in Bayou Royal, Mace realized; approximately the time he usually awoke, precondi-
tioned by the past. His late father's workday had begun
around then and he remembered opening his eyes to the murky
pre-dawn light, listening to the old man putting his breakfast
dishes on the kitchen sink directly beneath his bedroom.
Then there'd be solid footsteps moving away to the front
door. Then the front door slamming shut as James Duke
Mason left for the cannery to prepare for the shrimper fami-
lies, fathers and sons and even grandfathers, who'd be
returning with their early catches.

But, thanks to pollution, the disappearing marshlands, the
ruinous oil spill and cheaper imported shrimp from South
America and South-East Asia, the business had fallen off. And
the cannery had been sold and torn down and replaced by a
seafood chain restaurant run by thugs. And his father was dead.
And he was in Southern California, where it was nine minutes
before four, still very dark outside and inside their motel room.

He lay in bed, staring at the cracked ceiling, listening to
Angela's soft, steady breathing as she slept and the sound of
surf mixing with the light but constant traffic along the coast
highway. He'd assumed he was awake because of his body's
natural alarm clock. But the headlights that momentarily swept
across the ceiling made him wonder if some sixth sense hadn't
put him on the alert.

He slipped from the bed and moved to the window.

The source of the light was a vehicle that had turned into
the motel lot and was now parked behind the Mustang in a
way that blocked it. It was the black Bentley that had followed
him earlier.

He grabbed his pants and put them on while shaking the
bed, waking Angela.

'Huh?' she asked, blinking at him in the darkness.

'Visitors,' he said. 'We have to go.'

'What visitors?' she asked, getting out of bed.

'I don't know,' he said, forcing himself to stop watching her as she slipped on her shoes and searched the floor for her clothes.

The driver had turned off the Bentley's lights, but Mace could still see puffs of exhaust reflecting the blue of the neon motel sign. The passenger door opened and a large masculine figure separated from the machine. Stepping into the sign's neon glow, the blue-tinged man looked big and powerful and mean.

He stood there, apparently trying to select a likely cabin to invade. Mace was relieved they'd left the Mustang by the motel's entrance, but, as the big man trudged toward the manager's office, he was sorry about exposing the elderly Wally to their trouble.

Angela was nearly dressed. 'Give me your phone,' he whispered.

'It's in the car.'

'Of course it is. You ready?'

'For what? What's your plan?'

His plan. He moved quietly across the cabin to a screened window that looked out on a canyon road. It didn't matter where the road lead, as long as it was away from the motel.

Removing the screen from the window was about as difficult as zipping his fly, which Mace remembered to do just after helping Angela from the cabin.

There was a distance of about forty feet separating cabins seven and eight where they would be exposed as they headed toward the canyon road. Mace raised a hand, suggesting that Angela stay hidden while he checked the open area to make sure the Bentley and the searcher hadn't changed positions.

He doubted anyone in the sedan would be able to observe their departure. And even if poor Wally had been awake and fully toothed, with their location on his lips, he didn't think the searcher could have gotten a fix on their cabin so quickly. Still, he wanted to check.

He saw no movement in the semicircle in front of the cabins. Satisfied that they had a better than even chance of getting away up the canyon, he took a few steps backward until he was behind the cabin. He heard Angela emit an odd 'ahh' and was starting to turn when something very hard connected with his skull.

The surprise lasted only a bright and painful few seconds.

'Wake opp, you mees-ar-ab-al bastard,' a gruff voice ordered. Mace thought it sounded a little like the former governor of California. He could feel the man's breath and smell its chippino-and-cigar odor. He didn't want to open his eyes. Even though he'd enjoyed several of the ex-governor's movies, he really didn't care to see that lantern-jawed face glaring at him from just a few inches away.

'Slap him awake, Gulik,' another accented voice said.

'He is awake, Klebek, but I slap him anyway.'

Mace tried to raise his hands, to protect himself. When that didn't work, he tensed for the blow. It was not much of a slap, more like a pat. He opened his eyes.

The face in front of his was far from lantern-jawed. It was small for the attached massive body, and round, and featured a patchy black beard, bloodshot eyes topped by brows that were hairier and thicker than anything on his shaved but gray-stubbled head. Several of his teeth were gold. They glinted in the light of the cabin.

Mace's wrists had been tied to the rear legs of his chair by curtain pulls. His ankles had been tied to the chair's front legs. The bindings placed him in a difficult position in which his limbs were kept immobile by his own weight.

Gulik backed away, allowing Mace to see more of the room. Another big man, whom Gulik had called Klebek and who could have been his uglier brother, sat on the bed where, only a short time ago, he and Angela . . .

Gulik said, 'Your pussy in the car with Reiko. Reiko almost as handsome as me. Manhood like baby's arm. Maybe he fucking her. Maybe she sucking him. Either way, she now know what a real man is. Too bad for you.'

Mace surprised them all, including himself, by grinning.

'You think this funny?' Gulik asked.

'I just had a Popeye moment,' Mace said.

'What that mean?'

'Popeye, being threatened by Bluto. Olive Oil in danger.'

'This guy is moron,' Klebek said.

'We want coin,' Gulik said.

Mace looked down to see that his right pocket had been ripped from his pants, leaving the pants torn halfway down the leg. 'I'm guessing you know I don't have it.'

'You get coin for us, we give you back your pussy.'

'Why would I want her, after she's been doing all that stuff with Reiko?'

Gulik scowled. 'You foking with me?'

'I wouldn't fok with you. I leave that to Reiko and his baby's arm.'

It took Gulik a few seconds to get the gist of the comment. Mace was able to shift slightly on the chair, waiting for the punch. To his surprise, Gulik shrugged and pressed two kielbasa-like fingers against Mace's forehead, pushing him and the chair over backward.

Momentarily disoriented, lying on his back, he saw what appeared to be two Guliks towering above him. 'Get us coin, funny man, or we kill your pussy. We kill fat bastard you work for. We kill you.'

'I get it,' Mace said, his eyesight refocusing. 'You guys kill people.'

Gulik rested a foot on his chest. The foot was encased in the biggest Dr Martens steel-toe boot Mace had ever seen. 'Maybe I break your ribs,' the big man said. 'Stomp broken edges into heart.'

Mace had a sudden memory flash of Wylie's broken body. He blinked it away and said, 'That might make it difficult for me to deliver the coin. You should check with your boss Jerry Monte first.'

'Jerry Monte?' Klebek said in what sounded like genuine surprise. 'What's he got to do wit' any—'

'Shawt opp,' Gulik ordered his associate. He turned back to Mace. 'You think we work for la-di-da who sing and dance?' Gulik said. 'We work for Maxil Brox, you dumb mothofoker.'

There was something weird about the two of them, something off, but Mace couldn't get a fix on it. Something strangely familiar, too. 'What do you think Brox would prefer?' he asked. 'Me dead, or the coin?'

The big man glared at him, nodded and removed his foot. He took a cellular phone from his pocket and placed it on the floor next to Mace's head. 'What time?' he asked his associate.

The man on the bed looked at his wristwatch. 'Four twenty-eight.'

'OK,' Gulik said to Mace. 'You get coin and wait for call from Maxil Brox at exactly six a.m. He tell you what to do. You don't answer or you don't follow his instructions, we kill your pussy, we kill your comrade.'

The other man rose from the bed and they both headed for the door.

'It'll take me longer than an hour,' Mace said. 'Even if I wasn't tied up.'

Gulik paused, thinking about it. 'Mr Brox call you at *seven* a.m.,' Gulik said. 'No later.'

'Be sure to tell him you left me like this. My guess is he'll give you guys a special reward for making it impossible for me to do anything but lie here.'

Gulik paused at the door. He walked back to Mace. Giving him a wide, gold-tooth grin, he said, 'So helpless, huh?'

He raised his huge foot and brought it down hard and fast, breaking several rungs of the wooden chair.

Then, laughing, he followed his partner from the cabin.

FORTY

Even with the smashed rungs, it took Mace a while to splinter the chair enough to free his limbs. It was a quarter to five when he found Wally lying behind the counter in his office, unconscious; five nineteen, by the time he left the wiry old man sitting in a customer chair, mixing sips from what he called a 'breakfast brewski' with puffs on a double doobie to take the edge off his head pain and cursing the 'baboon who fucked me up.'

Mace ripped the tracking device from Angela's Mustang and tossed it into a pathetic little marijuana garden that Wally, or somebody, was tending next to the manager's office. Too impatient to put the top up on the convertible and ignoring the dew slick on the bucket seat and steering wheel, he started up the car and ground his teeth waiting for the wipers to clear the ocean-salty moisture from the windshield.

Then he was off to Paulie's house on Mulholland, using the drive time to pick at the scattered pieces of information he'd been given by Gulik and others and place them in context with what he'd already figured out.

He had decided, for example, that Paulie had to be the victim of the piece, the only participant who had played by the rules. The goat, in other words. There was no question but that his long-time rival, the late Tiny Daniels, had hijacked the coin with the formula. Mace knew this to be a fact. He'd gotten it straight from the horse's mouth.

If what Corrigan had told him was even a half-truth, Tiny had been partnered with Russian mobster Maxil Brox. The two clowns who'd taken Angela had said they were working for Brox. He should have realized that with the first accented syllables to spill out of Gulik's gold-toothed mouth. And yet there was something about the man with Gulik . . . Reacting in surprise to Mace's comment about them working for Jerry Monte, the guy on the bed had momentarily lost his Russian accent, had, in fact, substituted "wit'" for 'with'.

There was no rule saying Brox had to hire only his countrymen. But that didn't explain why the guy had pretended to have a Russian accent. Was it possible that Gulik had been faking his accent, too, but was a better actor?

Mace was keeping it at a cop-free fifty-five miles per hour along the nearly vacant Pacific Coast Highway, letting the cool, damp morning air clear his head. He understood that, by continuing to focus his thoughts on Brox and his two bully-boys, he was avoiding the one thing that meant the most to him: Angela's place in the puzzle. From the jump, he'd assumed she was not merely an innocent pawn in the plan to hijack the coin. Someone – the odds were on Tiny – had put her up to romancing Paulie to find out the shipping information.

But how deep was her involvement in everything that had happened since the theft? When Mace had walked in on her the night of Tiny's death, she'd been in bed, druggy and naked. But the silk panties he'd picked up from the carpet had been still warm from her body. Why had she stripped down just before he arrived?

At the time, he'd wanted to believe the gunshots had awakened her from a drug dream long enough to remove her clothes in anticipation of the arrival of her lover, Tiny's bodyguard, Carlos. Now he wondered if the whole thing hadn't been a charade to distract him from following Tiny's killer. Was it possible she had set up Tiny for the kill? If so, on whose orders? Brox?

His thoughts were interrupted by high beams filling his rear-view and lighting up the Mustang's interior. The vehicle was overtaking him much too quickly. He felt very vulnerable sitting in the topless car. He swung into the right lane and slowed a little, braced for the worst.

The speeder, an old souped-up Bonneville, zoomed past, twin exhausts roaring like a dragon in heat. About one car-length behind was a Highway Patrol sedan, it's red light flashing.

Just another LA car chase. But, because of the early hours and the light traffic, it would probably not even make the morning news. Still, it had spooked Mace enough that he stopped the Mustang at the side of the road and put up the top.

He was aware of how little protection a canvas cover offered. But it made him feel safer. He recognized this as a symptomatic trend. He was putting too much emphasis on feelings, too little on logic. That was courting disaster, with an emphasis on courting. He followed the PCH as it melded into the Santa Monica Freeway. With dawn drawing a bright white line along the horizon behind him, he forced himself to continue to rework the puzzle parts.

He knew Tiny, knew the fat man was greedy enough and arrogant enough to think he could slide a fast one past his Russian mobster partner, especially if Brox was a bit wary of setting foot on US soil. But Brox had evidently considered the coin worth the risk.

His presence helped to explain a thing or two. Sweets had

claimed that 'the fat man' had sent him to kill Paulie. But, as Paulie noted, if that had been true, it was doubtful that his limo mate, Thomas, would have accepted a contract on Tiny. If the limo trio were working for Brox, however, Paulie's murder would have made sense. The Russian could have seen him as a loose end that needed clipping. At the same time, Paulie's murder would have served as a warning to Tiny to stay in line. And, if Brox was thinking about opening a California branch, as some of his competitors had done on the East Coast, a weakening of Montdrago's operation would have made Paulie's removal even more appealing.

But Paulie hadn't been killed. And Tiny . . .

Mace was distracted by a jackass in a Toyota van behind him hitting his horn. He moved to the far right lane and let the guy zoom past. He noticed that the sky had gone from black to a charcoal gray and traffic was picking up.

He took the exit that carried him to the San Diego Freeway and even more traffic heading north.

Focus, he demanded of himself.

The attempt on Paulie's life had failed. And Tiny, who was trying to cut Brox out of an incredibly rich payday, had to be dealt with. How to do that and still tie Montdrago and Company to the fat man's murder?

He'd already considered the possibility that Thomas and his crew hadn't picked him up by chance at Point Dume. Sweets had seen Mace parked by the side of the road and recognized him as the guy who'd snapped his wrist. They'd grabbed him with the idea of setting him up for Tiny's death. If he hadn't escaped, he might have been left dead or dying at the crime scene accompanied by 'evidence' that he'd been hired to kill Tiny Daniels. Paulie would have been in the frame, too, the man who'd brought Mace to LA for the hit. Even Montdrago might have been ensnared, as an accessory before and/or after the crime.

Brox was the puppeteer, pulling all the strings, Mace thought. But where did that leave Angela?

Was she on the Russian's payroll? Had she been the one who'd knocked him out at the deserted motel where she'd insisted they stay? Everything he'd ever learned or experienced, behind bars or on the street, told him that the answer to both questions was 'yes'. But if she was playing it straight with him . . . or if he'd misread the signs, or forgotten something crucial . . .

No! Fuck the what-ifs. You spent a few hours with her. In bed, for Christ's sake, when everything seems possible. A week ago, you didn't even know she existed. Use your brain. Stop thinking with your dick.

FORTY-ONE

He almost overshot the Mulholland exit, had to swing in front of an early morning commuter who was lucky enough to have good brakes, but unlucky enough to have been drinking from a coffee mug. The Mustang was a peppy little car and Mace pushed it past the Skirball Center and up along the drive. He was going to have more than enough time to retrieve the coin before Brox's call, but he felt some need for speed.

He concentrated on the road, a good thing because it wound up beside a deep valley and some of its curves were extreme. He arrived at Paulie's shortly before six, just as dawn was breaking, painting the ranch-style home and the area with a warm golden glow that seemed so out of context it almost made him laugh.

He parked the Mustang on the cement slab beside Paulie's SL55 and Range Rover and a black Cadillac convertible with tinted windows.

The Caddy was locked up tight. There was a small pink rental sticker on the left hand corner of the windshield. The newborn sun hadn't begun to burn off the dew that covered the three cars. The Caddy had been there a while. Maybe it belonged to a lady Paulie had met in the night, but it made Mace cautious enough to avoid the front door.

He circled the house, taking quick peeks through the windows. There wasn't much of interest to see until he reached the glass doors that separated the living room from the red brick patio and the fake jungle pool and waterfall.

He'd been wondering why anybody would want a waterfall in their back yard. All that splashing. His current state of anxiety had been doing a good enough job of aggravating his bladder. The constant gurgling water was pushing the need to urinate past the need for caution.

Inside the living room, the too-modern chandelier was blazing.

He scanned the room – the darkened widescreen TV, the slightly rumpled carpet, the empty chairs and sofa. He had almost decided to move on when he saw the tip of a man's shoe poking out from behind the corner of the sofa.

Nothing stirred in the room.

Mace moved to the far edge of the glass door, but he could see no more than the whole shoe and an inch or so of the man's stocking. The foot was too large for it to be Paulie's.

Mace continued his tour of the building's exterior until he came to a door flanked by garbage bins. The door was closed but somebody had used a pry on it, leaving the frame splintered and the lock useless. He pushed the door open and several horseflies deserted the bins to try their luck inside the house. Mace followed them into a kitchen that smelled of lemons.

It was a smart, modern-looking room, complete with a skylight above a fancy food-prep island. There was pale wooden cabinetry, an empty metal sink, a shiny metallic space-age refrigerator. A stove/oven big enough to handle dinner for the UCLA football team.

The flat black floor tiles were made of a rubbery material that gave Mace's step a little bounce. Everything looked store-display new. He wondered if Paulie had ever fixed a meal there.

He checked his watch. 5:52 a.m., over an hour before Brox's promised phone call. He listened again for any stray sound. Just the buzzing of the flies, probably wishing they'd stayed with their friends.

He moved around the island and paused only briefly at a door leading to the rest of the house. A swinging door. He pushed it open soundlessly and carefully eased it back into position behind him. He followed the short hall to the entrance to the living room, where he stood, listening again.

The foot belonged to Drier. It and the rest of the man's body lay sprawled on the carpet beside the sofa. His head rested against the bottom of the sofa, twisted at an ugly angle. There were bruises on his neck. His eyes were open, but they weren't seeing much. The blood on his chin was not fresh.

Mace knew the man was dead, but he checked anyway. Cold corpse.

He turned from it and approached the giant TV screen. He ran his hand over the upper edge until he found the coin he'd stuck there, embedded in a wad of Wylie's chewing gum. The gum had dried out and popped free cleanly.

He moved back to Drier. The flies had found him. He shooed them away long enough to check the dead man's shoulder holster. It was empty but whoever had killed him had left his wallet, a small multi-bladed knife and a brass ring with an assortment of keys, including an electronic car starter with a Cadillac logo.

Mace pocketed the keys and used one of the knife's blades to scrape the gum from the coin. He put the knife and coin in his pocket. Then he flipped open Drier's wallet. He was surprised to find, hidden behind a French driver's license, an ID card with an angry eagle. Drier and – he presumed – Corrigan weren't ex-CIA. They were active agents.

He guessed he'd been wrong in assuming the men emerging from the van at the Florian had been private security.

But was CIA involvement a bad thing?

That depended on what the spooks were after.

He took the coin from his pocket and turned to the dead man whom the flies had again embraced. 'Level with me, Drier. Is this coin a real wiggle worm, or just a shiny lure to hook my pal Paulie? Or is Brox the big fish you were after all along?'

He stepped back and tried to postpone his bathroom visit long enough to get a sense of what had happened in the room.

The cushions on the leather couch were askew, but it didn't look as if there'd been a great battle. A beer bottle was on its side not far from the dead man, some of its contents forming a stain on the carpet. There was something under a table. He bent over slowly, more conscious than ever of his full bladder, and picked up the object.

He recognized the Samsung brand name, of course, but he didn't know much more than that. He thought it was a cellular phone but it was considerably sleeker and wider than the one Gulik had left him.

Paulie's Samsung. Probably performed all sorts of technological magic, he thought, placing it on the table.

He figured that Drier, and presumably Corrigan, had been paying Paulie a late-night visit, one friendly enough for them to park their vehicle out front. So, they'd been in the room, one of them drinking beer, when they'd been surprised by the sound of the back door being jimmied. Drier, the guard dog, would have gone to check it out. He'd been taken down, strangled and manhandled hard enough to break his neck.

Mace wondered if Gulik or his pal would be capable of that. His money was on Timmie. There was no lingering smell of cordite, ergo no gunfire, and it would take a lot to stop Drier's trigger finger long enough for someone to disarm and throttle him.

So, it had been Brox's hit squad – Timmie, Thomas and Sweets – that had crashed the party and departed with Paulie. And Corrigan? Had they taken him, too, or was his body somewhere else on the premises?

Not really his problem.

He checked his watch again. An hour before the call.

He used the guest bathroom to empty his bladder. He washed his face and then exchanged his torn trousers, filthy shirt and scuffed leather shoes for rumpled slacks, a black short-sleeve sport shirt and tennis shoes from his two-suiter. He placed the phone Gulik had left in his shirt pocket. Then he did the minimal packing necessary and closed and locked his single piece of luggage. Whichever way the day went, he wasn't going to be returning to this address. Definitely not with a dead CIA agent in the living room.

Looking at himself in the full-body mirror on the back of the closet door, he realized he needed sleep and a shave. He needed weapons more.

Forty-nine minutes to go.

He went to Paulie's bedroom, hoping to find a handgun. A rifle. Something. No luck.

Carrying his two-suiter, he returned to the living room and took a final scan of the room. He wasn't proud about leaving a corpse in Paulie's living room, but that wasn't his problem either. If Paulie came out of this whole thing alive and kicking, taking care of Drier would be a small price for him to pay.

He left the house by the front door and walked quickly to the black Cadillac. Using Drier's remote key, he popped the trunk and was about to place his bag in it when he saw an aluminum suitcase lying on its side.

He liked the looks of the metal case.

He found a non-electronic key on Drier's ring that unlocked the lid. Inside the case were a Sig Sauer P226 handgun and a BXP, a South African sub-machine gun, nestled snugly in a foam bed.

He thought the BXP an interesting choice, as if Corrigan and Drier had been expecting to bump into an army of terrorists. Or, to fit the craze of the day, zombies or vampires. The weapon was even capable of launching a grenade, though Mace didn't see either the launcher attachment or any grenades.

Too bad.

He pried the Sig Sauer from its nest, used the butt release to drop the magazine. He unlocked the slide and pulled it back, ejecting the round that had been in the chamber. The magazine had been at near full capacity, fourteen rounds. He snapped them back into place and fed the magazine into the gun, being careful to press the decocking lever.

He wondered if he should return to the living room to get the harness that Drier no longer needed. Forty minutes to go. When the call came, he wanted to be ready to roll. But he had time.

He ran back into the house with the Sig Sauer.

One look at the dead man's holster told him that it was too small. Annoyed, he tucked the weapon behind his belt.

And noticed Paulie's phone on the table.

Had Paulie been trying to call someone? Had he made the connection, said something to the other party that might help Mace?

He picked up the shiny gizmo and moved it around, trying to figure out how it worked. Reminding himself of King Kong studying a tiny automobile, he began pressing buttons along its side. A screen lighted up. On it was a picture of Al Pacino as Scarface. The 'Say hello to my little friend' pose. Typical Paulie.

Along the bottom of the screen was a drawing of an old reel-to-reel recorder. Mace did the King Kong thing and pressed his index finger against the drawing. There was a click. For a second or two, nothing happened. Then the screen was taken up by a larger reel-to-reel image and 'Voice 002'. At the bottom of the screen were two choices, a red button labeled 'Record' and a square filled with parallel lines labeled 'List.'

He opted for 'List.'

That brought him to a black screen with the line 'Voice 001' followed by the day's date and time stamp. Just a few hours ago.

He pressed the 'Voice 001' line and the screen changed once again. This time a glowing line began moving across the bottom of the screen and Mace heard a tinny, hollow-sounding voice. 'Don't kill him, Timmie.' Thomas's voice.

Then a voice that had to be Paulie's, begging Timmie not to kill him.

Thomas asked about the coin and a gruff voice, Corrigan's, replied that, he, Mace, had it.

That prompted a brief discussion about Mace's whereabouts and the probability of his being with Angela, which prompted Thomas to ask about the tracking device in her car.

Paulie refused to cooperate. There were screams. And then he told them what they wanted to know.

'You gonna kill me, now?' Paulie asked.

'Not now,' Thomas said. 'Your eventual fate will be up to Mister Mason. Come, Timmie, and bring our friends. Time to depart.'

'We going to the studio, Thomas?' Timmie asked. 'I hope so. I'm getting sleepy and that bed on stage three is soft as feathers.'

'You'll be on your feather bed soon enough,' Thomas said.

'And I don't like this costume any more. Tomorrow I wanna be a cowboy again.'

'What studio is he talking about?' Paulie asked.

'You'll find out soon enough,' Thomas replied.

That was followed by the sound of a door opening.

'Hey!' Paulie yelled. 'You don't have to shove. I can walk all by myself.'

The door slammed shut.

It would have been nice if they'd mentioned the name of the studio. But no matter. Southern California was studio central, but Mace thought he knew the one on Timmie's simple mind. And if he was wrong? Well, nothing ventured . . .

He left the house. At the Caddy, he removed the BXP from its case. Hefted it. It was way heavier than the Sig Sauer, probably carrying a full load. He checked, removing the magazine.

He was about to reload the sub-machine gun when he had second thoughts. He ejected the round in the chamber and then removed the shells from the magazine before snapping it back into place.

He'd considered using the Caddy, but he didn't like the idea of leaving Angela's car at the scene of a murder. Holding the BXP in his left hand, he closed the trunk. Then he wiped the trunk where he'd touched it, picked up his two-suiter and headed for the Mustang.

He put his luggage in its trunk, then opened the driver's door and slid on to the car's bucket seat behind the wheel. He leaned forward and placed the BXP on the passenger-side floor mat. Then he felt around under his seat and was happy to discover a small gap where the soft leatherette seat cover had pulled away from its metal clamp. He dug a finger in and opened the gap wider.

He checked the time. Brox would be calling in thirty-three minutes.

By then, with luck, he'd be within shooting distance of the Russian.

FORTY-TWO

He actually made it in twenty-nine minutes.

He was parked, sitting in the Mustang on Ferraro Street in Hollywood, staring at a vacant street and listening to The Sinatra Hour on an FM jazz station, when Brox's call came through.

The phone's ring tone was an odd little tune but also a familiar one. Da-dada-da-daaa-daaa, da-dada-da-daaa-daaa-da.

He turned off the radio, silencing Sinatra's transcendent version of 'Polka-dots and Moonbeams,' to better concentrate on the ring tone when it sounded again. Da-dada-da-daa-daa. 'A whooee-duh-whooee.' This time he was able not only to name the tune, *Blues in the Night*, but remember its personal significance. One of his earliest memories was of his mother crooning that song to him every night until he went to sleep.

It had been an oddly misogynistic maternal choice, he thought, a song about a mother warning her son that women were two-faced, troublesome creatures '. . . who'll leave you to sing the blues in the night.'

He wondered if Brox was trying to tell him something.

Time to find out.

He clicked the talk button on the phone and brought it to his ear. 'Brox?' he asked.

'Who else were you expecting, Mister Mason?' The accented voice was dry and unemotional.

'I don't know. It's not my phone.'

'You have the coin?'

'Are my friends OK?'

'One second.'

'Hi.' All Mace needed was the one syllable to recognize Angela's voice. 'I'm fine,' she said. 'We're all fine. I—'

'Enough,' Brox said. 'Mr Mason, are you familiar with Chandler Park in Hollywood?'

Mace had driven past it not ten minutes before. On Santa

Monica Boulevard, between Fairfax and LaBrea, a small neighborhood park featuring benches and a couple of tennis courts and a life-size bronze statue of its namesake, a meek-looking novelist in a suit and tie, wearing round glasses and a pipe in his mouth. He had a book under one arm and a cat cradled in the other. The sculptor had given his subject a raised eyebrow and a slight scowl, as if he were looking at something of which he didn't quite approve.

Mace always had the impression the statue was looking at him.

'I'm familiar with the park,' he told Brox.

'Good. Can you be there in half an hour?'

'I'm up on Mulholland Drive,' Mace lied. 'Let's say forty-five minutes to play safe. Where exactly do we meet in the park?'

'We don't,' Brox said. 'In forty-five minutes, I will call again with further instructions.'

He ended the connection.

Mace tossed the cellular phone on to the passenger seat. He didn't plan on using it again.

He wouldn't have expected their meeting to take place in the park. Or anywhere else beyond Brox's total control. The Russian wanted to make him jump through several hoops, softening him up, before luring him to a final destination. He was banking everything on that destination being on the other side of the freshly painted seven-foot wall to his left.

The old Brigston Film Studio.

He'd remembered Honest Abe telling him that a guy he knew had bought the studio to make porno films. Then there was Wylie's comment about seeing Timmie before, along with the corrupted titles of Elvis Presley songs and movies that no longer seemed to be the nonsensical ravings of a dying man.

He put the car in drive and toured the lot's outer perimeter. He made note of the bright red metal gate blocking the vehicle entrance and, a few feet away, a door of the same color for pedestrian use. He also noted the adjacent blocks, obviously zoned for commercial use and occupied primarily by rows of warehouses interrupted by an automotive repair garage here or a junkyard there.

He wound up back on Ferraro, parking in pretty much the same place where he'd started.

The sidewalk there was so bucked it probably discouraged foot traffic and the tall, faded and mottled yellow building that took up almost half the block across the street showed zero signs of human activity.

He looked at his watch. Thirty-nine minutes before the Russian would be calling. Thirty-nine minutes for him to get over the wall, check out the situation there and do whatever had to be done.

He'd never been a fan of elaborate planning. He was too impulsive. He preferred the fast, unexpected move. Sometimes it worked for him. Sometime not. But plans didn't always work out either.

He was suddenly struck by the not unreasonable fear that he wasn't fooling Brox, that, to the contrary, the Russian knew exactly where he was. Hadn't he read somewhere that there was a way of tracking people via their cellular phones?

He grabbed the phone and clicked it off. Much too late, of course, if Brox had been zeroing in on it. In a flash of anger, he tried to break the phone in two. He was only able to crack the plastic case and bend its inner workings a little.

'Fuck you,' he yelled into the now certifiably dead phone. 'Whatever you've got, bring it on.'

He lowered the passenger window and threw the damaged phone into the street. He raised the window and leaned back, taking deep breaths that were supposed to calm him. Eventually his heart stopped trying to beat its way out of his chest.

There were a few small things in his favor. He figured he could count on Corrigan, assuming that the CIA agent was in any position to help.

And he was vaguely familiar with the studio. Or rather, with what the studio had once been like.

He'd spent a little time on the lot about fifteen years before, when its then owner, Henry Gordon Brigston, decided to close the place down. Brigston had been an active B-movie and TV producer-director, who'd bought the property when he was in the chips. But ageism closed out his creative career and the slowdown in independent film production had turned the lot into a financial albatross.

He'd thrown a music, food, and booze-filled farewell party that Mace and Paulie had crashed, hoping to score starlets, which had not been that difficult. Mace and a big redhead, both several margaritas down, had staggered into what they'd thought was an empty bungalow but was, in fact, Brigston's office. They'd followed the sound of a movie to a small screening room, where his host was hiding out with a group of his cronies, watching a film.

The redhead, seeing it was old and in black and white, had tried to pull Mace away. But he was fascinated by the images on the screen. He took a seat in the theater's back row and didn't even notice that the redhead had gone. When the lights went on, Brigston, a bit surprised to find him there, introduced himself and asked if he'd liked the movie. 'Very much, what I saw of it,' Mace had replied. 'You made a great film.'

Brigston grinned and began laughing, as did several of his friends. 'Son,' he said, 'that was the nicest compliment anybody's ever paid me. The movie was made by a director *almost* as good as I was. His name was John Ford.' He then introduced Mace to the others, among them 'two reprobates you probably recognize,' an almost unrecognizable, aged Robert Mitchum, wearing huge dark-rimmed glasses, and a character actor named Anthony Caruso.

Brigston led them all into what appeared to be a sort of board room where a bar had been set up. He urged Mace to 'stick around and sip a few and listen to some of the biggest liars Hollywood has ever produced.'

So Paulie had wound up in a threesome at their beach apartment, which was fine with him, while Mace had awakened alone at dawn the next morning, lying on a couch in Brigston's office. Hung over, and possibly still a bit drunk, he'd staggered out of the bungalow to find himself facing four large sound stages, each marked with a giant identifying number. Out of curiosity, or maybe just to clear his head, he'd spent the next several hours strolling around the lot, walking through deserted sound stages and trying to keep out of the way of the clean-up crew that Brigston had hired to remove the party's detritus.

Now, sitting behind the wheel of the Mustang, he tried to recall everything he'd seen. Finally, he'd had enough of that. *Well, what the hell? It's an omelet situation. Time to break eggs.*

FORTY-THREE

Spying no activity on the street, Mace left the Mustang carrying the sub-machine gun.

The wall was about a foot thick, its top flat enough to hold the handgun and the BXP while he managed to hoist himself up and over.

His memory had convinced him that he'd be hidden behind a wooden building that had once served as a stable when black-and-white westerns filled much of television's prime time. Brigston had converted it into a garage.

It seemed that it was still being used for that purpose. He heard water splashing and a man humming a tune.

He lifted his weapons from the wall soundlessly and moved to the edge of the building. Beyond it, the lot seemed pretty much as he remembered, with the exception of wear and tear and some added construction vehicles – trucks, concrete mixers, backhoes, all idle. He scanned the area just long enough to convince himself that he and the humming man were the only creatures stirring.

He crept forward.

Sweets was standing with his back to Mace, looking very LA in baggy surf shorts and flip-flops, with a music player strapped to his upper right bicep and ear buds filling his head with sound. He was hosing off the Bentley with his left hand while extending his right arm with its electronic toy and plastered wrist away from the spray.

Mace tucked the Sig Sauer under his belt and ran forward, swinging the empty sub-machine gun against the back of the black man's head. He had to hit Sweets once more, while the suddenly freed hose snaked this way and that soaking his black trousers and tennis shoes. He cut off the water and looked out over the lot.

Satisfied that there was no one to observe him, he opened the Bentley's trunk, and, with some effort, lifted Sweets and tossed him in, getting wetter in the process. It took him no time at all to find a roll of duct tape on a shelf in the garage. He used Drier's knife to cut three strips and made sure Sweets wouldn't be getting out of the trunk or yelling. He wasn't in the least concerned with what the binding might do to the man's mending wrist.

He looked out over the lot and wondered if the construction machinery had been idled permanently. More likely, Brox had arranged for the crew to take an unplanned holiday. Mace's watch told him he had twenty-two minutes before the Russian made his phone call. He didn't know what the man would do when it went unanswered, but he didn't want to find out.

Better to take the bastard down now. But where, oh where, might he be?

Mace stared at Brigston's bungalow office sitting just past the construction toys, at the beginning of the backlot, facing the studio's four sound stages. Viewed from the rear, with its windows blocked by lowered blinds, it showed no sign of occupancy.

But it was the logical place for a self-important asshole to establish temporary headquarters.

It did not seem prudent to take the most direct route to the bungalow, since that would include crossing a wide expanse of open lot. To his right were a series of street facades constructed decades ago to substitute for on-location filming. They were creaky and their *trompe l'oeiel* effects were being severely undercut by peeling and sun-cracked paint. But they offered cover.

First up was the lot's western street, a relic that had probably been placed in that location to be near the working stable. It was breaking apart. The wooden rail in front had pulled loose from the rough-hewn post and the planks that had formed the walkway. A saloon sign and swinging doors had been placed in a pile waiting to be carted away.

But there was enough of the two-foot-thick facade left to hide Mace as he worked his way past its unpainted and rotting – but apparently well-constructed – foundation.

Next up was a peeling and partially deconstructed block of big city brownstones, circa 1940. Some of the stoops were missing and the real glass windows had broken long ago. Mace hopped over the braces that were keeping the whole thing standing and tried not to pick up any splinters.

He paused at the far end of the big city block. He was facing the right side of the bungalow. Six windows, four covered by blinds. The blinds were drawn up on the two windows near the front of the building and Mace could see into an apparently unoccupied room. But there was . . . something. A hum, coming from the direction of the bungalow. Very much a hum. He was surprised he hadn't heard it before.

An air conditioner.

Good. It meant that somebody was in the bungalow. And chances were they wouldn't hear his approach unless he kicked something. Like a gong.

He studied the bungalow for a few more seconds, then switched his attention to the numbered buildings. He imagined Timmie snoring away on his soft bed in Sound Stage Three, the one he'd mentioned on the recording. As long as Mace was fantasizing, he hoped Thomas might be asleep in there, too. Out of the way.

Seeing nothing more to discourage a visit to the bungalow, Mace was about to head for it when the sound of a gunshot trumped the air conditioner.

Mace ducked, but the shot had had nothing to do with him. It had taken place inside the bungalow.

He stood up, staring at the building. He saw some movement beyond the uncovered windows.

The front door opened and two men exited.

Mace took a backward step behind the facade, but was still able to see them standing in front of the bungalow, one offering the other a cigarette. Both were hiding behind designer sunglasses, but even without the glasses, it would have taken

Mace a few seconds to realize who they were. A clean-shaven
Gulik was wearing khaki shorts and a T-shirt that read,
'Keeping It Real'. His partner, Klebek, had on a pink, collared
pullover and lemon-colored shorts. Both wore sandals. They
didn't look at all Russian. They looked like two beefy locals
who'd been planning to get in a little beach or poolside time
but had been sidetracked.

Actually, Mace thought, they looked pretty much like the
two males in the threesome porno he'd glimpsed at Simon
Symon's apartment.

'. . . prepared for this bullshit.' Gulik was obviously
unhappy. Also obviously speaking without a hint of an accent.
He inhaled deeply on his cigarette.

'I tell you, dude, it was the fucking coldest thing I've ever
seen,' Klebek said.

'OK, so the guy *was* behaving like an asshole,' Gulik said.
'But still . . . Jesus!'

'The lesson is: you definitely don't want to piss these guys
off,' Klebek said.

'I think the lesson is: we get the fuck out of here,' Gulik
said.

'Without getting paid?'

Gulik's reply was interrupted by Thomas leaving the bungalow.
'If you gentlemen are finished blackening your lungs,' he said,
'let's collect my brother and take a little drive, shall we?' He
started walking in the direction of the sound stages.

Klebek looked at Gulik, evidently willing to follow his lead.

Gulik took another pull on his cigarette.

Thomas whirled on them and said, nastily, 'Hell-o. Was I
unclear? Did I not keep my words down to two syllables?
Perhaps I was impolite? I do apologize. Would you come with
me, please? Or should I . . . ?' He patted the bulge under his
tailored coat.

Gulik tossed his half-smoked cigarette away and Klebek
did the same. Both men followed Thomas.

Mace watched them walk toward the sound stages. He
wondered who'd just been shot. A guy who'd been behaving
like an asshole. He knew someone who fit that description.
He hoped he was wrong.

He'd find out soon enough. The grunts were all accounted for. It would take them a few minutes to get Timmie and head for the car. There they would discover Sweets' absence, maybe hear him banging around in the trunk if he had woken up by then. They'd kill another couple of minutes setting him free and trying to figure out what had happened to him.

At that point, Mace would be in the bungalow, in charge, holding a gun to Brox's head.

He saw Thomas pause at the door to Sound Stage Three, allowing the others to enter first. Then following them in.

As soon as the door closed behind Thomas, Mace was on his feet, running full out to the bungalow. He did not hesitate. Brox might hear him, but he'd assume it was one of the others returning.

He opened the door and, sub-machine gun in hand, stepped into a hall that ran the length of the building. The air conditioner was doing too good a job. The interior of the bungalow was freezing. That should have told him something, but his thoughts were focused on the Russian.

To his left was a room that might have served as a reception area. It was empty. The door to his immediate right was closed. That was where Brigston's conference room had been. At the far end of the hall, past rows of framed movie posters, were two other closed doors. As he recalled, the one to the right led to the screening room. Brigston's office had been to his left.

That's where he was headed. But the posters slowed him down a bit.

Fifteen years ago, they had been for serious small budget efforts like *War Bride*, which had won an Oscar for cinematography, and goofy exploitation flicks like *Cowboys from Mars* and *Dracula's Dentist*.

These had been replaced by posters from the new owner's production company, mainly porno permutations of Elvis Presley films. *Kid Gal-I-Had*, *Wild Sex in the Country*, *Roust-a-butt*, *King C-hole*. Each poster featured an assortment of naked ladies clinging to a shirtless, and, in one instance, also pantless, Timmie, who was billed as 'The Supersized Elvis. When his pelvis swings the girls all sing.'

At another time, Mace might have been amused. But not now. Especially after noting the director of the movies. Simon S. Symon.

Mace took a deep breath, raised both weapons, kicked open the door to the office and stormed in.

The small, pale man in a tight, gray business suit who sat behind the desk was unmoved by his entrance. He was leaning back in his chair, his head titled slightly so that his pale blue eyes seemed to be observing a corner of the ceiling. The bullet that tore a hole in his forehead had made a messy exit, splashing blood and gray matter over his chair and a section of the wall and giving his luxurious mane of brown hair an odd upsweep at the back.

'And who the fuck are you?' Mace asked the corpse.

He didn't expect an answer. But he got one.

'That would be the late Maxil Brox, Mason,' a familiar voice said behind him. 'A gent who wasn't quite as smart as he thought he was.'

He turned to see Corrigan lying in a heap on the carpet. 'Gimme a hand, would ya?' he asked. 'In this position my arthritic knees are as useless as feathers on a fox.'

Mace tucked his handgun away and rested the BXP on the desk. He grabbed Corrigan's arm and helped him to his feet, wondering if the CIA agent really had arthritis or was using that to get him to disarm.

'Thanks, Mason,' the stocky man said, pressing a spot under his white hair and wincing. He looked at the weapon resting on the desk. 'Is that mine?'

'Not anymore,' Mace said, picking up the sub-machine gun. 'What happened here?'

'The Brit plugged Brox and whacked me on the noggin. Thought he'd put out my lights, but he underestimated the thickness of my skull.'

'Why the violence?'

'I'm not sure exactly. Brox's boys woke me up a short time ago and led me over here. Brox said you were bringing him the coin and he wanted my advice on putting a deal together with the right distributor.'

'You told me you didn't want to deal with him.'

'I didn't. But I was willing to lie a little to get out of here in one piece. I didn't get the chance.'

'Why not?'

'Seems the Russkie had a silent partner who got wind of our meeting and didn't like being excluded. So she sent the Brit to put a hole in brother Brox's head.'

'She?'

'Yeah,' Corrigan said. 'I hate to be the one to break it to ya, Mason, but the love of your life isn't the sweet, young innocent we all thought she was.'

FORTY-FOUR

'You're saying Angela Lowell was partnered with Brox and had him killed?'

'That's my understanding,' Corrigan said.

Mace circled the desk without turning his back to Corrigan.

'She, ah, inherited Tiny Daniels' position in his deal with Brox,' Corrigan continued. 'But she let the coin get away from her. And that's when Brox decided to take a hand. You listenin'?'

'Sure,' Mace said. He used the barrel of the gun to edge the blinds an inch or so from a window, giving him a clear view of the backlot and the garage where he'd left Sweets. The Bentley was gone. That surprised him. It also gave him hope that the crew hadn't been too concerned about the black man's absence and had gone on their errand with him still unconscious and undiscovered in the trunk.

That scenario meant he had a little more time to find Paulie . . . and Angela.

Corrigan flopped on a leather couch against the far wall and let out a long sigh. 'So, brother Mason, I imagine you're smart enough not to be carrying the coin in your pocket.' When Mace didn't reply, he added, 'But I bet you can lay your hands on it anytime you want. That's why you and I have to have a mutually rewarding cha . . . What the hell are you doin'?'

Mace didn't bother to answer because it was clear what he was doing. He'd reached into the corpse's inner coat pocket and withdrawn a well-used leather wallet that was packed with cards and a few bills.

He studied the driver's license under the glassine window, the small color photo of its owner indicating that he didn't look any more rosy-cheeked when he was alive. He shook out the cards on to the desktop, separated them with the gun barrel. Apparently satisfied, he used the tail of his shirt to wipe his prints from the wallet and tossed it on to the desk, too.

Then he looked at Corrigan who was wincing in embarrassment, probably feigned. 'OK,' the stocky man said. 'So the guy wasn't really Brox.'

'Horace Pender. That's the name on his driver's license, on his SAG card, on his AFTRA card. He was an actor who lived in goddamned Pasadena. What the fuck's going on, Corrigan?'

'I haven't quite figured out the big picture. I knew this mutt was a ringer. I actually saw the Russkie once in Prague. A bruiser, meaty, bald as a baboon's ass. I know for a fact he was financing Daniels' play for the coin. I'm only guessing, but I think the dame was worried she didn't have the, ah, gravitas to reclaim the coin and close the deal on her own.'

'Why not use the real Brox?'

'He may have been too cautious to risk a trip here to the States where he is persona non grata. Or la Lowell may have been afraid to tell him all was not well.

'In any case, she hired a stand-in who, as it turned out, wasn't up to the job. Wasn't hungry enough, or crooked enough or smart enough. He didn't figure the money was worth getting involved in murder and he wanted out. And . . . that's what he got.'

Mace frowned. 'If that's the truth, what are you doing here?'

'They brought me here to have my brain picked by a guy I was supposed to think was Brox. I, ah, confronted him, told him I knew he was a fake. It shook him, so I pushed it. I asked if he knew he was mixed up in an international conspiracy and that people had been murdered and . . . he started shaking like a leaf.

'The other two blokes may have been hard cases but they

were a little shook themselves. I don't think they'd been given all the facts. Anyway, the little guy mentioned something about going to the cops. He'd barely got the words out when the Brit danced in and, without a "by your leave", plugged him. Then he slugged me. He thought I was down for the count, like I said. I imagine he'll be showing up shortly to drag my ass back to keep your pal Lacotta company.'

'Lacotta still alive?'

'Last I saw. They're hoping to trade him for the coin.'

Mace hoped that wasn't a lie.

'Before we get interrupted,' Corrigan said, 'let's take this discussion to another room. That stiff is making me a little queasy.' He made the finger-to-the lips quiet gesture. Then he tapped his ear.

Mace nodded that he understood the charade. 'Sure,' he said, picking up the BXP.

In the hall, he moved toward the screening room, but Corrigan thought it was too cold in there and they wound up in the conference room.

'Let's get down to business, Mason,' Corrigan said when they'd taken seats across the table from one another.

Mace stared at him.

Corrigan had waited much too long to clue Mace in about the bug in the other room. So he was now, officially, a part of the problem. And the conference room, which was no less chilly than the rest of the bungalow, had to be just as wired at the one in which they'd left the dead man.

Mace supposed that Corrigan may have been brought to the bungalow to be quizzed by 'Brox'. And it was probable that he saw through the substitution. But after that, nothing in his story was certain, except that Pender did something to incur the wrath of his employer. And, with the ersatz Brox out of the picture, and Mace on the way, the improvisation had begun.

Goodbye fake villain Brox, hello fake friend Corrigan.

The other thing about the improv was the fact that it had been put into play so quickly. It meant that they'd known Mace was only minutes away. They'd been tracking him, thanks to the damned cellular phone.

What galled him even more was that they were assuming

him to be too thickheaded to realize he was being overheard by probably more listeners than the Sinatra Hour.

'What's your plan?' he asked Corrigan, resting the empty sub-machine gun on the table.

'Like I said, the present deal is a straight exchange, the coin for Lacotta's life. I think we can get that sweetened a bit.'

Mace cocked his head and asked, 'What kind of deal would you have made for Drier?'

The question hit Corrigan like a punch. He flinched, blinked and was momentarily silent. Finally, he said, 'I . . . wasn't given that option.'

'I guess you two were pretty close.'

'He was my partner for nearly twenty years, for God's sake. I . . . he was closer to me than family. Thrown away, discarded like a . . .' Corrigan clamped his mouth shut and stared at the table as if searching for a message in its wood grain.

He began moving his lips. Mace had seen people do that in silent prayer, but he doubted Corrigan was praying. He had been baiting the man, trying to see what effect, if any, Drier's death had had on him. Now he was concerned that he'd pushed him too far to be of any use in a showdown.

'You OK?' Mace asked.

Corrigan took a deep breath and gathered his thoughts. 'Sure. Past history.' He stared at Mace. 'I assume you're ready to negotiate?'

'I'm not here to get frostbite from the air conditioner,' Mace said.

'Good. Hand me that weapon and we move to phase two.'

'I don't think so,' Mace said, placing a proprietary hand on the unloaded sub-machine gun.

'I can assure you, possession of the coin is a greater weapon than any gun.'

'Tell that to the guy who had the coin before me, Tiny Daniels.'

'Daniels' death was a monumental mistake; the kind of stupid, thoughtless act that will not be repeated.'

'It's not just Tiny. Look at the poor sap in the next room. Or your pal Drier. '

Corrigan had hardened himself. No momentary mental drift

this time. Just knotted jaw muscles. 'That's not going to happen to you.'

'That's right,' Mace said. 'Because I'm hanging on to this.' He pointed the weapon at Corrigan's chest. 'I think it's time now for you to take me where they're keeping Paulie.'

'It would be a mistake, Mason. Your girlfriend won't let 'em kill you. But you step out of this building with a weapon and you'll lose a kneecap or an elbow.'

He was fairly certain Corrigan was lying about Angela being the villain of the piece. Their location suggested a much more likely candidate. Just after Honest Abe had told him about a 'friend' buying Brigston Studio, Jerry Monte had appeared at the coffeehouse. Then, in the game room at the castle, Angela had mentioned Monte's purchase of a property in Hollywood.

He was convinced that Jerry Monte was behind the whole charade. Monte owned the lot. Monte had put Timmie in his movies. Mace bet the porno he'd seen at Symon's, featuring the fake Russian tough guys, had been one of Monte's, too. And, most damning, he'd seen with his own eyes that Monte and Corrigan were poised to cut a deal with the US-approved arms dealer Enrico Acosta. The whole Brox thing had been a distraction.

What Monte and his pals needed was the coin. And he had it.

Mace stood suddenly, keeping the gun aimed at Corrigan's chest. 'I'll tolerate no more bullshit about Angela. Understand?'

Corrigan shook his head. 'You seem like a pretty smart operator, Mason,' he said. 'Don't let your willie get you killed.' He slid back his chair and stood slowly. 'I'll admit, I may have exaggerated the lady's status a bit. But please believe me when I say that she's who we'll be dealing with.'

Was this more bullshit, Mace wondered, or was he fooling himself with some romantic fantasy? Paulie believed Angela had betrayed him to Tiny Daniels. She'd been at Tiny's the night of the murders. It was not unthinkable that she'd set the fat man up for . . . Jerry Monte. She was Monte's girl. Mace was not conceited enough, or self-confident enough where women were concerned, to think that one night could change that. Her affection and profession of love had seemed real, but . . .

Enough! It was time for him to find out where everybody stood.

He handed Corrigan the unloaded sub-machine gun.

Corrigan grinned. 'Smart lad,' he said. 'Let's go see the lady.'

FORTY-FIVE

As they left the bungalow, Thomas was approaching from the direction of the sound stages. The gun pointed at him was definitely a Spitfire, Mace decided.

'I'll carry that for you,' Thomas said to Corrigan, holding out his free hand for the sub-machine gun.

Corrigan hesitated before giving up the weapon. He evidently wasn't feeling all that trusting of his associates.

Mace waited for Thomas to misplace his reliance on the BXP and holster the Spitfire. But the Brit opted to keep his hands full and both weapons in play.

'Shall we, gentlemen?' he said.

Thomas herded them in the direction of Sound Stage Three. Mace remembered, from fifteen years before, that some of its interior space had been taken up by a courtroom set used in a once-popular lawyer series. When he'd gone on trial a few years later, he'd been surprised by how similar the real courtroom had been to the fake.

He half expected to see that same pale-wood construction, untouched by time. Instead, he found something quite different. The courtroom had been replaced by two smaller sets. One was a very feminine boudoir, all pink and white satin. The other was a different sort of bedroom; blood-red and black silk. A tall onyx armoire sat with its doors open to a bright-red interior and an assortment of hooks from which dangled various implements employed in bondage games.

Both sets were well lighted. The rest of the vast space was either dark or in shadows.

The bondage room's king-size bed and shiny black duvet

were being tested by Timmie's massive weight. The giant was stretched out, wearing a plaid shirt and tight Levi's, à la Elvis in *Roustabout*. Paulie was sitting on the floor leaning against a bedpost, hands bound behind his back, eyes covered by a sleep mask, mouth silenced by metallic tape. He looked weary and miserable. But alive and, as much as Mace could see, not too badly damaged. He was wearing a spiked dog collar with a chain leash strapped around Timmie's thick wrist.

Fifteen or twenty feet from the set, Sweets and one of the fake Russians, Klebek, were sitting on director's chairs, staring at him. Angela, at a slightly lesser distance, was also in a director's chair, facing a card table, on which she had laid out a game of solitaire and a .45. She was wearing oversized, dark-framed glasses.

Mace continued to scan the area but saw no sign of Jerry Monte's presence, either physically or electronically, though he supposed an elephant could have been dozing in the darker corners.

He turned again to the three people on chairs. Their moods were varied. The fake Russian seemed apprehensive, taking nervous sips from a cardboard coffee container. Sweets' narrowed eyes conveyed a homicidal anger, which Mace granted was partially justified. And Angela . . . her magnified eyes seemed alert, but he couldn't quite read the rest of her face. Resigned? Remorseful? Minus his romanticized spin, maybe just annoyed.

She'd exchanged her party nightwear for something a little more practical – tight black slacks and a white pullover. She turned to Klebek, who was sitting next to her. 'I'd appreciate it if you would give Mr Mason your chair.'

'Sure,' Klebek said, rising so swiftly, he nearly knocked the chair over. Reacting to her outstretched arm, he placed the chair across from her.

Mace took his time approaching, eyes focused on Angela.

He moved the chair slightly, so that he wouldn't have to crane his neck too much to get a glimpse of the action on the bondage set. When he was seated, Angela asked, 'Ready to get down to business?'

'Sure,' he said.

Paulie was squirming, trying to make himself heard through
the tape. Mace had to look away. He considered using the
handgun, but there were just too many to kill. And Timmie.
He could use all his ammunition on him alone and maybe still
get pounded to death.

'Paulie's not looking so happy,' he said to Angela. 'Can't
you get the blindfold and collar off?'

She told Sweets to take care of it. He stood and used his
left hand to awkwardly draw a small gun from his pocket, as
if he expected Lacotta to give him trouble.

Mace turned to the fake Russian. 'Where's your buddy
Gulik?'

Klebek lowered his head. Sweets, who was halfway to Paulie
turned suddenly and pointed his gun at Mace. He said,
'Chickenshit got what *you* deserve, motherfucker.'

When Mace offered no reply, Sweets obeyed the orders he'd
been given. Once Paulie's blinders had been removed, he began
blinking, then rolled his eyes around as if he were having a
seizure.

Sweets couldn't remove the collar one-handed and the fake
Russian was employed to help him complete that task.

'That's my evidence of good will,' Angela said to Mace.
'What's yours?' She added a whispered plea, 'Trust me.'

That twisted his head a bit, which, he supposed, could have
been its purpose. He decided to react as if he hadn't heard it.
He turned to Corrigan. 'You gonna cut my deal for me?'

'I think Mr Corrigan has cut his last deal with me,' Angela
said. 'A success, considering he's still breathing. If that's the
deal you want for yourself and Paulie, hand over the coin now.'

'I don't have it on me.'

'We should make sure of that,' Thomas said.

'When I want your advice, I'll ask for it,' Angela said. She
stared at Mace as if trying to read his face. He gave her a
blank page. 'Where is it?' she asked.

'If I told you that, I'd have to kill you,' he said.

She gave him a brief, wintery smile. 'No more jokes,' she said.

'All right. Serious and from the heart. I'm concerned that
as soon as you get the coin Paulie and I will go the way of
Pender and my old friend Gulik.'

She frowned. 'They said some rather foolish things and Thomas reacted in his usual hasty manner.'

'They said they were going to the police, madam,' Thomas said. 'Should I have stood aside and wished them "*bon chance*"?'

Angela gave him a bored look, then said to Mace, 'I think we can assume neither you nor Paulie is likely to run to the police.'

'Not our style,' Mace said.

She lowered her eyes to his beltline. 'Glad to see me?' she asked.

He looked down and saw that the Sig Sauer was causing his shirt to tent slightly. He shifted on the chair and the shirt flattened out.

She was now staring at him, eye to eye. It had been a warning, but could he really trust her? Could he trust himself?

'Sweets,' Angela said, not breaking eye contact, 'place your gun against Mr Lacotta's forehead. If Mr Mason has not told us the location of the coin before I reach the count of ten, pull the trigger.'

Mace heard Paulie yapping like a muzzled mongrel. His eyes and Angela's were still locked. 'It's at Paulie's house up on Mulholland,' he said. 'I used gum to stick it to the back of his TV screen.'

'If this turns out to be a delaying tactic,' she said, 'it'll get very ugly, very quickly.'

'Nobody likes ugly,' Mace said.

FORTY-SIX

There were several things Honest Abe Garfein preferred to be doing that morning, lolling about in bed with a nasty brunette being first and foremost. He could not think of anything he'd less prefer doing than rattling along Santa Monica Boulevard in Simon Symon's Cherokee clunker.

The faded color of the vehicle reminded him of a ghastly vat drink called Purple Jesus. Symon's personality and conversation were on a par with his hygiene, which was wanting in every possible way. And Abe was depressed by the section of the boulevard they were traveling through, which had been a bar-and-grill, hooker-rich hipster playground during his young adulthood, but now had been transformed, apparently overnight, into a family-oriented, super-malled neighborhood that looked considerably cleaner than the man sitting beside him at the steering wheel.

'What's this meeting all about anyway?' Symon whined. 'I was planning on hanging out in Burbank this morning, trying to get a shot of Brad and Megan during their break.'

Abe had answered that question several times already, but he figured he might as well give it another try. 'As I was told, Jerry wants to discuss the sequel to *Kid Gal-I-Had*.'

'I get that,' Symon snapped. 'What I don't get is: what's there to discuss? Either we shoot the fucking porno or we don't. It's not like we're making *Green Hornet Two*.'

'I believe we still have to sell him,' Abe said, staring sadly at a corner where he'd once received oral sex from a beautiful, black hooker with bright platinum hair. Now there was a crossing guard helping an old lady across the street.

'It's the way of the world,' he said.

'Shit. It's not like I'm getting DGA pay, Abe. And I don't like working with that big freak.' They'd made several movies with the huge Elvis-like man-boy, Symon behind the camera, Abe producing, Jerry Monte financing on the QT.

'Timmie's OK, as long as you stay on his good side,' Abe said. 'And you have to admit, the boy does have a million-dollar package.'

That seemed to quiet Symon for the moment.

As they turned right on Formosa, Abe stared wistfully at a restaurant on the corner that still matched the image in his memory. It used to be one of the few places where you could be sure of getting an excellent gin martini. He wondered if that was still the case. 'Ever go the Formosa?' he asked Simon.

'Jesus, Abe, do I look like Army Archerd? How old do you think I am?'

Abe sighed and said nothing more until Symon started to turn into the former Brigston lot. 'Watch out for the dog!' he shouted.

Symon hit the brakes and a mutt, apparently unhurt but frightened, slunk from under the front of the Cherokee, his ribs showing beneath his mottled and patchy coat.

'Fucking dog,' Symon shouted, hiding his own fear. 'Kill yourself on your own time.'

The dog gave them a furtive backward glance before trotting off and Abe, ordinarily not one to put much stock in signs or portents, wondered if this might be a bad time to visit the lot.

'Simon . . .' he began, and paused.

'What?'

This was foolish, Abe thought. There was business to be done. 'Let's go close the deal,' he said.

Symon coughed, rubbed the underside of his nose with a finger and drove on to the lot. His first sign that something wasn't quite right was the absence of sound. No roaring engines, no cement mixers, no grinding, rending, collapsing.

'What the hell?' Symon said. 'What happened to the construction? Where are the workmen? Tell me Jerry hasn't tapped out.'

'The country will tap out before Jerry,' Abe said. 'Some kind of holiday, maybe.'

'My fucking bank is open,' Symon said. He slowed down the Cherokee, looking right and left for a sign of . . . something. 'Dead as old man Brigston,' he said. 'You sure Jerry wanted to see us today?'

'So the broad said.'

'He took her back, huh? Last night it looked like the romance was over.'

'These things ebb and flow,' Abe said.

Symon parked the vehicle in front of the office bungalow. 'Don't see any of his cars,' he said. 'Don't see Rufe's black ass anywhere. You ever know Jerry to go anywhere without Rufe?'

'Actually, no,' Abe said, looking around now himself.

Getting out of the car, he saw the door to Sound Stage Three open. Two men exited the building. 'Here's somebody,' he said to Symon.

'The fucking Brit and Sweets,' Symon said with some disgust. 'Key-rist. Don't tell me they're gonna be at the meeting?'

The black man was taking his time, but Thomas marched hurriedly toward them. 'Hello, chaps.'

Symon shot a nervous look past him and Sweets. 'That whack-job brother of yours around somewhere?' he asked.

'He's in building three –' Thomas said genially, removing his gun – 'my whack job brother, as you so quaintly put it, you insipid, odoriferous little vermin.'

'Hey, look, I—' was about all Symon was able to articulate before Thomas blew the top of his head off.

He turned the gun on Abe. 'Comment?' he asked.

For the first time, Abe realized that, while it had not been obvious before, Thomas was as much a whack job as his brother. He shook his head and said nothing.

'What the hell you doin', Thomas?' Sweets whined.

'Ridding the world of one more impossibly rude cretin,' Thomas said, as unruffled as a calm sea. 'Care to make it two?'

Sweets blinked and immediately dropped his attitude. 'Uh, I better get goin',' he said.

'Put this garbage somewhere out of sight, first,' Thomas said, indicating Symon's corpse.

Sweets started to hold up his plastered wrist, but thought better of it. 'I'll stick 'im in the workmen's with the other one.'

Looking at the man's narrow face and wide fearful eyes, Abe was reminded of the dog at the entrance to the lot. It had been a portent after all.

FORTY-SEVEN

There had been some discussion about who should retrieve the coin. Since the least crucial member of their group, the man known as Klebek, was deemed a bit less than trustworthy, Sweets was tapped for the trip.

Angela told him to phone in as soon as he found the coin. 'Or, more likely, as soon as I don't find it,' Sweets said.

He crossed the room and opened the door. He started to

exit, then stepped back. 'Car parked by the office,' he shouted. 'Somebody out there.'

Thomas' face lit up.

'Know them?' Angela asked.

'Didn't get a good look,' Sweets said.

'I'll find out,' Thomas said with a grin.

'No, wait a—' Angela began.

'Timmie, take this,' Thomas interrupted her, holding out the sub-machine gun. 'Keep our friends at bay.'

His brother lumbered toward him and accepted the weapon. 'Bang-bang.'

'Use it only if you must,' Thomas said and left with Sweets to check on the newcomers.

Mace thought this might be the time to make his move, with Timmie holding the useless weapon, the other two men more than halfway on his side. And Angela . . . ? He might as well find out where she stood.

He dropped his hand to his lap.

'Don't,' Angela whispered. 'Not yet.'

He was being foolish but he decided to play along. He was gambling his life and Paulie's. Not all that much, really.

He settled back to wonder who'd just arrived and if or how it would alter the dynamics of the situation.

'I like guns,' Timmie said, distracting him. 'But pistols are my favorite. Cowboy pistols.'

Mace shifted in his chair to observe the big man. Corrigan was doing the same. Standing slightly behind Timmie, he glared venomously at the giant.

'A man strong as you doesn't really need a gun, Timmie,' Mace said. 'You do pretty well bare-handed.'

Timmie smiled. 'I am strong. I lifted two pretty girls in *Wild Sex in the Country*.'

Mace was about to drop the late Drier's name into the conversation when a popping sound made its way through the soundproofed walls of the building.

'Gun,' Corrigan said.

'Thomas,' Timmie said gleefully. 'He only needs one shot.'

Mace looked at Angela, who seemed troubled. 'Expecting someone?' he asked.

'You never know who'll drop by,' she said. Her mind seemed to be working furiously.

When the door opened, all of them but Timmie turned toward it.

Two men entered, one holding a gun, the other with his arms raised. The gunman was Thomas. The other, tall, weary-looking and wearing a loud Hawaiian shirt, looked the room over. His eyes locked on Mace's.

'Hi, Abe,' Mace said. 'You here on business or pleasure?'

'I . . .' Abe seemed shaken. He shifted his attention to Angela and said, 'He just killed . . . Simon.'

'Vermin eradication,' the Brit said.

'Damnit, Thomas,' Angela said, getting to her feet. 'That shoot-first attitude is what got us into this mess.'

'No big loss, I assure you,' Thomas said. He casually gestured toward Abe with his gun. 'It's not as if I kill everyone I see.'

'Don't be mad at Thomas,' Timmie told her. The big man was now facing Angela, as if trying to decide if he should use the weapon in his hand. She leaned forward, her hand just inches from the pistol on the table. Thomas was walking toward his brother. None of them was paying attention to Corrigan.

The stocky man picked that moment to attack Thomas, knocking the gunman off his feet. They struggled on the ground. It wasn't much of a contest. Thomas had age on his side, but that was no match for Corrigan's weight, strength and experience at hand-to-hand combat. Avoiding the Brit's kicks and flailing, he concentrated on his goal, which was getting and using Thomas' gun.

But Thomas refused to release the weapon. Corrigan tore it loose, accompanied by the sound of finger bones cracking.

Thomas let out a scream of pain as Corrigan rolled free of him. He rose on one knee, the gun aimed at Timmie, who was still transfixed by the image of his brother writhing in agony. Corrigan's first shot was high, tearing a ridge in the big man's upper arm.

It did little damage but it caught Timmie's attention. He swung the sub-machine until it was pointed directly at Corrigan, who was halfway to a standing position. Timmie pulled the trigger. When nothing happened, he looked down at the gun, perplexed. He shook it and tried the trigger again. Nothing. 'Is this a real gun?' he asked.

Corrigan was standing now, apparently cured of arthritis. He sent his second shot into Timmie's right side. It angered the giant, but didn't seem to do much else. 'That hurt Timmie,' he said, running toward Corrigan.

The CIA agent fired another bullet into the big man's body. But it wasn't enough to stop his advance. Timmie drew back his useless weapon and smashed it against Corrigan's face.

Mace saw the blood spray from Corrigan's broken nose as he fell backward, losing the gun.

Thomas, holding his hand with broken fingers close to his body, reached out his other hand for the fallen weapon and scooped it up. He tried to get a clear shot at the man who'd hurt him, but his brother had Corrigan wrapped in a bear hug, crushing him. The Brit then turned his gun on the fake Russian, Klebek, who'd had more than enough and was running for the door. 'Quisling bastard,' Thomas shouted. Before he could pull the trigger, Mace placed a shot in the center of his back.

Mace had drawn the Sig Sauer to use on Timmie. He wasn't sure why he'd switched targets. Maybe it was because he felt the fake Russian deserved the assist more than Corrigan. Maybe it was because he believed an armed Thomas posed a more serious threat than his already wounded brother.

He didn't have time to give it a lot of thought.

Timmie, responding to his brother's death cry, tossed the now-lifeless Corrigan aside. Emitting a wail of sorrow mixed with fury, he turned and stomped toward Mace, his big Elvis-like head swinging from side to side.

Mace held his ground and placed two bullets into Timmie's chest. They forced the big man to take a few backward steps. 'That really hurts,' he said and continued forward.

Time for a head shot, Mace thought. But he missed by inches. And Timmie was on him, wrapping his massive arms around him until they met, then squeezing, lifting the smaller man off his feet.

Mace couldn't breathe. The Sig Sauer was still in his hand, but it was trapped in a flat position between their bodies. With a final struggle, Mace was able to angle it slightly toward Timmie and fired.

He felt the big man react as the bullet tore through a fleshy portion of his gut. But his squeeze intensified and Mace was too weak and too woozy to try for another shot. He knew his ribs were at the cracking point. He was struggling for breath.

And the old familiar anger kicked in.

With a growl of fury more animal than human, he shoved his head forward, pressed his mouth against Timmie's chest and bit hard enough to tear through the big man's shirt and remove his right nipple.

Timmie screamed and relaxed his hold for just a beat. But it was long enough for Mace to spit the torn flesh in the giant's face, lower his weapon to his pelvic area and continue firing until he was out of ammunition.

With a screech, Timmie unwrapped his arms and Mace fell to the floor, not quite realizing what was happening. He was trying to breathe, but the effort was too painful. Gasping, he let go of the gun and pressed his hand against his chest.

His own touch seemed to have some therapeutic value.

He calmed a bit. That allowed him to inhale a little in spite of his aching ribs.

As his mind cleared, he became aware of the huge figure still standing just a few feet away. Standing, but swaying. Timmie's huge hands, covered with blood, were squeezing his ruined penis and testicles. 'Where . . . are . . . you . . . Thomas?' he yelled. 'I hurt baaaad.' He began crying like a baby.

Which is what he was, Mace supposed.

Suddenly, Timmie sat down hard on the concrete. He looked surprised. He whimpered and fell over on his side. His breathing was ragged. Then it stopped.

Mace pushed himself to his feet. He stumbled toward the card table. He leaned on it and when it began to slide on the concrete floor, settled back on his own two feet.

He heard Paulie making a keening sound through his tape gag and recognized it as a warning. He looked up and saw Angela standing several feet away. She had her gun in her hand, pointed in his general direction.

'Wait,' he said, but she fired anyway.

If he'd been in any better shape, he might have realized she'd meant him no harm. Instead he was still gawking at her when he heard the male half cry, half grunt just behind him. Followed by a soft thud.

He turned to find Honest Abe lying on his back on the concrete floor. Angela's bullet had pierced his chest at an evidently fatal location. Even after the fall, he still clutched the gun he'd been about to use on Mace.

Angela moved to Abe, stepped on his wrist and used her other foot to kick the gun away.

'He's dead,' Mace said.

'Thanks for the affirmation,' she said sarcastically. 'The problem is, he's no fucking good to me dead.'

'I don't understand,' Mace said.

'Clearly. We needed this piece of crap to help us nail the real Brox.'

'We?'

'I'd show you my ID,' she said, 'if I was lame enough to be carrying one into this snake pit. I'm a member of the same club as the late Mr Corrigan, only I pay more attention to the rules.'

Mace was experiencing chest pains when he breathed. He felt dizzy. Mainly, he felt like a fool. 'I . . .' he began. But he wasn't foolish enough to finish the very personal thing he was thinking. Instead, he improvised, 'I thought the rules said your club wasn't supposed to play in this country.'

She turned her blue eyes on him. If there was a hint of warmth in them, he couldn't see it past the frost. 'Mason,' she said, 'you and I shared a memorable night of fucking. And I just blew my assignment by saving your life. So don't be a putz.'

He suddenly realized she was right and, in spite of everything, he felt like laughing. But the joke wasn't quite complete. 'Brox was your assignment?'

'Eventually. My original orders were to . . . become friends with the two Southern California entrepreneurs who were bidding on the formula. When I reported my discovery that Tiny was being backed by Brox, I was told to forget him and concentrate on Paulie, specifically to verify that he intended to set up a deal with a USA-approved weapons manufacturer.

'When the formula – the coin – was hijacked, it was assumed that Tiny was the culprit. *Au revoir*, Paulie. Hello again, Tiny. My assignment from Langley was to verify his possession of the formula and to reclaim it. I found that Tiny had the coin, but I wasn't able to discover where he was keeping it.'

Paulie began making loud mumbling noises. He evidently didn't like being bound and muzzled. Or maybe he just wanted to hear what they were talking about. Mace considered cutting him free but he didn't want to break the confessional mood. And, in truth, he felt Paulie deserved the inconvenience.

'How did Abe get involved?' he asked Angela.

'We've known for some time that Brox wanted a toehold on the West Coast and that Abe was running several small operations for him. Employing young Russian émigré hookers, of course. Supplying pornos and bootleg DVDs and CDs for Brox's international distributors. Nothing worth our immediate attention. But it seemed logical that he was at least peripherally involved in the deal between Tiny and Brox.

'One night out at Point Dume, I overheard Abe and Tiny getting hot and heavy over the coin. Tiny was holding out for a bigger cut of the deal. Abe was threatening him to play nice.'

'And you became friends with Abe,' Mace said.

'Yes,' she said, defiantly. 'My supervisors felt he could be used to induce Maxil Brox to set foot on US soil illegally. Brox's arrest would have not only removed a world-class villain, it would have given his good friend Putin a serious kick in the ass, diplomatically speaking.'

'Did you set Tiny up for Abe's hit man?'

She hesitated, then replied, 'I had no proactive involvement. But I knew it was going down. I was ordered to, and I quote, "sit tight and see what develops".'

'They thought the coin would surface after Tiny's death?'

'Or it wouldn't,' she said. 'Either way, with Abe trusting me, I'd be in a position of control. Then you arrived, Mason, to screw things up royally by taking the coin. Where is it, by the way? I know where it isn't: the back of Paulie's TV.'

'I don't have any idea,' he said. 'I never had it. Maybe Tiny ate it.'

She stared at him. 'If it shows up and you are in any way

connected, I'll make sure you get your old cell back. And you'll be sharing it with your fat friend.'

Mace looked at Paulie who was staring at them, red-faced, eyes bulging in indignation.

'You'd better untie him and get the hell out of here before my associates arrive. When they see this temporary graveyard they'll want to blame somebody and it won't be me.'

'What about Monte?' Mace asked.

'Jerry? What about him?'

'Wasn't Abe working for him?'

She gave him a sad, disdainful look. 'My God, weren't you listening? Jerry knows less about all this than you do.'

'What about the pornos being made on this lot? He owns the place, right?'

'The only pornos Jerry knows about are the ones starring him. He's never set foot on this lot. And he won't until all this is torn down and his West Coast offices are up and running. It was all Abe.'

'It's hard to believe,' Mace said, getting out Drier's knife to use on Paulie's bindings. 'Nine years ago, the guy was a happy whoremonger, sitting life out on Sunset. I wonder what made him decide to go for the gold?'

'Running whores, making pornos and selling coffee most not have given him enough creative satisfaction,' Angela said. 'Who'd have thought?'

FORTY-EIGHT

'Shit. You ripped the goddamn skin off my lips,' were Lacotta's first words after Mace pulled the tape from his mouth.

'Get a chap stick,' Angela told him, walking away.

Lacotta wiggled his freed fingers. 'Oh, man, got those little needle pains.'

Mace handed him Drier's knife and suggested he use his needle-pained fingers to cut the tape from his ankles. He approached Angela who was kneeling beside the now-silent Timmie, checking for signs of life.

She stood, looked at Mace and said, 'Dead as Hillary's dream.'

He shook his head in wonder. 'You may be the greatest actress I've ever seen.'

'Better than Heather Locklear? I always figured if I could achieve that . . .'

'You were way beyond her last night,' Mace said.

She gave him a half-smile. 'Suppose I said I wasn't acting then? Where would that leave us? The agent and the ex-con. Tune in next week for more hilarious adventures.'

'Might be a long-running hit.'

'Wouldn't last even a mini season,' she said.

'Hey, Cisco,' Paulie called out, 'let's went.'

'Good plan,' Angela said.

'I get the deal about you following the formula,' he said. 'That explains your hooking up with Paulie and Tiny and Abe. And me.'

'I didn't fuck *them*,' she said. She began walking him to the exit, where Paulie was waiting impatiently.

'Good to know,' he said. 'But my question is: if Monte wasn't a major player in—'

'What's your thing with Monte? He was just a bankroller Corrigan hoped to use if we got our hands on the formula. An afterthought.'

'That being the case,' Mace said, 'why were you hanging out with him?'

Her smile was patronizing. 'You may find this hard to believe, but sometimes our caseload includes two, even three, separate jobs. Monte is . . . ass-deep in negotiations with certain Chinese businessmen. We are interested.'

'Then you're still . . .'

'His main squeeze? Yep. That's me.'

'Won't he be pissed off about last night?'

'Pissed off? Yes. But more interested than ever. He's left dozens of phone and text messages for me. He's a guy who likes to win. Don't you know anything about men, either?'

'Not Monte's kind,' he said as they reached the exit.

'He's a job,' she said. 'Easier than most. It's what I do. If the agency ordered me to get close to Al-Zawahiri, I'd give it a shot.'

'I sure never figured you for a spook, Angie,' Lacotta said.

'Are you asking me to kill you?' she said.

He held up a halting hand.

'You should leave,' she said. She tapped her right ear where a tiny shard of clear plastic was not quite hidden. 'My crew picked up Sweets on Mulholland about a half hour ago. They'll be here any minute now.'

'I don't suppose they, uh, cleaned up my place while they were there?' Paulie asked.

'We claim our own,' she said. 'Unlike some.'

'So long, Angie,' Lacotta said, heading out. 'It's been fun. *Not.*'

'Before I go . . .' Mace began, but she put a finger to his lips.

He removed her finger. 'Before I go,' he began again, 'I left the Sig Sauer on the table. I'd appreciate it if you'd give it a wipe. You might want to stick it in Corrigan's hand. It belongs to him.'

'I was expecting sweet talk,' she said.

'OK. Then here's a little: I'm going to steal your car for a few hours. Paulie will get it back to you.'

She moved against him, stood on her toes and kissed him.

It was a good kiss, as farewell kisses go. More than he'd expected.

FORTY-NINE

'Have you been fucking her?' Lacotta asked as they got into the Mustang.

'Why would you want to know that now?'

'I don't know. Because I'm an asshole? Have you?'

'No,' Mace said.

'Good. I didn't think so,' Paulie said, watching him. 'Something the matter with the seat?'

'Nothing. I just wanted to adjust the tilt a little.' Mace wondered how many more lies he'd have to tell before his plane took off.

He put the top down on the car and they roared away, looking like two LA guys showing off their classic wheels.

They were stopped by a red light on Santa Monica Boulevard, a few blocks west of Formosa. The light changed and, as Paulie began another of his romanticized milestones from their past, a black van glided by heading toward the studio. It looked like the same vehicle Mace had seen at the Florian. Angela's crew. Another of his mistaken assumptions. Whatever else the nearly fatal trip to LA had or hadn't achieved, it had given him a few needed lessons in humility.

They drove west on Olympic Boulevard.

It wasn't until the air started to cool that Paulie realized they'd passed the San Diego Freeway. 'Where you going?' he asked.

'To the ocean. Then LAX.'

'What's the hurry to leave? Everything's taken care of. Except the coin, of course. But fuck that. Now we can just have fun.'

'That's my plan,' Mace said. 'But not here.'

'Here's where it's all happening.'

Mace smiled and enjoyed the feeling of the wind and the sun.

When they arrived at Lincoln Boulevard, he took a right and eventually a left and headed to the pier.

'I used to love the beach,' Paulie said. 'Until they started dumping all that industrial crap into the water and the life-guards began showing up in cancer wards.'

He gestured to somewhere on their left. 'Remember that night in Chez Jay's, Mace?' The reference was to a restaurant on Main in Santa Monica. 'We were with some Hollywood bimbos and, who was it, Ann Margaret or somebody like that, strolled in and Jay ran from behind the bar and gave her party the table that was meant for us. And when you complained, he said, "The lady's an actress." And your broad, or maybe mine, stood up and yelled, "And what are we, fuckface? Didn't you see *Slasher Two*? Victims four and five, right here."'

Paulie began to laugh and Mace felt surprisingly happy, himself, as he steered the Mustang slowly past the pier's pedestrian traffic to the parking area.

'Honest Abe, Jesus,' Paulie said. 'I sure underestimated the prick. He was a goddamned joke, the pimp who looked like Lincoln. And he had Tiny snuffed.'

'Among others,' Mace said.

'I'll say. That sound stage looked like the end of *Macbeth*.'

Mace thought he meant *Hamlet*, but it wasn't worth the mention.

'Christ, you know something, Mace? If Tiny hadn't ripped me off, Abe's killers might have been on *my* case.'

The thought actually brought Paulie to a point of introspection. It lasted less than a minute, when he realized that Mace had parked the car and was getting out.

'Where the hell you goin'?' he asked.

'To say goodbye to some friends of my family.'

'Oh, yeah. I remember. The show biz couple that played the clubs with your folks?'

'Yeah,' Mace said. 'I won't be long.'

'I'll . . . just check out the pier.'

Paulie got out of the car and watched Mace walk away. He turned toward the Ferris wheel, which was stalled between rides. Then he was distracted by squeals of fear and relief coming from the roller coaster. It had been years since he'd been to the pier. And, in point of fact, it really wasn't his thing. A little too carnival-like. He preferred the entertainment available at an upscale gentleman's club.

He strolled past the noisy arcade where people, kids mainly, fed quarters into gaming machines that paid off in prizes worth pennies. Not a bad scam, but nothing he'd want on his resume.

At the end of the pier, near the tackle shop, he paused beside a group of old, sun-baked fishermen who sat on boxes or fold-out stools, clasping poles they poked past the railing, their long lines dangling down to the ocean. 'How you doin'?' he asked the nearest fisherman.

The grizzled old guy was wearing khaki shorts, a

sun-bleached purple T-shirt and an ancient, faded Yankees baseball cap. The last time he'd shaved had been maybe never. He gave Paulie a suspicious glance and said, 'Go fuck yourself.'

'Lemme guess. The Bronx?'

'Yeah. So? Buzz off, fatso. I'm busy.'

Paulie buzzed off, amused at one more reminder of why he'd decided to make Southern California his home. That, and the broads.

Mace was waiting behind the wheel of the Mustang.

'Everything OK?' Paulie asked, getting in.

'They're old,' Mace said.

As they drove off the pier, Mace hung a right and headed in the direction of Venice. He didn't seem to want to talk and Paulie went along with that, though he was curious about where the hell they were headed. It was a very roundabout way of getting to the airport.

Traveling along Speedway, Mace took a sudden right, as if on a whim, and drove into a beachfront lot.

He got out of the car and Paulie followed, though for the life of him he couldn't figure out what Mace was up to.

It was nearing noon and the sun was at its strongest. The beach was surprisingly populated for a workday. People with dogs. Nannies with little kids. Young women in bikinis, tanning their wax jobs. The occasional couple, stretched out, catching rays.

Mace strolled through them, heading for the ocean.

'Slow down, for Christ's sake.' Paulie had paused to pull his shoes off. He hopped a little on his sockless feet, rushing to catch up.

Finally, they arrived at the hard-packed sand near the water. Mace took his shoes off, tied them together and draped them around his neck. He pulled off his socks and stuck them in his pocket.

'Beautiful, huh, Mace,' Paulie said, puffing a little from the trudge through the sand. In case he was being misunderstood, he waved the hand not holding his shoes at the ocean, the rippling waves, the cloudless blue sky.

'Definitely beautiful,' Mace agreed.

'Level with me, pally,' Lacotta said, 'If you'd had the goddamn coin, you'd have given it to me, right?'

'Why wouldn't I?' Mace rolled his trousers knee-length and walked into the water.

'You get weird ideas, sometimes,' Paulie said, rolling up his pant legs with one hand and doing a bad job of it. 'And when I heard you and Angie . . . oh hell, forget I mentioned it.'

'Forgotten,' Mace said, walking out further, the water just below his knees.

Lacotta stared at him, frowning. 'How far out are you gonna fucking walk?'

'Not much further,' Mace said. His hands were in his pockets. He withdrew his right hand and tossed something far out into the darker water of the ocean.

'The fuck was *that*?' Paulie asked.

Mace returned to the shallow water. He put his arm around Paulie's thick shoulders and led him back to the sandy beach.

Paulie kept twisting his head, as if he were trying to fix an image of where the object had entered the water. But all he saw was ocean. 'I could come back with one of those giant fucking metal detectors,' he said.

Mace smiled. 'If there's something a metal detector turns up out there, let me know.'

'You fucker. Tell me you didn't just do what I know you did.'

Mace didn't bother to reply.

'Fucker,' Paulie said again, but with no anger behind it. He grinned. 'Maybe that was the right move,' he said.

At an outdoor public shower, Mace watered the sand from his feet. Paulie tried to copy him but forgot he was holding his shoes. 'I wet my goddamn Maglis,' he groaned. 'This has definitely not been my day.'

'You're alive,' Mace reminded him.

'Yeah. There's that.'

It wasn't that long a drive from Venice Beach to LAX.

'Maybe I'll return this car to Angie personally,' Paulie said.

He was trying to get a rise out of Mace, but, instead, his friend said, 'I'm sorry about the money you blew on the formula. How are you going to handle Montdrago?'

'I'm guessing I'll skate on that. When Tiny's "insurance" surfaces, the big M is gonna have other things on his mind, like how he'll look wearing orange.'

'Maybe Tiny was bluffing about the insurance,' Mace said. When Lacotta's smile went shark-like, he added, 'I get it. You're gonna make sure something surfaces.'

'My uncle's been good to me,' Lacotta said, 'but nothing lasts forever. You gotta keep one step ahead. That's why I want you back here, Mace. My number one man.'

'That's not gonna happen.'

'It'll be like the old days, amigo. You and me. Only now, we'll be large and in charge.'

'You'll do fine on your own.'

'If you stuck around, maybe you and Angie . . .'

Mace stared at him, all signs of humor gone from his face. 'You should know me better than that,' he said.

'I swear, Mace,' Paulie said, 'sometimes I think I don't know you at all.'